Annie Laurie

Lawrence Gulley

This is a work of fiction. The characters, events and places in this novel have been inspired by true events, but the details and arrangement of them are products of the author's imagination and are used fictitiously.

Gulley, Lawrence.

Annie Laurie / Lawrence Gulley—1st ed.

ISBN: 979-8-9881499-5-8

First edition: May 2025

10 9 8 7 6 5 4 3 2 1

Annie Laurie

Chapter 1
1927

It seemed that Annie Laurie was born at a disadvantage. Times had always been hard for her. First of all, the person she loved more than anyone else in the world came down with a bad cold and wound up coughing herself to death when Annie Laurie was barely three years old. Annie Laurie didn't quite know what death was until her Mama was dead and buried for a week.

Her mama's name was Laurie, or that's what her daddy referred to her as.

Annie Laurie's mama was wrapped from head to toe in a quilt and buried in a wooden box her daddy had made. The homemade coffin was placed outside near the back door. Her daddy carried the thin body of her mama out of the back door. Once he'd placed her mama's body Inside, he nailed the top down. The mule was hitched to the coffin, and it was dragged to the edge of their property line, near the forest and buried in a deep red clay hole. There were several more mounds there with a cross at each end.

Annie Laurie's daddy's name was Franklin Reed, or that's what folks said. Her mama called him Frankie. It was cold weather, so the holly trees were loaded with red berries. Her daddy broke a few of the holly branches and stuck them into the soft red clay around the grave. The only words that were said over the grave were, "You've been a good wife and mama Laurie. I hate that none of yo folks could be here."

Annie Laurie and her daddy then followed the mule back to the stable. Annie Laurie had to almost run to keep up with her daddy.

She had very little concept of what had happened, all she knew was that she was hungry, as her mama had been sick for a week. About all her daddy could cook was baked sweet potatoes and fried salt meat. Of course, he could make coffee, but she was told she had to be twelve before she could drink it. "It'll stunt your growth," she was told.

The iron stove they cooked with burned wood. After they'd returned to the house, her daddy took the key and removed one of the top stove eyes.

After putting a few pieces of wood on top of the hot charcoals, he put the eye back into the opening and grabbed the heavy frying pan.

She knew what was coming next, fried salt meat.

The salt pork was kept in wooden barrels in the pantry.

Several foods were kept in the pantry, salt meats, sugar, flour, meal, rice {when they had it}, sugar, tin cans of syrup, honey, and a few other food items, such as seasonings. The pantry was also stocked with all kinds of homemade medicines. Annie Laurie didn't know the names of the medicines then, but she would later learn. There was mullein weed for cough and colds, blackberry leaves to purify your blood, sassafras bark that was used for several things, including a laxative. Annie was required to drink it once a month. "It'll kill the worms in your belly" her daddy once said. There were also cedar balls, they would clear your kidneys. Willow bark was used for fevers.

Luckily, they had a clear water creek that ran through the northern corner of their land. An old spring house was built at the edge of the spring, and that's where they stored the goat milk and butter. The cold water kept things from spoiling so fast. The only milk that Annie Laurie had ever drank was goat milk, as they didn't own a milk cow. The nanny goat wasn't like a cow, that only needed milking twice a day. The goat needed milking every two or three hours, which really interfered with working in the fields. Of course, Annie Laurie's mother kept the goat milked, along with all of the household chores. Annie didn't realize the change that she was about to face in her life, but she would soon find out.

There wasn't much to do in the fields in the winter months but come spring, things really picked up. There were collards, and other greens that grew in the winter months, but that was it.

While they ate their sweet potato and salt meat, then forcing it down with the goat milk, Franklin was worried.

He suddenly realized their lives were about to change. He knew Annie Laurie was too young to realize it, but she'd be spending a lot of time alone inside the house. He'd never spanked her, that had been her mama's job. He'd just have to start getting up earlier to feed the chickens, which were kept in a pen, due to varmints. Gather the eggs, milk and feed the goat and milk it, then feed the two hogs, and Pete, the mule. Too, Franklin knew he was going to have to learn to cook. He had watched Laurie cook a few things, so he knew they wouldn't starve, but God, how he missed her already.

Franklin's 40 acres of land was surrounded by forest, which was owned by big timber companies. All but the front, for a wagon trace of a road ran across the entire front. No lane left the "So called" road that led to his land though. Franklin had cut a curving path from his house to the road, making it impossible for anyone to see his house from the road.

The old house was made of logs. He'd inherited it from his Pap, and his Pap had inherited it from his. The cabin was well built. It had a huge living room, with two bedrooms on the side. In the rear was the kitchen/dining room, and of course, the pantry. The house had both a front and back porch, they ran the entire length of the house. The cabin once had cypress shingles, but Franklin had replaced the leaky roof with tin. A huge stone fireplace adorned the living room, but they seldom stayed in there, especially during the winter months. They preferred the warm cozy kitchen area.

Franklin only plowed about ten acres of his land, it was enough to sustain them and about all he could work. Most of it was planted in corn. It took a lot of corn to feed them, the mule and chickens. The goat ate very little corn, she favored grass or fodder. Franklin also planted butterbeans, peas, both sweet potatoes and Irish potatoes, tomatoes, cabbage and other greens. Very little fertilizer was bought, there simply wasn't money for it. Manure from the animals was used for fertilizer.

For cash money, Franklin weaved split white oak and made baskets. He sold the assortment of baskets at Kelly Mercantile in Dottelle or Excel, Alabama. With the money he bought tea, coffee, flour, clothes, including shoes. He also helped at Dottelle gin, during cotton ginning time. There were eight big pecan trees that encompassed the house, they shaded the house during the hot summer month. In the fall of the year when the nuts started falling, they were gathered and sold, so the pecans were another source of income. The other 30 acres was used for hunting or gathering wood. Franklin wondered how he would be able to do all that and tend to a small child. He'd already put off weaving the baskets due to Laurie's sickness, then death.

Franklin wasn't a church going man, except for when Laurie pushed him. He believed in God and every word in the Bible, but he felt that he just didn't fit in at church. After they'd eaten their meager meal that afternoon, Franklin prayed to the good Lord for help, and to just show him the way. He prayed for little Annie Laurie too. She was a pretty little thing and seemed to be very bright. Her one drawback was she just couldn't talk. She was "Tongue tied" or something and he couldn't understand a word she said.

Therefore, she pointed to what she wanted or to where she wanted to go. *"Maybe she'll simply grow out of it,"* he thought. There wasn't anything wrong with her hearing though, for she could understand every word that was said. It was just her words came out all twisted and jumbled.

After they'd eaten he told her to stay inside while he fed the hogs and mule, and she nodded her head that she would.

Annie Laurie, knowing that it would soon be bedtime, ran to the bedroom doors and opened them, so that some of the heat from the kitchen and dining room could go into their bedrooms.

"Smart girl," Franklin said, then patted her on the blonde head before he went out of the back door.

There was a junk pile down the road from their house. Her daddy had found her several things to play with there, but she loved the thick catalogue the best. When Franklin returned Annie Laurie was sitting on the floor near the warmth of the stove looking inside the weathered old catalogue.

Franklin pulled off his thick denim coat and hung it on a nail near the back door, then locked it. He then put some more wood in the stove and dipped some warm water out of the reservoir of the stove and began to wash the dishes.

He poured the grease from the salt meat into a metal container, then replaced the lid, as lard was a precious commodity.

Laurie and Annie Laurie had a habit every night. When it was the child's bedtime, they'd get on their knees by the child's bed and pray. Laurie prayed orally, so that Annie Laurie would know what was going on. At the end of the prayer, Laurie would say Amen, and Annie Laurie would repeat with an, "Anen." Laurie would then kiss her on the forehead after she'd helped her in the bed. The last thing she'd do before she left the room would be to turn down the wick in the kerosene lamp. She always left the door ajar whether it be summer or winter.

Franklin didn't know quite what to do after he finished the dishes, but he told his daughter to use the slop jar in her room, then put on her pajamas.

"When you're ready for bed come back in here and I'll help you in," he said.

Carrying the catalogue with her, Annie Laurie went into her bedroom.

Annie Laurie returned in a few minutes wearing a pair of flannel pajamas that her mama had sewn.

"I'll help you to bed, but let's do our praying in here," Franklin said, as he pulled his daughter into his lap.

"Now, bow your head," he said, so she did.

"Dear God in heaven, I'm praying to you tonight to look after my little girl, Annie Laurie. Give us strength to go forward and face life without her mama. In your name I pray, amen," Franklin said.

"Anen," Annie Laurie muttered.

Franklin followed her into her bedroom, then after swinging her into the air, making her squeal with delight, he helped her into bed.

He knew the routine, so he kissed his daughter's forehead, told her "Good night," and left the room, after turning down the wick on the lamp.

After sitting back down at the kitchen table, Franklin wondered how he was going to make it without Laurie. He'd gathered all the pecans and sold them. All the cotton had been ginned for that year. The only other income he could fathom was the money from the split oak baskets. Nearly all the money he'd made was spent on staples already.

He thought they had enough flour, sugar, meal, and salt to last for two or three months.

"Maybe, I can sell enough baskets to make it until next fall," Franklin thought. *"If only Annie Laurie was a couple of years older,"* Franklin continued to think.

Franklin then counted the money in his pocket and found that he had sixty-three dollars and thirty-five cents. *"It'll have to do us until I start selling my baskets,"* he thought.

Before Franklin realized it, he found that his head was on the table, and he was silently crying. Not for himself, or Annie Laurie, but for Laurie. She'd never did a harmful thing to anyone, and he prayed that her body wouldn't be cold, for he

knew that red clay dirt was bound to be
chilly.

Chapter 2
December 1929

Things hadn't changed very much, except Franklin had learned they could survive. They just had to make some adjustments. First of all, Franklin learned that Annie Laurie had to be with him at all times. *"If she could only talk,"* Franklin had thought, he wouldn't be so afraid to leave her alone in the house. He'd tried at night to teach her by writing words or pointing at objects in the catalogue that she loved. When the words came out of her mouth, they'd be all twisted and garbled. The talking sessions made Annie Laurie very anxious and sometimes she'd cry. It would wind up with Franklin holding the child in his lap or rocking her in the rocking chair until she settled down.

Annie Laurie was learning though, from just watching her daddy. She'd learned to fry or scramble eggs. Make pancakes, that would be covered with cane syrup and were so delicious at breakfast time. She didn't plow the mule, but she figured she knew how to rig one up In order to plow it. Another thing she'd learned was to weave baskets, they were small, but she'd learned the trade.

Franklin had given her some small strips of the split white oak, some leftovers that were too small for him to use. He even taught her how to put good sturdy handles on them. They were more than less a novelty, but Miss Earnestine, at Kelly Mercantile bought everyone that she made. While Franklin worked at the gin house, Miss Earnestine, who was the store owner's daughter, kept an eye on the child. She'd give Annie Laurie small tasks to do, like dusting items on the shelves, or sweeping the front porch. Annie Laurie was rewarded with cold drinks or lollipops. Due to the cotton ginning, small particles of cotton swirled everywhere, so Annie Laurie kept busy. The main highway ran directly in front of the store. The gin was on the opposite side. Mules and wagons, trucks with trailers loaded with cotton formed a long line, waiting for their cotton to be ginned. The farmers didn't mind though, for the cotton meant money. The cotton was long hot arduous work, but it was what fed and clothed families for another year.

Due to the depression that had hit the country, the price of cotton had dropped from 35 cents a pound to 7 cents. To some of the farmers it would be their last year of planting it. They'd have to resort to peanuts or some other cash crop.

One afternoon, while coming back from the gin, Annie Laurie noticed that someone had thrown away a black puppy at the junk pile. Franklin stopped the mule and wagon long enough for his daughter to get the puppy.

"Alright now, the first time he digs a hole under the chicken fence and catches one of our chickens, away he goes," Franklin said.

Annie Laurie muttered something as she held the puppy next to her. Franklin noticed that he was a male, as he put the puppy in the back of the wagon, then helped Annie Laurie in the back with her puppy.

Laurie's maiden name was Lewis. Her people, a sister and brother lived in the northern end of the county at a spot in the road known as Old Texas. Franklin had written Laurie's sister a letter telling about her death. It had taken nearly two years for them to show up, but her sister and husband were sitting on the front porch when they returned home.

Franklin was glad that he had everything locked, for he'd heard that Paul Lee, or Rat, as he was commonly called, his brother-in-law was a thief. Laurie's sister was referred to as "Sister Sarie," but her name was Sarah Lee. She and Paul had a house full of children, but they were either in jail or married and had left home. Sarah was ten years older than Laurie.

Franklin acknowledged them by removing his hat as he passed by the porch. Paul did the same, while Sarah nodded her head.

The first thing Franklin noticed was the carriage and boney mule in Pete's lot. He saw that the starved mule was chowing down on Pete's corn and fodder. After putting the wagon in the barn, then corralling Pete, Franklin removed the meager amount of groceries that he'd bought. Both he and Annie Laurie entered the back door, after he'd unlocked it.

"Sit on the back porch with your puppy until we can take him to the creek and wash him for fleas and ticks," Franklin told his daughter. He then gave her a piece of salt meat that was left from breakfast, and the black puppy gladly followed her back to the porch.

After putting the groceries on the table, Franklin went outside to join his in-laws.

Sarah's nickname was Sarie, while her husband's name was "Rat." Franklin figured it was because he was tall and very skinny. His mouth also protruded, and he had pointed teeth. Rat had inherited a few acres and a ramshackle shack. It was said that he'd sit on the porches with his feet propped up while he watched his wife and children work.

Sarah, who had once been very pretty, now looked older than her years. She had sandy red hair like Laurie's but now he saw a few gray streaks in it, and she had it pulled to the back of her head and fashioned in a ball. Most of her teeth were missing. Franklin thought that their way of living really showed on them.

Franklin, not caring for "Rat Lee" didn't bother to shake his hand, and Rat didn't bother to move from his position, sitting on the front porch.

Rat, like Franklin was dressed in a pair of overalls. Both were also wearing high-topped brogan shoes.

Poor Sarie's pale green dress looked as though it had been run through a wringer. Her long skinny breast looked as though they hung to her navel.

"Frankie, Little Annie Laurie shore looks like you. I don't see any Laurie in her," Sarie said, breaking the ice.

"Thank you, Sarie. She found herself a new puppy on the way home, so she's spoiling it right now," Franklin said.

Rat rolled a Bull Durham cigarette, struck a match to light it and inhaled a long drag.

"I don't know how long y'all are planning to stay, but there'll be no smoking inside the house," Franklin said.

"I don't blame you, Lord, Paul and the boys stink up everything in the house. We just came to spend one night. I'd come sooner, but the law caught Paul making "Licker" in a swamp near our house and they gave him a year. I don't know how they expect us to make a living, starve I guess," Sarie said.

"Yeh, Christmas is less than a week away, I need to be home making a living. I been promising Sarie ever since I got out of the slammer that I'd brang her to see her sister's grave," Rat said.

"I've packed up all of Laurie's clothes to keep Annie Laurie from seeing them. You can have them if you wish," Franklin told Sarie. {In reality Franklin wanted them out of his sight. He'd be doing alright, then he'd see one of her dresses, coat, or some other personal item and he'd break down again.}

"Look, I've got to go wash a puppy, milk a goat, feed the chickens, gather eggs, feed the hogs, and Pete, the mule. If you'd like we can visit Laurie's grave, then I'll wash the puppy and get some milk out of the spring house while we're down there," Franklin said.

"Follow me down there, I already have a bar of octogen soap at the spring," Franklin said.

Franklin always kept twelve feet of the grass hoed around his house, in case of fire. The rest of the grass was kept mown by the goat, or Franklin's sling blade.

"Rat," slid off the porch, threw his cigarette on the ground and stomped it.

"Alright ole gal, you've been nagging me for a year," Rat said, as Sarie got up from the chair and followed Franklin down the doorsteps.

Annie Laurie was playing with the puppy in the backyard when Franklin introduced her to her uncle and aunt.

The child smiled and nodded her head at them. Sarie hugged the pretty little girl and held her hand while they walked across the field toward Laurie's grave.

"It's just not fair," Sarie said, as she read the inscriptions on the wooden cross at the head of her sister's grave. She was beautiful," Sarie added, as she wiped the tears away from her cheeks with the palms of her hands.

"A good woman and mama too," Franklin said, as he picked the puppy up and walked toward the spring.

Franklin kept a bar of the strong soap on top of the spring house, so he grabbed the puppy and walked downstream from where he'd be getting water for the house and began to scrub the puppy.

Annie Laurie stayed with Franklin while Rat and Sarie tarried around the grave. They stayed there long enough for Franklin to finish everything but gather the eggs.

Franklin was really surprised at Sarie's reaction, it made him feel better about her, for the time being.

"My goodness, what do you do with so many eggs?" Sarie asked as she looked at the big basket of eggs.

"Sell most of them to the store in Dottelle, and we eat a few," Franklin replied.

"I'd be eating some chicken," Sarie said.

"Well, to be frank, I know how to dress one, but I don't know how to cook it. I tried once but the chicken still had blood in it when I put it in the platter," Franklin said. Then he added, since none were killed, they just keep multiplying."

"Do you have lard and flour?" asked Sarie.

"Sure," answered Franklin.

"Let me in that pen, we'll have chicken and dumplings for supper," Sarie said.

That would be good," said Rat, as Franklin opened the door and Sarie went inside the pen.

She picked a big fat red one, grabbed it around its neck, then stepped back outside, and began to wring the chicken's neck. After making sure the chicken was dead, she added, "Now go pluck the feathers out of this sucker and bring it back to me."

Franklin remembered Laurie pouring hot water over the chicken before she plucked it, but he didn't say anything. He carried both the chicken and basket of eggs to the back porch. He set the eggs down on the back porch, then went to the barn for a croaker sack to put the feathers in. He didn't want to just throw the feathers on the ground for two reasons, it looked bad, and they'd attract varmints.

The back door was still locked, even though it was near Christmas the weather was still warm enough for them to be outside. Besides, Rat was busy smoking his cigarettes.

After plucking the feathers, Franklin took out his pocket knife and cleaned the chicken, throwing the intestines and feet on the ground for the puppy to eat.

Franklin kept a bucket of water and dipper sitting on a table on the back porch, so he washed the fat hen, then handed it to Sarie so he could unlock the backdoor.

"Bring me a clean dishpan," Sarie said.

After bringing her the pan, Franklin invited everyone in, then he began to build a fire in the stove.

Sarie commenced washing the chicken again, then began to cut the chicken into pieces.

In a few minutes she said, "Now watch me Franklin Reed, and you'll learn how to boil a chicken."

"All you need to do is cover the meat with water, then measure a teaspoon of salt In it. If you want a thick broth sprinkle about three heaping spoons of flour into the water after the chicken is done.

"Now, I'm going to make dumplings, so where is your flour and lard. I'll also need a pan to mix it in and a rolling pin," Sarie said.

"It's all in the pantry," Franklin said, as he pointed in the direction.

Sarie plundered inside the pantry.

"Oh boy, can I cook some of these dry butterbeans too?" she asked.

"Sure, cook what you want," Franklin replied.

"You have plenty of flour and lard, so I'll roll us out a big pan of biscuits too. My oh my, at the salt pork in here," Sarie said.

"Yeah, I butcher two hogs every thanksgiving," Franklin said, as he got the cast iron pan off the wall that Laurie cooked biscuits in and put it on the table.

"Can you read?" Sarie asked, as she brought the items out of the pantry.

"Sure I can read, if it's simple," Franklin replied.

"Good, I'm going to write down some simple recipes for you tonight, so you'll know how to cook some of this food. Now get this dog from under my feet so I can get this going," she said.

Franklin picked up the puppy and told Annie Laurie to follow him into the living room.

He closed the door after they were all in the big room.

It was late in the afternoon, but still light outside, so Rat said he was going to sit on the porch to smoke.

Franklin built a small fire in the fireplace, then went outside to join him.

The front of the house faced west. On a clear day Franklin and Annie Laurie loved to sit outside and watch as the sun set behind the tall pine trees in their yard.

"You shore have a nice place Franklin. Give me the country any day. I don't see how the folks in Monroeville live like they do, all jammed up together," Rat said.

"Yeah, this old place is old, but it was good enough for me, my folks, and their folks," Franklin replied.

"What's wrong with the little girl's talking?" asked Rat.

"We didn't know, she was born that way. She understands everything, even knows some words, but when she tries to talk everything's all jumbled up. She's about quit trying to talking all together," Franklin said.

"It's just not fair, for her to be so pretty and all," Rat replied.

"We used to try, but it made her so anxious, we just quit. I keep hoping I can come up with the money to send her to a specialist in Mobile. Money is scarce as hen's teeth around here though," Franklin said.

"How well I know the feeling. Folks around Old Texas don't even have money for a pint of good moonshine," Rat said.

"Well, at least she has a puppy now, something to play with. I've thought about it before, but heaven knows we just don't have enough scraps left over to feed a dog. I'm learning though," Franklin said.

"Hmph, there's not many scrapes at our house either, especially since all the young'uns are gone. There's a passel of dogs at my place too, if they don't catch it, they don't eat it. I'll swear I got a hound that can climb a tree as good as a coon," Rat said.

"Gracious," Franklin said.

"Then, I have a dog named Randy. You know folks trade things to me for shine. They'll be in sich a shape till they'll swap thangs for the stuff. I'd be willing to bet I have fifty shotguns, and no telling how many pistols. They'll swap dey wives sewing machines too, jist anything. One feller wanted to swap his wife, but I tole him Sarie wouldn't go fer that." Rat then chuckled.

Rat was more of a talker than Franklin, so he continued.

"Heck, we ain't even had no way of going till last week. I swapped old man Kearley a whole gallon fer that mule and raggedy carriage. You know it takes a feller a while to git back on his feet after he's been in jail for a year. You can't let the law rule yo life though. It took me a little while to git up they cash, but I went right back into bizness. Anyhow, I put a lot of that stuff I git into my corn crib, and Randy guards it wif his life. I'll have to admit, I feed him," Rat said.

Franklin knew Rat, and he figured he was stealing some of those things, it was just in him to steal.

"Are you still off the licker?" Franklin asked.

"Oh, yeah. I seen what it can do fer you. That stuff is meant to sell and not to drank," Rat said, as he rolled himself another Prince Albert.

It was getting dusk when Annie Laurie came out of the house holding her puppy.

They could smell the things that Sarie was cooking when Annie Laurie opened the door.

Forgetting the child couldn't talk, Rat asked her what her puppy's name was.

"Blocky," Annie Laurie said. With a struggle.

"Blacky, that's a good name for him," Rat said.

Annie Laurie nodded her head and repeated, "Blocky."

"Honey, you need to put Blacky on the ground so he can use the toilet," Franklin said.

The men could tell that Annie Laurie seemed distressed, then she made a motion with her fingers that he would run away.

"He might run around in the yard some to stretch his legs, but he'll come back, you can bet on that," Franklin said.

Annie Laurie let go of her grasp on Blacky, He gingerly made his way down the doorsteps, sniffed around outside, then peed. That was enough for the child, she ran down the doorsteps and picked Blacky up.

The two men laughed.

"Franklin looks like you have a dog," Rat said.

Rat then told Annie Laurie after Blacky ate the scraps leftover from supper, he wouldn't be going anywhere.

Annie Laurie smiled.

It wasn't long before Sarie opened the front door and hollered, "Alright, y'all can come and get it!"

Sarie had lit a kerosene lamp in the living room, so they didn't have trouble finding their way through the house.

The table was steaming from the hot foods.

"Boy, we haven't seen food like this since Laurie passed," Franklin said. He also noticed that Sarie didn't bother taking things from the boilers, as Laurie did. She'd just set the hot boilers on folded rags onto the table.

"I've never made biscuits from goat milk, no telling what they'll taste like," Sarie said.

"They look delicious!" Frank said.

They all sat around the table, while Franklin blessed the food, which was alien to Rat, for he had already reached for the handle of one of the hot boilers.

Sarie had already prepared Annie Laurie's plate, so it wouldn't be so hot. She made sure that the child had a drumstick, plus dumplings, butterbeans, and a biscuit.

In a small while nothing could be heard at the table but spoons as they hit the plates, for everyone was hungry. Soon as Annie Laurie had eaten most of the meat from the drumstick, she slipped the bone to Blacky, and he ran under the table with it.

Sarie didn't notice who ate the most, but she was mighty pleased with both Rat and Franklin.

After the main course had been eaten, Sarie gave each one of them a saucer. She didn't have to tell them what to do, they each got a biscuit and drowned it with cane syrup.

"Boy, this is some good syrup," Rat said.

"It was made right here on the farm by Annie Laurie and me," Franklin said.

"Yeh, I saw your cane mill out there," Rat said.

Rat continued, "I just don't see where you find the time," Rat added.

"Well, the sugarcane is the last thing to make, so I have the time. I cook the squeezing's, and Annie Laurie skims it. I'll give you a can of it when y'all go home," Franklin said.

"Franklin probably finds the time, because he's not laying around on the front porch waiting on the next customer," Sarie said, as she licked her saucer clean. "It is some good syrup, to be sure," she said.

After seeing everyone had finished eating, Sarie said. "Now you menfolks make yoselves scase, while me and this girl clean-up this mess. As the old saying goes, a man's work is from sun to sun, but a woman's work is never done."

The men went back to the front porch, while Annie Laurie helped her Aunt Sarie scrap the plates into one of the boilers.

"Now you take this boiler of scraps out on the front porch. The puppy will follow you after he smells it. He'll be right outside when you get up in the morning," Sarie told Annie Laurie.

Annie Laurie didn't like the idea, but she did as her Aunt said, besides, she sort of reminded her of her almost forgotten mama.

Sarie saw the extra bed in the corner of the living room and imagined that's where she and Rat would be sleeping. So she threw a small piece of wood in the fireplace, then she and Annie Laurie went outside to join the men. She discovered they were talking about President Hoover, and Model T trucks.

"Yessir, Hoover ain't worth the salt that goes in his bread. He's the very reason we're driving in that carriage out there. If it wasn't for him, I'd be driving me one of them new Model T trucks," Rat said.

"You're right, cars and trucks are getting mighty popular around here too," Franklin said.

"Well I'm gonna cut this baby's hair before we leave tomorrow, when it's hanging down to her behind, it's time to cut it," Sarie said. She had grabbed Annie Laurie and pulled her into her lap. "I don't believe this child's hair has been brushed since her mammy passed," she added.

"Probably hadn't," Franklin answered.

"Chile, a lady brushes her hair one hundred strokes every night, and you have such pretty blonde hair too. We'll get your hair really soaped up in the morning after breakfast and brush those tangles right out of there. That is, after I trim it up some, " Sarie said.

Aunt Sarie's strokes on her back and shoulders were so soothing. Annie Laurie had forgotten how good a woman's touch felt. With a full tummy and the female affection, it wasn't long before Annie Laurie was yawning.

Sarie rocked her a little more and she felt her go limp in her arms.

"Franklin Reed, you can put your baby to bed now. She's already gone to sleep, so she can get her bath in the morning," his sister-in-law said.

Franklin did as he was asked, and he was amazed at how clean and orderly the kitchen and dining room were. For he had to walk through it to get to Annie Laurie's room.

After he'd eased her into her bed, he said a small prayer over her and kissed her tenderly on the forehead. He made sure to turn down the wick in the kerosene lamp at the door, before he went back outside to join his company. He noticed that Sarie had slipped inside and put on an old worn sweater, but she was still rocking away.

Franklin resumed his spot on the doorsteps.

"It sure is quiet and peaceful here. All you can hear are the whippoorwills," Rat said, then he blew a cloud of smoke out of his mouth.

"Yeah, it is. It's the only place I've ever known," Franklin said.

"It's an old house, but solid. Franklin, you need to put some window panes in, instead of those shutters. My Lord, these old shutters went out with Methuselah. Windows are air tight too. On cold days you can look outside and not have to open the shutter," Sarie said.

"Well, I'm sure they'd be fine, but what little amount of money I can save back I'm planning on sending Annie Laurie to a doctor. Maybe he can do something with her tongue. It looks like it's twisted side-ways," Franklin said.

"Poor baby, she's as cute as can be too. She has your looks though. I don't see a smidgen of Laurie in her. Laurie was slim too, while this child is stocky like you. Yes sir, blonde hair and all. Another thing, while I'm at it. Why do you dress her in those long dresses, they're out of style," Sarie said.

"Well, since Laurie passed, I've been getting Mrs. Peacock to sew her clothes for her. She's a sweet old lady. She has a grandson, his name is Lee, he lives with her. He and Annie Laurie sure play well together. They live down the road from the store in Dottelle. Mrs. Peacock wears the same type dresses, with bonnets to match," Franklin said.

"She must be of the Holliness faith," Sarie said.

"I don't know what she is, all I know is she's a sweet old lady, Besides, Laurie made them like that, and my daughter seems satisfied with the dresses and bonnets she wears.

Rat could tell from the sound of Franklin's voice, that he was getting peeved about what the child wore, so he told Sarie to shut up about it.

"Sarie, you raised our girls, let Franklin raise his," Rat said.

Sarie didn't say anything else, but she got up from the rocking chair and went inside.

"Women," Rat said, after he was sure Sarie was inside.

The men didn't tarry long after that before they too went inside.

Franklin woke up the next morning before anyone else. He put on clean clothes, then turned the lamp off in Annie Laurie's room. The morning was cool and brisk, as he made his way outside to milk the goat and do his morning chores.

After milking the goat, he grabbed the water bucket off the back porch. After reaching the springhouse he swapped the warm container of milk for a cold one, then dipped the bucket into the spring for some fresh water.

He went back into the kitchen and put the cold milk on the table, hoping Sarie would make them some more biscuits. He then made a fire in the stove, checked the reservoir in the stove and found it needed water. He then got both buckets out of the kitchen and headed back to the spring. He filled both buckets, pouring one in Pete's trough and the other into the hog's trough. After that he threw the animals some corn in their pens.

The last thing he did was go back to the spring for two more buckets of water. He poured the chickens a little water through the wire fence, then shelled eight ears of corn and threw it inside for the eager chickens to eat.

After he'd finished with the chickens, he went back inside with the two buckets of water. It was getting daylight outside, so he dipped into the reservoir for some warm water to shave, then poured the half full bucket of water into the reservoir, which filled it. The other bucket of water he set on the table beside the milk.

Franklin shaved on the back porch with a straight razor. He had nailed a piece of mirror against the wall, along with his razor strap.

He soaped the blonde stub on his face and neck, whetted the razor on the leather strap a few times, and commenced to shaving. Franklin was a clean shaving man, but Rat had a long swooping red mustache. Really, Franklin's big hurry was to watch how Sarie made those biscuits.

After he'd washed and dried his face and walked through the kitchen he saw that Sarie was washing her hands from a pan of warm water that was on the back of the stove.

"Good morning," he said.

She returned the greeting. "If only I had a pantry full of food like y'all, I'd be cooking for a spell," she said.

"Well, just help yourself to it, cook all you want," Robert said.

Franklin's next task was he took a pan of warm water, a cake of soap and bath cloth into Annie Laurie's room.

She was awake, but still drowsy.

"Alright, bathe from head to toe while the water is warm. By the time you're finished, Aunt Sarie should have breakfast on the table," Robert told her.

Annie Laurie smiled and struggled to say something. It sounded like she said, "Aunt Sarie reminds me of meme. She cooks good too."

"Yeh, she reminds me of your mama too, and she is a good cook. Now you wash good and put on some clean clothes. Show Aunt Sarie what a big girl you are," Robert said.

Annie Laurie smiled and nodded her head.

Franklin went back into the kitchen for a cup of the coffee he smelled brewing.

Rat and Sarie were sitting down at the table, enjoying a cup of the black brew.

"Good morning, Rat," Franklin said. Rat acknowledged his greeting by throwing up his hand.

"I always enjoy a cup of coffee before I start with the breakfast," Sarie said.

"It sure makes a difference, and I'd like to say that it's so nice having someone here to talk too," Franklin said in a low-keyed voice, so Annie Laurie couldn't hear him.

Franklin took his normal seat at the head of the table, and Sarie shoved a cup of coffee his way.

"Well, it's been nice, but we have to load up and head back to Old Texas after breakfast," Rat said.

"I'd be the first to admit, a fellow does what he has to do, but y'all visit more often. I stay too busy to visit y'all," Franklin said.

"Shoot, I don't see how you get around to everything," Rat said.

"I stay busy, especially in the spring and summer, then in the fall, I'm at the gin, making syrup, making baskets and cutting wood to burn in the stove and fireplace. We seldom go into the living room though. We stay right here in the kitchen and dining room," Franklin admitted.

Sarie soon smacked her lips, as she set her empty cup on the table and headed toward the pantry. It wasn't long before she returned with a big sack of hominy grits and the biscuit bowl.

"We'll be having grits, fried eggs, salt meat, and biscuits for breakfast, if that suits you," Sister Sarie said.

"Yeh, sounds good to me," Franklin said.

Franklin noticed every move that Sarie made.

First, she sliced the salt meat and put the sliced pieces into a boiler of water to boil.

"If you'll start smoking this hog belly, you won't have to drown it with salt. That way you won't have to boil the salt out," Sarie said.

Franklin didn't tell her that he'd been frying it without boiling it first, and it was nigh impossible to eat.

Next, she poured some flour in the biscuit bowl, then dipped her hand into the can of lard, putting the lard into the middle of the flour. Next, she poured about a pint of the goat milk into the bowl, and with her right hand she began to work the ingredients into the flour until it formed a big ball.

She'd already greased two frying pans. She then dusted her left hand with the flour and rubbed her hands together until all the dough from her right hand fell into the garbage pail. She then dusted both hands with the flour. Mashing the flour dough with her left hand, she got enough dough into her right hand to make a biscuit. Then dusting her hands again she began to roll up the dough into a ball and put the balls of dough into the pans. She'd mash the ball down with the back of her hand and start rolling another one.

Each pan held twelve biscuits. How Sarie knew how much flour to pour into the bowl to make precisely twenty-four biscuits, Franklin didn't know. He guessed it was from experience.

While the biscuits were baking she put the water on to boil for the grits.

He watched her with the grits too, for he and Annie Laurie were tired of eating salt meat and flap jacks.

The grits were simple, she simply poured a small amount of salt into the water, then about two cups of grits. After stirring them good, she moved the grits to the middle of the stove to reduce the heat.

Next, she forked the boiling meat out of the salt water, after rinsing it in water, she put it into a frying pan and commenced to frying it.

"Boy, this meat has enough fat in it to fry the eggs, and that's what she did, she fried eight of them.

The whole ordeal didn't take Sarie over twenty minutes. By then, Annie Laurie was up and had already gone to the back porch to check on her puppy.

In a few minutes, Sarie had everything on the table. Franklin thought everything looked good. The biscuits turned out a golden brown and the grits weren't cooked so thick, they were sort of soupy, the way Franklin liked them.

The filled syrup pitcher was setting on a plate in the middle of the table.

The grownups drank coffee with their meal, while Annie Laurie drank the goat milk, only her Aunt Sarie stirred a little cane syrup into it.

As the night before everyone ate heartily, then ate biscuit and syrup as a dessert.

"Boy, if you lived here, I'd be too fat to work," Franklin said.

"Oh, I don't know about that, look at me, I stay slim and trim," Rat said.

"Hmph, in your case I need something to cook," Sarie answered.

"Ah, stop your complaining, we have enough," Rat answered, as he drank the last of the coffee.

"Well, if you're determined to get home before dark, I'd better get up from here and clean up this kitchen," Sarie remarked.

Annie Laurie helped her aunt scrape out the dishes, then went to the back porch to feed Blacky.

The men went outside to get Rat the can of syrup. While they were out there, Rat asked Franklin if he could have a sack of corn to feed his mule. Franklin obliged him.

"If there was room in that carriage, I could use some of the fodder too," Rat said.

After Sarie finished getting the kitchen in order, she was bound and determined to trim Annie Laurie's hair.

She asked Annie Laurie about some scissors and comb, so she went into her daddy's room and returned to the kitchen with them.

Sarie poured all of the water that was remaining in one bucket into the other, then dipped warm water out of the reservoir into the empty bucket.

"Now, follow me to the back porch," Sarie told the child.

Annie Laurie was told to hold her head over her daddy's shaving pan, which she did.

It was a struggle, but Sarie finally got the ends of Annie Laurie's hair into the pan.

"Now close your eyes and don't open them until I tell you to," Sarie told her.

Sarie started at the nape of her neck and slowly began to pour the warn water over Annie Laurie's hair until the pan was full.

After that she began scrubbing her head and hair with the strong octagon soap.

"Now hold your head up but don't open your eyes," Sarie said.

After soaping the ends of her hair, she took the towel that was around Annie Laurie's shoulders and held it against Annie Laurie's face.

"Hold the towel against your face," Sarie said, as she began to twist the ends of Annie Laurie's hair.

"Annie Laurie has never had bangs, so this should be easy," Sarie thought.

After wringing most of the suds out, she wiped Annie Laurie's face, then, sitting on the top doorstep with Annie Laurie between her legs she began to comb her hair.

The wide tooth comb slid through Annie Laurie's blonde hair, except for a couple of tangles, which she cut out with the scissors, cutting as little hair as possible.

Sarie would just sling the soap suds from the comb on the ground.

After Sarie had finished she told Annie Laurie to stand up, she then began to cut.

It was so easy, she cut the tangled ends off about six inches. She'd combed all of Annie Laurie's hair to the back, making it easy to cut.

After Sarie had finished, she said, "Now stand right there with the towel against your face and I'll be right back," Sarie said.

Annie Laurie did as she was asked, as Sarie went back into the house for more warm water and a dry towel.

When Sarie returned, she poured the clear water over Annie Laurie's head and hair, until it was rinsed.

"Now, wipe your face and hair where you are," Sarie said, as she began to comb the child's hair straight back.

"Now, see, no tangles. My, my, you're a lucky little girl. Them old gals of mine would kill for hair this color," Sarie told her.

After Sarie was satisfied, she said, "Now go look in your mirror how pretty you are. Remember to give it a hundred stokes a night. Can you count to a hundred? Sarie asked.

Annie Laurie smiled and nodded her head that she could.

"Good, your Uncle Rat can only count as high as twenty."

"Pull that damp dress off and put on a dry one. Just hang it across a chair or something, it'll dry pretty fast that way," Sarie told her.

It didn't take Sarie long to put what clothes she'd worn back into the sack that she'd brought. After making the bed, she ran to the toilet, and she was ready to go.

Rat was anxious to go, or she would have stayed longer. For at least, if it was only for a night, she'd left the trouble of her wayward children behind her.

Rat had lain the sack of corn in the bottom of the carriage, and their knees were almost up to their face. Having little room inside the carriage, Franklin had tied the big cloth sack of Laurie's things to the back of the carriage.

Sarie jumped out of the carriage when she saw Annie Laurie standing on the front porch. She hugged the child's neck and whispered, "I love you," before she ran back to the old carriage.

"Franklin Reed, I left you some cooking do's and don'ts on the bed in the living room," Sarie shouted back.

Annie Laurie waved at them as they zig zagged through the pines to reach the road.

Franklin walked over to his daughter and said, "My, my, just look how pretty you are," as he ran his rough hand over her hair that ran down her back.

Chapter 3

Soon as Rat and Sarie left, he poured water into the big black cast iron pot in the back yard, then built a fire around it. He really felt dumb. He'd never noticed that Laurie only sprinkled the bacon with salt, then hung it in the smoke house to smoke. He knew the hams were smoked, and he was saving one for Christmas and one for Easter.

After he'd brought all the salted hog belly out of the house and put it into the boiling pot, he hooked the ground slide to Pete.

Annie Laurie, as usual was watching everything he done.

"Hop into the ground slide and let's see if we can find a Christmas tree," Franklin said, so Annie Laurie climbed in.

Franklin had spotted a small cedar tree in the woods near the springhouse, so off they went, with Blacky following them.

Franklin had the reins in one hand and the axe in the other.

In a small while they were headed back to the house, only this time Blacky was riding in the ground slide with the tree. Annie Laurie hung to her daddy's back pocket on the way back.

Franklin laid the Christmas tree on the back porch, then unhooked the ground slide and put Pete back into his pen.

Next, he built a small fire on the dirt floor of the smokehouse, then using the pan that he'd brought the salt meat out with, he used a pitchfork to retrieve the bacon from the black pot, putting it in the pan.

This time, after opening the smokehouse, he noticed one of the hams was missing.

"Why that Rat, just when I was about to change my mind about him," Franklin thought.

He used the sharp pitchfork to put the slabs of hot bacon on the wire hooks above the fire. He then went to the woodpile and brought two big pieces of oak and put them on the fire. The green oak would smoke until the next day, then he'd put some more in.

Annie Laurie was anxious to get to the Christmas tree, so he filled a foot tub nigh full of dirt, then using the axe he trimmed the limbs from the bottom of the cedar tree.

Since the tree was so prickly, he used some gloves to jam the tree into the soil of the foot tub, and it stood up straight as a judge.

"Now, we'll put it in the living room away from the fireplace, then we'll decorate it," Franklin told the grinning child.

The only decoration that Annie Laurie had to decorate with was cotton balls. The cotton Franklin had brought from the cotton gin in Dottelle.

While Annie Laurie was having a good time decorating the tree, Franklin was reading the notes that Sarie had left for him on the bed.

Franklin grinned, either Sarie thought he was a dumb oaf, or she was near illiterate, for the words were very simple and most were misspelled. He made the recipes out though.

Some of the foods were so simple to make. Now they could have cornbread, beans, peas, assorted greens, simple cobblers and puddings. Even cornbread dressing, which he was going to attempt for Christmas dinner. Even though it looked so simple for Sarie, he knew he couldn't make biscuits, so they'd have to stick with pancakes.

Franklin folded Sarie's "cooking" papers up and put them in his back pocket. He then told Annie Laurie he was going outside to do the chores while she decorated the tree. She nodded her head, so he walked into the kitchen and grabbed the water buckets.

The first thing he did was to milk the goat, then feed the animals and chickens.

He walked to the springhouse and exchanged the milk, leaving it on the top of the springhouse, he dipped the buckets into the water and watered the animals and chickens.

Returning down the well-worn path, he returned to the springhouse and filled the two buckets.

The milk container was a wide mouth fruit jar with a lid on it that tightened, so after making sure it was tightened, he simply dropped it into one of the buckets.

After carrying the water and milk into the kitchen, he returned to the chicken pen and gathered the eggs. Blacky followed him to the spring, then back to the house and chicken pen.

Franklin noticed that the shadows were getting long from the pine trees. So, he hurried to put stove wood on the back porch. After finishing that, he carried the eggs into the kitchen.

After building a fire in the stove, he walked into the living room to see how Annie Laurie was doing with the tree. Surprisingly, Franklin thought she was doing very well, most all the cotton balls were about the same size. Franklin did his usual. He went outside and sat on the doorsteps to watch the sun set. He didn't know why but it seemed relaxing to him. Of course, he always thought of Laurie, but more so in the afternoons, sitting there on his doorsteps, observing the remnants of the day. He hoped that Rat and Sarie would make it back home.

Blacky soon discovered where Franklin was at and laid across his shoes hoping he'd get a stroke down his back.

He wasn't there long though, for Blacky heard the chickens making a racket as they flew on their roost, so with a growl, he went to investigate.

Franklin got up to begin supper. Sarie had cooked them an extra baker of biscuits, so he was glad of that.

The simple directions on cooking that Sarie left seemed so easy. Franklin had wished so many times that he'd been paying closer attention to Laurie when she cooked. The two were sick of salt meat, pancakes, and syrup three times a day.

That night for supper they had rice Which he'd never cooked}, two fried eggs each, biscuits, and syrup.

They each ate heartily too.

Franklin knew that night that he wouldn't be selling as many eggs to Kelly's Mercantile.

"Just think, we'll be having smoked bacon in a few days, and that's not including the smoked ham we're having for Christmas dinner," Franklin told his daughter.

Annie Laurie replied by rubbing her stomach.

They each made sure they left a little leftover to stir in with the rice remaining in the boiler for Blacky's supper. Franklin dared to put the remainder of the biscuits in the dog's food though. *"We'll have them for breakfast the next morning,"* he thought, for he knew he'd never be able to make a biscuit.

Annie Laurie helped her father to clear away the table, then she took the few scraps of food to the back porch to feed Blacky, while Franklin did the dishes.

At some time or other, Annie Laurie had found a good leather belt in the junk pile that someone had thrown away. The belt was too small for her daddy, but she'd brought it home anyway and put it in her room.

After feeding Blacky and giving him a couple of hugs, she brought the boiler back into the kitchen to be washed, then ran to her room for the belt.

She waited patiently at the table for her father to finish with the dishes, then she got the smallest butcher knife she could find.

Franklin noticed her and asked what she was up to.

"Blocky," she answered, as she pretended to cut the leather.

"Oh, you're wanting a collar for your puppy," Franklin said.

Annie Laurie nodded her head. "Fa Sandy," she struggled to say.

"A Christmas gift for Blacky?" Franklin asked.

Annie Laurie smiled and nodded her head.

"Ok, but I'm just guessing at it," Franklin said, as he cut the leather, then began to bore holes in it.

Annie Laurie ran back into her room and tore out a colorful page from the catalogue, and along with some red thread, she ran back into the kitchen.

"Oh, so now you want it wrapped," Franklin said.

Again, Annie Laurie nodded her head.

After Franklin had did the best he could do with it, he gave it to her and she ran into the living room, then placed it under the tree.

"It's a fine thing when a dog gets the first gift under the tree," Franklin said, while his precious daughter smiled and nodded her head.

"Brr, it's chilly in here, I say we go back into the kitchen where it's warmer," Franklin said.

There was one old rocker in the dining room. The two had grown accustomed to Franklin telling her Christmas stories at Christmas time.

Franklin sat down in the rocker and patted his lap. Annie Laurie remembered what was about to take place, so she crawled into his lap, waiting for the story to begin.

Franklin always made up the Christmas stories that he told his daughter. Some would be about her and Santa Claus, and others would be in a faraway land with plenty of snow and mountains. Santa would have a heck of a time getting around to everyone's house, but if they'd been good, he always made it.

Franklin told her two stories before she began to yawn.

"No, no, you're not going to sleep without a bath. Don't you know that Santa won't visit children that doesn't take baths?" he asked.

"I'll build a fire in the living room and sit in there awhile. You can take your bath right here in the kitchen, where it's warm. I'll dip you a pan of warm water out of the reservoir," he said.

Annie Laura slid out of his lap and ran to her room to get her pajamas, while Franklin got her a bath cloth and bar of soap. He placed all the items on the table, then walked into the living room to build a fire in the fireplace.

He hadn't enjoyed the warmth of the fireplace long, before Annie Laurie came in looking clean and smelling good. He kissed her on the forehead, patted her on the back and told her sweet dreams. She rubbed her tummy, indicating that she had enjoyed her supper, then ran toward her bedroom.

Franklin continued to sit in his rocking chair, thinking of the future. At one time he'd thought about remarrying, but he knew he'd be marrying for the wrong reasons. To begin with, he didn't see how in the world he could raise a small child, farm, and do his other things. Things to make money. They literally lived off the land, but there was money needed to buy clothes, shoes, flour, sugar, coffee, salt, and so many other things. The good Lord that he prayed to every night had seen them through it though, and he thanked him right there in his rocking chair for it.

They had plenty of sweet potatoes in the bank, {A sweet potato bank was a hole dug on high ground, with sweet potatoes and pine straw in the hole.} It was covered with a shelter to keep the rain out. The shelter had a small door on one end, so you could get to the potatoes. The corn crib was full of corn, for the winter months. There was plenty of fodder in the loft of the barn for the mule and goat. Plenty of meat in the pantry and smoke house. Preserving the meat is what took so much salt. While butchering a hog, he'd put a layer of meat and a layer of salt in the barrel. You had to wash the salt off the meat before you could cook it. Since Sarie's visit he'd learned to boil the salt out of the meat.

Franklin loved planting things and watching them grow, but he'd also learned that farming relied strictly on the weather. Luckily he had good rich soil, and it slopped, making it nearly impossible for his crop to flood. He loved his jobs on the farm, all except gathering the fodder.

Gathering fodder was a hot arduous job. While the stalks and leaves were still green, you had to crook one arm, then walk between the rows stripping the leaves, or blades off. You'd lay seventeen blades in the crook of your arm, then with the eighteenth one you'd loop it around the bundle and tie it. By the time he'd get to the end of the rows his left arm would be bleeding, as the blades were very sharp.

Franklin had scars up and down the inside of his left arm from years past.

Making the syrup was another task. Squeezing from the stalks of cane was used for that. The tops of the stalks were cut off, then buried, and that's what you'd plant the next year.

It took three containers to make the syrup, they were all hooked together. The first container was the largest, the containers, or vats were made of metal. A big fire was used for the big container. A smaller fire was used for the second container. Franklin would stir and dip the foam off the top. When the syrup would become ropey, he'd pull up a small door, allowing it to get into the second container. Both he and Annie Laurie would steadily dip the foam off the top, he didn't want foam in the syrup. When the liquid turned thick and there wasn't any foam on top, the third door was opened, and the syrup would pour into it. Later, after the syrup was cooled down, they put a can beneath the last vat, the plug was pulled from the outside of the vat, and the golden colored syrup would soon fill the can.

Franklin would usually store ten-fifteen half gallons of syrup into the barn.

Franklin thought of several things that night, but as usual his thoughts always returned to Laurie and Annie Laurie.

He heard rain as it hit the tin top of his house and he knew what that meant, cold weather was coming.

Franklin went into the kitchen and brought back a pan of water. He placed it on the hearth of the fireplace.

He checked on Annie Laurie, then turned down the wick in her lamp. He then stripped down to his Union underwear and bathed in the kitchen.

Franklin couldn't sleep with a light in his room, so he made his way into the bed by feeling with his hands.

After saying his prayers and thanking the Lord for his many blessings, he went to sleep thinking they'd have grits and eggs for breakfast.

The next morning Franklin couldn't help but feel proud of himself, he thought he'd did a good job with the grits, and he found that frying eggs was a whiz. After breakfast and Franklin had cleaned the kitchen, he told Annie Laurie to put on her coat, for they were going to the store.

Annie Laurie wondered what was up, because usually they just walked to "Miss Earnestine's," but today they were going by mule and wagon. The store sold everything from baby items to caskets. The store, which was about a mile and a half away from their house was now commonly known as "Miss Earnestine's" even though her father owned it. Her father, who was a senator. He also owned Kelly's Mercantile in Excel, which wasn't but about two miles away from Dottelle. Senator Kelly owned a world of land in the area and several rental houses. He, his wife, son, and Miss Earnestine lived in a beautiful home in Excel.

Whereas, Dottelle only had the store, gin, and a Methodist church, Excel had several smaller stores, three churches, a bank, two boarding houses, dentist, doctor, two barbers, and a new brick school. Excel also had a couple of bootleggers that lived at the edge of town, one toward Jones Mill and the other toward Monroeville. Since Franklin was a teetotaler, he never frequented the places.

Franklin had been right the night before the weather had turned colder that morning. As they left Blacky followed behind the wagon, so Franklin stopped the mule, jumped from the wagon and put Blacky in the back of the wagon. The puppy quickly made his way to Annie Laurie, and she picked him up.

"Alright, you're gonna have to tend to him at the store, Miss Earnestine won't allow a dog inside," her daddy said. He then continued, "Maybe I can find a place on the side of the store, it'll help block the wind and you can sit in the wagon. That way only your head will be sticking up."

Annie Laurie nodded her head, as her teeth shattered, not totally from the weather, but sitting on a plank in a wagon was a rough ride.

In about fifteen minutes they passed Woodlawn Methodist Church, so Annie Laurie knew they didn't have far to go. They had met several vehicles on the narrow dirt road and Franklin pulled over to let them have the road.

Finally, Franklin reached the place. He saw the trusted black man that worked at the store standing on the porch, his name was Columbus, but most folks referred to him as "Lum."

Franklin asked Lum if he could keep an eye on Annie Laurie while he was inside the store.

"Yassuh, I'll look out fah hur, long as Miss Earnestine, she don't calls me," Lum said.

"Thank you Lum, I'm just going to do a little Christmas shopping," Franklin told him.

When Franklin went inside, Lum told Annie Laurie, "I gots a little fye bunning in the back of the sto, ifs you wanna go back dare."

Annie Laurie waved her hand from side to side, indicating that she'd stay out front. She then reached into the wagon and picked up Blacky.

Lum smiled, then reached into the bib of his overalls and brought out a big fat cigar and lit it.

"Maybe eyes can git a lick or two of dis fo Miss Earnestine send fuh me," he mumbled to himself. He then added, "Lawd, folks sho is buying in dare todays."

Annie Laurie could tell by the amount of mules and wagons, carriages, and vehicles that Mr. Lum was right.

The happy acting people came in and out of the store, but she didn't know any of them, for she seldom left the house.

Mr. Lum stayed busy too, helping the shoppers carry their purchases to their vehicles. He never took the cigar out of his mouth, but it looked like the fire had gone out and he was chewing on it.

Once, when he came out, he brought her a 7-up and five oatmeal cookies.

After about an hour of sitting on the porch, Mr. Lum walked across the road to a warehouse and brought back a long metal pole and two rolls of wire. He put it all into the wagon. The pole slid up and down or the wagon couldn't have held it.

Soon, her daddy and Mr. Lum came out with a cardboard box and three big paper bags. Annie Laura had no idea what was in the box and bags, but her daddy sure looked happy.

Without turning Blacky loose, her daddy grabbed her under the arms and put them both back into the wagon.

After they had made their way from the store and were headed back toward home, her daddy said, "I have you a special treat in one of those bags."

Annie Laurie looked at him with a puzzle look in her eyes.

"It's called Kool Aid. Everyone is drinking it. I got two flavors, grape and orange. Miss Earnestine said she sold the steam out of it. Now, when I'm drinking my coffee, you can be drinking your Kool aid," her daddy said.

Annie Laurie was anxious to try it out, but of course, she didn't attempt to say anything.

She didn't believe in Santa Claus, or else she could talk, but she wouldn't dare admit it to her daddy. She just hoped some of the things in the paper bags were things to go under the tree. She was pretty sure one of the bags had apples in it, for now and then, she could get a whiff of them.

She noticed they were moving mighty slowly and carefully on their way home. Franklin admitted to her that he had bought a radio, "I've been paying two dollars a month on it, but I paid it off this morning. Now when your Aunt Sarie comes back for a visit, she can teach me to dance," he said.

Annie Laurie rarely Laughed but she did at her daddy's last statement, she just couldn't see her daddy dancing with Aunt Sarie or anyone else. They soon passed the junk pile. They saw there was a pile of new junk thrown into the growing heap, but they passed on by. Annie Laurie knew her daddy was anxious to get the radio up and running. Her young mind didn't know much about a radio. She had seen them in her catalogue, and on one page a couple was dancing in front of one.

She could hear the goat bleating, wanting to be milked as they crossed the ditch that led to the lane to their house.

It had turned out to be a cold clear day. Franklin stopped the mule in front of the house. The chores would just have to wait until he got a fire going for Annie Laurie and the radio inside, plus the food items that he had purchased.

The first thing that Franklin did was pick Annie Laurie up out of the wagon and placed her on the front porch, then ran up the steps and unlocked the door.

"Leave Blacky outside; you come on in out of the cold while I get a fire going in the fireplace. Now, don't look Inside any of the bags I bring in," he told her.

Annie Laurie put Blacky down and he ran down the doorsteps into the yard, while the two raced into the living room.

By using a large amount of kerosene, Franklin soon had a roaring fire going. After bringing everything in the wagon inside, he went outside to get the wagon into the barn and unbridle Pete after he was in his lot.

It was still too early to feed everything, but he knew he had to milk the goat in order to quieten her down.

Before long the room was warming, so Annie Laurie pulled off her coat and was enjoying the warmth of the fire. She could hear her father as he dug a hole with the hole diggers and the rattle of the long pipe. Before long he was poking a wire under the shudder in the living room.

"Grab the wire and pull it to the middle of the room," he shouted from outside, so Annie Laurie did as he asked.

In just a few minutes her daddy came through the front door holding the big cardboard box.

"Close the door behind me," he asked, so she did.

Franklin used his sharp pocket knife to cut around the top of the box. He then reached into the box and pulled out the radio.

It was without a doubt the most beautiful thing she'd ever seen. It had a sharp oval top, with knobs in front and a soft cloth like front.

Franklin soon had the wire attached to the back. He set the radio on top of a centerpiece table and turned a knob.

"The tubes have to get warmed up before we'll hear anything," he told his daughter. Soon they heard static, then her father began twisting one of the knobs. The first song they heard was, "Aint Misbehaving," and Annie Laurie squealed with delight. The next song was "Tiptoe Through the Tulips." The announcer soon announced that the music was coming from WCKY, Cincinnati, Ohio.

"My, my, I'll bet it's cold up that far north," her daddy said. He then added, "It's about time that we move into the twentieth century."

Franklin allowed Annie Laurie to continue listening to the radio while he fetched water for the house and animals, and of course, do his other chores.

In about forty-five minutes Franklin came through the back door with a basket of eggs and started a fire in the stove.

Annie Laurie heard him in the kitchen, but she was so enthralled with the magic sound of the radio until she stayed in the living room.

Bessie Smith was singing, "Saint Louis Blues," and Annie Laurie thought, *"Oh, if I could sing like that!"*

Franklin was still wearing his thick denim jacket when he came into the living room and threw another piece of wood on the fire.

"It's gonna be a cold one out there tonight, you better wear your thick flannel pajamas to bed that Mrs. Peacock made you," he told his daughter. He then added, "That radio operates off a battery. I'll have to turn it off until we eat supper, then we'll turn it back on."

Annie Laurie nodded her head that she understood.

After turning the radio off, he grabbed the bags and went into the kitchen. He put two of the bags on top of a tall cabinet, and the other he opened. She saw the two bottles of Kool Aid. One was dark blue and the other orange. Both had labels that had a smiling child on it.

"So, what would you like to drink, orange or grape?" Her daddy asked.

Annie Laurie pointed toward the bottle with the purple liquid.

"Ok, grape, it will be," he said, as he read the directions on the label.

She watched him carefully as he dipped two teaspoons of sugar and put it in a glass, then measured the Kool aid with the cap that came off the top. Last, but not least, he poured water to nearly the top of the glass and stirred it all up.

"Let me know what you think?" he asked, as he laid the glass on the table.

Of course, she was anxious to try it, so she picked the glass up and took a small swallow.

"Umm," she said, as she licked her lips.

Franklin smiled, then turned toward the bag and brought out a can of spam.

The can had a key glued to the top.

Franklin took the key and opened the can of processed meat.

"Now don't you do this until you're older. The metal strip I took off is razor sharp and so is the top of the can," he told her, as he shook the loaf of meat into a saucer. He then cut the meat into thick slices and began to fry it.

The stove wasn't that hot, so he had time to hang his coat on the nail by the door and go to the pantry for the flour.

Flap jacks, or pancakes, were used as a substitute for biscuits. After pouring a little used grease into the flour bowl and adding the goat milk he began to stir the mixture. After stirring the flap jacks, he turned over the spam in the frying pan.

Eggs were another staple of every meal, except for when dried vegetables were cooked, so lastly her daddy fried them four eggs. One for her and three for himself.

Annie Laurie had never eaten spam before, but like the Kool Aid,

She liked it. The Kool Aid didn't have the fizzle that the 7up had though.

Annie Laurie couldn't help but wonder what was in the bags on top of the cabinet while she ate.

Franklin had thrown together a quick meal, for he had heard about "The Grand Ole Opry," and he wanted to listen to it.

After they had eaten, the scraps were raked out on the back porch for Blacky's supper and quickly washed the dishes.

"You'd better be watching me, you'll be doing this one day," Franklin said, as Annie Laurie drank the last of her Kool Aid, so her father could wash the glass.

The fireplace didn't warm the living room like the stove did in the kitchen and dining room, but they managed it without their coats.

Franklin turned the first knob on the left until they heard music. He then turned the knob on the right to WSM 650, and the announcer introduced Deford Bailey. Annie Laurie had never heard of DeFord Bailey, but he could sure blow a harmonica. She enjoyed watching her daddy, for she could sure tell he was enjoying listening to the Grand Ole Opry.

They listened to the radio until eight o'clock. After that, the station had so much static until the music was hardly legible. Franklin feared something might be wrong with the radio until he turned the knob back to WCKY and found that it was still clear.

Franklin then turned the radio off, being satisfied there wasn't anything wrong with the instrument, he said, "Well, we need to save the battery anyway. It was good while it lasted though."

The fire in the fireplace was still burning well, so Annie Laurie crawled into her daddy's lap, and he told her more stories about Santa Claus until she went to sleep.

That year for Christmas she got a baby doll from under the tree, and some new underwear, clothes, shoes, and fruit.

For Christmas dinner, Franklin boiled a chicken then baked it, along with the ham. With the broth of the chicken, he chopped up an onion and made cornbread dressing. Both Annie Laurie and Franklin thought everything turned out good.

Chapter 4

1934

It was September, Annie Laurie would be ten years old the next month.

She was now doing most of the household work, which involved most of the cooking, washing all of the dishes, and keeping the house clean. She washed and ironed her own clothes, but Franklin took care of his. She'd noticed that her daddy was beginning to stoop, but it didn't seem to slow him down. They had gathered everything in the fields, except the sugarcane, it was always cut, and syrup was made in October.

Since Annie Laurie was doing most of the housework, Franklin and Blacky had time to go hunting. Blacky had turned into a good hunting dog, plus watch dog.

There wasn't much to hunt, except rabbits, quail, squirrels, racoons, and "Possums."

Franklin had sewn him a thick canvass bag with a shoulder strap on it, and that's what he'd put the bounty in.

Blacky loved squirrel hunting and chasing the rabbits more than anything else. When Franklin came home to skin and clean the animals, he'd always give Blacky the head from the squirrels and rabbits. The dog didn't seem to have a bit of trouble crushing the skulls and gobbling them down.

Franklin had told Annie Laurie that a snake didn't stand a chance with the dog. "He'll wait until the snake strikes at him, and that's when Blacky will grab him behind his head and shake him to death," her daddy said.

Franklin and Blacky only hunted in the winter months. Franklin always hunted with a single shot .22 rifle. He had a .12-gauge shotgun, but said the shotgun damaged the animal too much, plus the shells were too expensive.

Franklin always cooked what he killed, and Annie Laurie had to admit, it sure beat eating pork all the time.

It was in September when the hurricane came.

The day was dark and windy when they made their walk to Miss Earnestine's store. They were out of sugar, flour, and Franklin's coffee. That's where they found out about the hurricane in the gulf.

They'd just walked into the two-story place of business when a gust of wind blew in a downpour.

Miss Earnestine told them about the hurricane that might come their way, so they hurried to buy their items, which also included a quart of milk and two bottles of Kool Aid.

The goat had died the year before, and Franklin said the goat was more trouble than it was worth. "It's always wanting to be milked, so I'd rather to just buy it," Franklin told Annie Laurie.

After their purchases, Miss Earnestine asked Lum if he would carry them back home, which he did.

Since there wasn't a lane that led from the road to their house, Lum just pulled as near to the culvert as he could. When the rain slowed down to a drizzle, Lum helped Franklin to carry the bags to the front porch.

Annie Laurie ran ahead of them with the key to the front door.

"Thank you Suh," Lum told Franklin, then he hurried back to his truck.

"Whew, what a blessing he is," Franklin said, as they rushed their things into the house.

A gust of wind hit the house and blew rain through the door, so when Franklin rushed in with the bags, Annie Laurie slammed the door closed.

It was so dark outside until the chickens went to roost by midday. In a short while the winds really picked up. Annie Laurie wondered how the house and out-buildings stood it.

Blacky had holes dug under the house on each side of the building, plus one under the middle of the house. He slept in the hole in the middle of the house in cold or rainy weather. Annie Laurie heard him bump his head at the middle of the house during the storm.

Annie Laurie checked the water buckets in the kitchen, then the reservoir in the stove and saw they had plenty of water to last them through the night.

By the middle of the afternoon she could tell that her daddy was worried, the storm just didn't let up. They couldn't look outside, due to the shutters in the windows and they sure weren't going to open a door. All they could do was wait as they listened to the howl of the wind as it swirled around the house. Occasionally they could hear as a tree made a thunderous crash to the ground, and things blowing across the yard. Thank God the house held, and the almost constant lightning didn't strike it.

It was too early to start a fire in the stove, but as usual they both congregated in the kitchen, so Annie Laurie built a small fire in the stove. Somehow or other things just seemed cozier with a fire in the stove.

Annie Laurie set two of the smoothing irons atop of the stove, then went into her bedroom and brought back some bed sheets and pillowcases. She thought if she'd get busy at something it would take her mind off the terrible storm outside.

Franklin started a pot of coffee, while he wondered how the other people in and around the community was doing from the storm.

Annie Laurie wrote on a piece of paper and handed it to her daddy, asking, "Do you ever remember another storm being this bad?"

"No, not one to last this long," her daddy replied.

Annie Laurie quickly wrote back. "Well, I'll be glad when it's over, I want to see what it's done outside."

As serious as the situation was outside, he couldn't help but smile, for Annie Laurie hadn't gone to school a day in her life but could spell and write better than he could. He gave their little sessions at night, and her looking in the catalogues and magazines that were found in the junk pile the credit. *"Her urge to learn doesn't hamper either,"* he thought.

Franklin thought it seemed crazy but when the winds, rain, and lightning let up, he could see the setting sun in front of his house.

He donned his boots and slicker to go outside to check on things before it got completely dark.

Annie Laurie stood on the porches to see too. She knew she didn't iron too many pieces, but she wanted to see too. It was still raining, so she had to stand next to the wall of the house. In the front of the house she could see several of the trees were blown down or mangled.

She then ran to the back, that way she could see the cribs, barn, and toilet.

The toilet stood so far from the house, but it looked like it had blown over, the cribs, chicken pen, and barn looked to have stood the awful winds and lightning. She noticed that most of the sugarcane had blown over though.

Franklin noticed the trees in front too, but his main concern was the house. After walking all the way around the house, checking the tin roof, he found that everything looked okay. The chickens had already gone to roost and Pete had already gone into his stable, so all he needed to feed was the greedy hogs.

Franklin was met in the back yard by Blacky. After stroking the frisky dog a few times, he climbed the steps that led to the back porch. He too had noticed the sugarcane and toilet.

Franklin sure gave praise to the Lord that they were safe, and things weren't worse than they were.

He sat down on a bench to remove his boots, then hung his slicker on a nail.

He knew better than leave his boots on the porch, for Blacky would head straight for them.

Franklin didn't dare tell Annie Laurie, but he was scared. He knew he was drawing over, just the wee task like pulling his boots off nearly killed his back. He wondered how much longer he'd be able to do the hard work on the farm.

"Oh, well, I'll go as long as God's will," he thought.

When he walked in the back door, holding his boots with one hand, Annie Laurie had started supper.

After putting his boots back in his room and changing socks, Franklin went into the living room and turned on the radio. He felt damp, so he started a fire in the fireplace. As usual the only station he could pick up was **WCKY** from Cincinnati, Ohio. He wished they had a local station so he could find out about the storm.

It was nice listening to the music though, but it still wasn't as good as **WSM** and the Grand Ole Opry. Franklin liked the Carter family, or anything with a banjo and fiddle.

Franklin thought of many things while he sat there. He thought of Kelly Mercantile and hoped it had survived the storm. He thought of all the locals that were still in the store when they left and wondered if they hunkered down inside the store or made their way home. He was glad that they didn't go in the mule and wagon, for they'd never made it home before the storm hit. He also hoped that Lum made it back to the store safely. He knew he had a few days of hard work ahead of him, from the looks of things, with all the trees being blown down. *"One good thing about it,"* he thought, *"We could always use the wood to burn in the house, especially the oak."* Pine trees had too much tar to be used for firewood. He guessed he'd just saw it up in sections and have Pete pull it to the back of their property.

Franklin didn't have time to check things out very well before dark. He thought he'd give everything a good going over the next morning. Of course, the main thing was the house had held.

His mama's maiden name was Knowles. It was her daddy that had built the house when he returned home from the war between the states. His name was Robert Harrison Knowles. His wife was Minerva Phillips Knowles. It was the only house that he had ever lived it. Franklin grinned, he thought of the time that he'd asked Laurie to marry him, but she turned him down. She said her parents were old, and they needed her because Sarie had married Paul "Rat" Lee and had moved away. Her parents lived near Monroeville in a rented house. Her daddy's name was Al Lewis and her mama's name was Pearl. They seemed to like Franklin, and when they found out the reason Laurie wouldn't marry him, they scolded her for it. They said they'd miss her, but she had her life to consider, and they could take care of themselves. Just two weeks later they were married and Laurie moved five miles down the road. Franklin's parents had recently died from the flu, so they had the house all to themselves.

If Laurie ever regretted her decision, Franklin never knew it, for he was as loving as a husband that he knew how to be.

They married in the spring of 1919, the busiest time of the year for a farmer.

For a while, Laurie left things just as they were in the house, but as time went on, she arranged things to suit her.

Franklin learned that she was a good cook, and that sure suited him. For a couple of years they'd hitch-up the mule and wagon and visit her folks, usually on a Sunday. Laurie would always take a picnic lunch with her, and they sure seemed to enjoy it.

Both her parents had died though by the time Annie Laurie was born on an October morning 1924.

Franklin had written all the names down in the Bible, so Annie Laurie would know a little something about her ancestry.

Before long, Annie Laurie came to the door and motioned for her daddy to come eat supper.

Franklin's mind and thoughts snapped back to the present. Still walking in his bare feet he headed toward the kitchen.

To his surprise he saw that his daughter had baked cornbread, and there was also something in a boiler. Franklin could smell onion. Instead of plates on the table, there were bowls.

After blessing the food, Franklin sat down and cut him a big slice of the cornbread. With both hands, Annie Laurie set the boiler and ladle on the table. Franklin didn't say anything as he dipped the ladle into the boiler. To his surprise he found that Annie Laurie had cooked some macaroni stew. He saw that she had opened a can of tomatoes and chopped some pork into small pieces. Even more to his surprise it was delicious enough until he ate two servings.

"It sure beats salt meat and flap jacks," Franklin said, as he pushed his bowl to the side.

Franklin saw the smile that came across his daughter's face.

"It was the perfect meal, after the storm we went through this afternoon," he said.

Annie Laurie nodded her head, then placed her clasped hands under her chin.

"I can hardly wait to see how everything around here came through the storm. I know I'm gonna have some sawing to do, in order for us to get to the road. It was so dark by the time I could get outside until I couldn't check things out properly, and boy, I sure hope Mr. Lum made it back to the store safe and sound," Franklin said.

"Oh, Blacky made it just fine. He followed me out to the barn," Franklin told his daughter.

Annie Laurie couldn't respond to her daddy, but she had seen her dog when she was on the back porch, so she just smiled and nodded her head.

Franklin saw his daughter as she begun to crumble some of the cornbread, then dipped a ladle of the stew to pour over it. He knew that she was anxious to feed her dog, so he surprised her by getting up to clean the kitchen.

Annie Laurie waited until the dog wolfed down the food, before she stroked him on his head, for the rest of his body was muddy.

She locked the door behind her when she came in. She noticed that her daddy had poured the remainder of the stew in a quart jar and had washed everything but the bowl in her hand.

"Shoot, I'm gonna put the leftovers in the springhouse in the morning," her daddy said. He then added, "You keep on and you're gonna make as good a cook as your mama."

Those words really pleased Annie Laurie, so she smiled from ear to ear.

"Hey, whatcha say we go listen to the radio a small while before we turn in?" he asked.

"Uhmm," Annie Laurie responded.

They didn't listen to the radio long, for they were anxious to get up by daybreak and see about the storm, so they went to bed early.

Chapter 5

The next morning, Annie Laurie was cooking grits and eggs by lamp light. About the time things were ready to eat her daddy came into the kitchen. "I hope you have something in my coffeepot, I'm like your Aunt Sarie, I just can't seem to get moving until I've had my coffee," Franklin said.

Annie Laurie placed a cup in front of him, then grabbed a thick potholder to pick up the hot coffeepot, in order to fill his cup.

Once, Annie Laurie had secretly tried a taste of the bitter brew and she didn't see what all the hoopla was about. *"Besides,"* she thought, *"I don't believe that one small taste would stunt my growth."*

Annie Laurie decided against cooking flapjacks that morning, she thought they'd just settle for the grits and eggs. Franklin didn't say anything about it, for he was eager to get out and about too.

It wasn't long before Franklin was putting on his lace-up boots, and Annie Laurie was feeding Blacky. The morning was foggy, so she still couldn't see much.

"One thing about it, all my life I've heard that a foggy morning means it will be a sunny day," she thought.

After loving on the starving dog, Annie Laurie came back inside to wash the dishes, and she met her daddy going out.

She thought as she was washing the dishes, *"There's one thing about Blacky, he accepts me as I am. He doesn't care if I can talk or not. He loves me as I am."*

Annie Laurie didn't have an old pair of shoes that she could wear, so she cut the toe of the shoes out and squeezed her feet in, then went outside.

She heard her daddy hammering on a piece of tin, so she followed the sound and saw that her daddy was hammering down a piece of tin on Pete's shed.

Blacky reared up on her, wanting to be petted, but his feet were muddy due to the soaking wet ground, so she pushed him away.

He didn't seem to mind her actions, for he began to run around in circles as if he was chasing his tail.

"Old Blacky sure seems like he's glad the storm is over," her daddy said, as he took a break from the hammering.

91

"So far, all I can see damaged is this one piece of tin, the trees, and the sugarcane. It's almost matured, so I believe with a few sunny days the sun will pull it back up. Another thing are the pecan trees. Most of them were ready to fall from the trees, so we'll have to search for them, they're blown everywhere," Franklin said.

"Tat baid," Annie Laurie said.

"I thought when I finish this we'd zig zag out of here and see how things are in Dottelle, I sure hope they fared as well as we did," Franklin told her.

Instead of trying to verbally answer again, Annie Laurie clasped her hands together and put them under her chin.

Franklin was through with all the chores by nine o'clock, which included bringing water to the house. He had told Annie Laurie that her job was inside of the house. "Besides those two buckets of water are too heavy for you to tote," he said.

By nine thirty, they were dressed, then went under and around trees until they reached the road. They had to scold Blacky to prevent him from following them.

By the time they reached the junk pile they found two big oak trees across the road. Franklin had brought five dozen of eggs to sell at Miss Earnestine's store, and already he regretted it. He and Annie Laurie would take turns climbing over the trees, then handing each other the eggs.

They could look across the fields to where the forests began and see whole sections of trees blown down.

"Boy, all I can say is the good Lord was looking out for us," Franklin told Annie Laurie.

They finally reached Woodlawn Methodist Church and saw that some men were busy cutting a big black gum tree that had blown down in front. The quaint little church didn't seemed to be damaged, though, and Franklin was proud of that.

Before long they reached the intersection that led to the store. Even though it was about two hundred yards away from them they could see that the store had survived. The store had one single gas pump, and they could see that Mr. Lum was pumping gas into a pick-up truck.

"Whew, thank God, he made it," Franklin said, as they continued their trek toward the store.

Mr. Lum had finished pumping the gas by the time they made it to the store. He was smiling from ear to ear by the time they made it to the store.

"Mister Frank, Missy, It'[s sho good seeing y'all are alright," Lum said. "Yeh, we came through it alright. We've been worried about you though, because the thing hit about the time you left," Franklin said.

"Lawd, I had time enough to goes home and gits Miss Octavia. Miss Earnestine wuz worried abouts de sto, so we'se spent de night heah," Lum told them.

"Well, I hope your house is alright," Franklin said.

"Yassuh, it be's alright. Lucky fuh us, deys fields on both sides of de run, jest about all de way home. I tooks Miss Octavia home at daylight and eberthang looked okay at de house," Lum told them.

"Well, I know you're bound to be worn out, not sleeping and all," Franklin told Lum.

"Wese slept on de flo, adder dat wind started to settle down some," Lum replied.

"I sees dat you brought some eggs, Miss Earnestine will be glad to git dem, you knows dem city folks don't habe chickens," Lum said.

Franklin and Annie Laurie climbed the wide steps that led to the double doors and entrance into the store.

Miss Earnestine had hired a lady helper in the store, her name was Lois, and the two were in deep conversation about the havoc of the hurricane.

Miss Lois and Miss Earnestine were two opposites, and Franklin wondered why Miss Earnestine had hired her. Lois kept her short blonde hair cured and dyed. She wore plenty of make-up, rouge, and lipstick too, she always made sure to wear dresses that accented her shapely figure too. Miss Earnestine was plain and simple. She was slender, with straight black, and never wore any kind of make-up. She was friendly and had a good heart, yet she was all business, and everyone knew it.

Miss Earnestine's brother, Riley jr. had nothing to do with the business of the store or the gin. He had a nice office built off the side of the building where he wrote poetry and short stories all day. Franklin believed that Mr. Kelly kept Riley jr. in the store, just to say there was a man inside.

Franklin broke up their conversation when he laid the basket of eggs on the counter next to them.

"Mr. Reed, sure good to see that you and Annie Laurie made it through the storm. Lois and I were just talking about the devastation in the area. Of course, the further south you go the worse it gets," Miss Earnestine said.

"Yes mam, we made it. I'll admit, it was rough going there for a while, Franklin replied. He then added, "I had to nail down a piece of tin on the mule's shed, and we have trees down in the yard," Franklin said.

"So, how did Excel come out?" Franklin asked.

"Believe it or not, I didn't see any structural damage, neither there on the way here, just trees down everywhere," Miss Earnestine answered.

"So, I guess it's time to stop gossiping and time to get back to business. So, how many eggs did you bring me this morning?" Miss Earnestine asked.

There were two long glass top counters down each side of the store. Miss Lois was in charge of the one on the right, which sold clothing, shoes, perfumes, and other bodily items.

Miss Earnestine stayed behind the other counter, which sold food items, kitchen utensils and just about everything else, including seeds, and fertilizer. The fertilizer was kept in a shed across the road, next to the gin.

Miss Lois quickly walked across the store and got behind her counter.

"Yes Mam, I brought you five dozen this morning," Franklin answered

Without counting them, Miss Earnestine shifted the eggs from Franklin's basket to hers. She then pushed a button on the cash register and handed Franklin a dollar.

"Now, is there anything I can do for you?" she asked.

"Yes mam, I'll need a half pound of oleo, a bag of macaroni, a quart of milk, a bottle of liniment, five oatmeal cookies, two bottles of grape Kool Aid, and a can of tomatoes," Franklin answered.

Miss Earnestine put all of the items into a cardboard box and pecked each item into the cash register.

"Now, that'll be three dollars and twenty cents, tax and all," she replied.

"I just hope I can get this Oleo into the springhouse before it melts," Franklin said.

"I double wrapped it for you, and if you'll keep the lid to the box closed, that'll help," she said.

Franklin paid for the items, thanked her, then handed Annie Laurie the small bag of cookies.

Someone else had driven next to the gas pump, so Lum snapped to attention and went down the steps to help them.

The walk on the way home didn't take as long, as the County had sent a big bulldozer out to push the trees out of the road. Workers were then sawing the trees and limbs into sections.

"One good advantage about living on an unpaved road. We can get our dozers in and clean the mess up fast. There are trees down everywhere," Mr. Chandler, the supervisor told Franklin.

Franklin didn't take time to socialize though, he knew they needed to get home. He had work to do and he needed to get the oleo into the springhouse.

Once they reached home, and he took care of the trivia things around there, Franklin took the buck saw and axe to the blown down trees and began.

Usually, they just ate a small dinner, making supper their main meal. Annie Laurie knew her daddy would be hungry after such hard work, so she fired up the stove.

She knew that syrup always gave him energy, so she waited for a small while then fried three pork chops and a stack of flapjacks.

Franklin could get a whiff of things cooking now and then and knew what his daughter was up to. He smiled, thinking what a sweet daughter he had.

When Annie Laurie finished in the kitchen, she sat on the front porch watching her daddy work.

"Poor thing," she thought, *"He is really bowing over."* She then thought of the

bottle of liniment that morning and wondered if he had bought it to rub on his back.

He finally looked her way, and she motioned for him to come to the house.

Franklin didn't tarry, for the grits and eggs they'd eaten at breakfast had long ago worn out, due to the strenuous work.

"Oh boy, flapjacks, and pork chops, and I'm gonna pour plenty of syrup over my flapjacks," Franklin said.

Annie Laurie smiled and nodded her head, meaning she was too.

Franklin washed his hands, and they sat down to eat.

While they were eating, Franklin mentioned that maybe the next day the ground would be dry enough for them to search for the pecans. "Heaven knows we need every penny we can get, things are sky high," he said.

As usual, they both saved some of their meal for Blacky.

Franklin hardly waited for his food to settle before he was back outside sawing and chopping.

By the middle of the afternoon he hitched-up Pete, and with a chain he pulled the trees that he had cut out of the way and made their lane visible again. The one oak tree that had fallen, Franklin had Pete pull it to the woodpile, to be used for heat inside the house.

As soon as he had Pete in his stable, he fed him, the hogs, and the chickens. He gathered the eggs and after stomping his boots on the doorsteps, he took them into the house. He saw that Annie Laurie was cooking.

"Shoot, it might be a little cool outside, but I've sweated so today, I'm gonna take me a bath in the spring," Franklin said. He then added, "I'll bring back the two buckets of water."

Annie Laurie nodded her head, wishing she could jump into the cold water as she had done in the past.

Franklin went into his room and brought out some clean overalls, and a pair of red "Long handles."

Annie Laurie had already emptied the buckets of water into the reservoir, so with his other hand, Franklin grabbed the vails of both buckets and headed out the back door.

Annie knew that he'd also wash the clothes that he pulled off while he was down there, as that's where their clothesline was situated.

For supper, Annie Laurie had cooked some dried beans, baked cornbread, and three more pork chops. She had gone into the smokehouse and cut off a piece of smoked meat to season the beans with.

Annie Laurie had everything on the table when her daddy returned with the two buckets of water.

"Umm, I'm hungry as a wolf," Franklin said. He then blessed the food, and they sat down to eat.

Franklin didn't waste time filling his plate.

"Goodness, everything is so good," he said, as he dipped him a second portion of beans.

Franklin always drank water with his meals, then afterwards he'd savor a hot cup of black coffee.

After pouring his cup of coffee, Franklin turned on the radio, and in just a few minutes, Annie Laurie could hear Rudy Vale singing.

After cleaning the dishes, on a piece of paper, Annie Laurie wrote, "I'm going to take a bath, then I'll come in here too."

As usual, Franklin had made a small fire in the fireplace and was enjoying the radio and his rocking chair.

Annie Laurie showed him the note, and he nodded his head.

Franklin sat in his chair and considered things. *"Boy, it's a big difference in the weather tonight, compared to last night. For a while there I believed we were goners,"* he thought.

As usual, almost every idle moment he had, which was rare, his thoughts always returned to Laurie. To be sisters, she and Sarie were exact opposites.

Whereas Sarie was loud and cheap looking, Laurie was quiet and always dressed in starched and ironed clothes. Whatever Franklin said was the law, and she never argued with him. The only make-up Laurie wore was a little lip gloss. *"She was a lady in every aspect,"* thought Franklin. The only regret he had was they never produced a son.

He knew that Laurie would never have believed that he and Annie Laurie could never have pulled it off, and with such harmony. He had to admit that things were rough there for a while because Laurie had them both spoiled. He wondered what Laurie would think about the radio, for in the background he could hear, "I only have eyes for you." Franklin took a deep breath and knew that he'd love Laurie to his dying day. *"If I can only hold out to get Annie Laurie grown and able to take care of herself."*

His thoughts were interrupted when Annie Laurie entered the room wearing clean pajamas, and he saw that she had even washed and combed her hair.

He had noticed that she'd quit sitting in his lap, instead she pulled up another rocker next to him and they listened to the radio together.

Annie Laurie had gotten to where she carried a notebook and pencil with her nearly everywhere she went. On a page she wrote, "A big difference from this time last night."

Franklin smiled and nodded his head, then poked at the fire with the fire poker.

"I really enjoyed supper tonight," Franklin told her.

Annie Laurie's simple reply on the notebook was, "I'm learning."

Franklin smiled and patted his daughter on the back.

Franklin knew that the next month, Annie Laurie would be ten years old. "He wondered how many other ten-year-olds could write and spelled as well as she could and not have spent a day in a classroom." Words were beyond compare how proud he was of her.

They listened to the radio for a short while, giving time for the fire to be just charcoals when Franklin said, they'd better turn in. "Old Pete and I have got to turn the toilet back upright tomorrow."

Annie Laurie quickly wrote in her notebook.

"Yuk, you can do that, while I start picking up the pecans."

The next day started out like all the others, they ate a hardy breakfast of grits, eggs, and a pancake with syrup.

Franklin had done all the chores outside while Annie Laurie cooked breakfast.

It was when Annie Laurie was picking up the pecans, when things happened that would affect the rest of her life.

She thought she'd heard something, so she looked up and saw Lee Peacock and another young fellow with coal black curly hair, come through the gap on their bicycles.

They came to a skidding halt in front of Annie Laurie as she was picking up pecans.

"Hey Annie Laurie, this is my friend Jesse Jordan," Lee told her.

"Hi, Annie Laurie," Jesse replied.

Annie Laurie, who was dirty from picking the wet pecans off the ground, simply waved and nodded her head.

"Oh, I forgot, Annie Laurie can't talk, she can hear though, and knows how to play ball,"

"Do you have a bicycle?" Jesse asked.

Lee answered for her, "No, but they have a mule, and his name is Pete."

Franklin had finished with the toilet and was picking up pecans on the other side of the house, thus he'd put the mule back in the stable.

"Jesse's folks will soon be your neighbors, his daddy bought eighty acres of land across the road from the cemetery.

They're living in the old house until they get their new house built," Lee told her.

Again, Annie Laurie nodded her head and smiled.

"She means, she is pleased," Lee told his friend.

"I believe you've been around her long enough to understand her," Jesse told Lee.

"Yeh, we've been friends all our lives," Lee responded.

"Well, we were just riding around seeing what the storm done. We're holding you up from your job, so we'll be seeing you Annie Laurie," Lee told her.

"Nice meeting you Annie Laurie," Jesse told her, as they began to turn their bikes around.

After they had left, Annie Laurie continued to pick up the pecans, thinking, "There's something different about Jesse. She couldn't quite put her finger on it, but whatever it was, she liked it."

Annie Laurie continued picking up pecans until she figured it was time to started on supper. As she'd filled her foot tub, she'd carry them to the back porch and pour them into a big sack. She noticed that her sack was almost full.

She brushed herself off the best that she could, thinking she'd wash her hands and arms at the spring. She thought she'd get the left-over macaroni stew and add something else to it.

After getting there, she thought if it was a little warmer, she'd get the bar of soap, at least pull off her cumbersome dress and take a bath.

She made it to the house and set the cold jar with its contents on the back porch. She then thought she'd help her daddy, who was still busy with the pecans, so she got four ears out of the barn. She shelled them one ear at a time, throwing the corn through the wire fence and fed the chickens. After that she gathered the eggs. She counted twenty-five of them. *"Not a bad day,"* she thought.

They sold the baskets and most of the eggs to Miss Earnestine, but Franklin learned years ago that the pecan man paid more for them. He was a jolly old fellow from Andalusia, Alabama. He came around two times in the fall of the year buying pecans and paid top price. His name was Mr. Booker.

Annie Laurie suddenly thought of what she could cook to go with the macaroni stew. After carrying the stew and basket of eggs into the kitchen she went back outside. While she still had her soiled dress on, she climbed into the sweet potato bank and brought out four potatoes. She decided she'd slice them and fry them. *"That ought to go with the stew,"* she thought.

She saw that her daddy was still picking up pecans. She smiled at him when she went by him and vice versa.

Annie Laurie knew how important it was for them to gather all the pecans they could. With the pecan money they bought the salt that was used to preserve the pork meat, and next month would be time to slaughter the two hogs.

Annie Laurie changed clothes before she started supper. She just hung her dirty dress over a chair for it to dry, for she knew she'd be wearing it for a couple more days, at least.

She hurried into the kitchen to start supper. Of course, the first thing she had to do was get the fire going in the stove. The oven had a temperature gauge on it, until it reached three hundred degrees, she started peeling the potatoes, being very careful with the knife. Slicing the hard potatoes was a task. She got them sliced though by hitting the big knife with a stick.

Next was making the pan of corn bread and getting it into the oven. If the oven got too hot, she'd have to open the damper to cool things down. She'd used the stove long enough that she'd learned about how much wood to put in it.

Next was the sweet potatoes. She put about eight tablespoons of Lard into the cast iron frying pan and fried them on top of the stove. When she wound up, she had a heaping platter of them. She checked the cornbread and saw that it was ready to take out of the oven. She dumped the bread into a plate, then put the sizzling pan into the dishwater, along with the one she'd fried the potatoes in. Last, but not least, she thought about one of the cast iron frying pans, knowing it would cut down on the things she had to wash. She rinsed and dried the pan, and poured the stew in it, after she'd put the pan back on the stove top.

It was so hot in the kitchen until Annie Laurie opened the shutter in the kitchen. She saw that her daddy was feeding the animals, so she began to set the table.

Annie Laurie loved sweet potatoes as much as her daddy, so while the stew was getting hot, she sat down at the table and began to nibble on a slice. Suddenly, she laughed. She was glad that Jesse and Lee didn't witness her daddy as he and Pete were putting the toilet back in place.

Chapter 6

1938

Annie Laurie was fourteen that October. Mrs. Peacock, who still made all her dresses, made the remark that her shapely figure wasn't fair to the other young girls in the neighborhood.

Annie Laurie felt as though Mrs. Peacock paid her a big compliment, until she said, "It's a crying shame you have that infirmity, you just can't talk honey," Mrs. Peacock said, forgetting that Annie Laurie could hear. "I'll have to make this a little large, I know your daddy wouldn't want to see you in anything that would show off your figure. Another thing, you need to see Miss Earnestine about a brassiere Honey, you're big as a grown woman up there," the old lady said.

Annie Laurie thought, *"Lord, I'm costing my daddy enough as it is!"* She remembered when she started her menstrual cycle a couple of years ago. She read a lot, but she didn't know a thing about a girl having a menstrual cycle every month. All she knew was she was bleeding down there, and she was scared to death. Trying the only thing she knew to do was tie a clean rag down there and hoping it would stop. After the third day, she hinted to her daddy that she needed to see Miss Earnestine. Franklin could tell from the expression on her face that she was scared about something, so he hitched Pete to the wagon, and they left.

Luckily, no one was in the store but Miss Earnestine, Miss Lois, and Mr. Riley, but as usual he was in his office banging away on his typewriter.

Annie Laurie had brought her notebook and pencil. She walked up to Miss Earnestine and showed her what she had written down. "I'm bleeding down there," Annie Laurie had written.

Miss Earnestine tapped on Mr. Riley's door, then opened the door and asked her brother if they could borrow his office. Mr. Riley smiled at Annie Laurie cordially as he stepped out of the office.

"Sit down young lady," Miss Earnestine told her, as she pointed to a straight back chair.

Annie Laurie did as she was told.

"To start with, you're not a child anymore, you're a young lady. I know you don't have a mother to talk to, so you probably don't realize what's happening to your body. When a lady gets mature enough to produce children they have a period each month. There's not a thing we can do about it but get pregnant to stop it and you don't need that. Just keep your seat and I'll be right back," Miss Earnestine had said.

Annie Laurie breathed a sigh of relief, knowing she was like every other young lady.

Miss Earnestine soon returned with a bag. She pulled two items from the bag.

"Now this is a sanitary pad, and this is the sanitary belt." She then showed Annie Laurie how to snap the pad to the belt. "You see this little clip right here you slide it up or down in order for it to fit your body. Make sure your pad is good and tight, you don't want any leakage," she told Annie Laurie.

Annie Laurie nodded her head.

"There, you see you're just like the rest of us, and if you have anything else in the future that you're in, feel free to come to me," Miss Earnestine had said.

Annie Laurie's mind returned to Mrs. Peacock, when Mrs. Peacock said, "Honey you need to start putting just a pinch of baking soda under your arms in the morning. It'll cut down on the odor."

"My goodness, what's next, first, my breasts are too big, and now I stink under my arms," Annie Laurie thought. Even though she had to admit, she did get a strange whiff of herself at times.

Mrs. Peacock did compliment her though. After she'd finished measuring her for her birthday dress, she said, "You know honey, you're so lucky in many ways. You have the most gorgeous complexion, not a pimple anywhere. The perfect figure for a young lady your age, and you're the prettiest girl around these parts."

Annie Laurie blushed.

Mrs. Peacock laughed at her, causing Annie Laurie to blush even more.

After the measuring and advice, Annie Laurie redressed, after Mrs. Peacock told her she'd need to trim her hair before long. {For Mrs. Peacock was not only a seamstress, but also a barber. She kept both her daddy and Annie Laurie's haircut.

Before Annie Laurie left, Mrs. Peacock wrote on a piece of paper, Brassier size 36, C cup, one box of baking soda.

"Here, give this note to Miss Earnestine," Mrs. Peacock told her.

Annie Laurie read the note on the way to the store and wondered how much more money she was going to cause her daddy to spend on her for personal things.

It was a cool clear day, and they had walked to the store, toting a few of their first weaved baskets. She saw that her daddy was sitting on the porch, and he was carrying one of the larger baskets back home, filled with groceries. She only hoped he had enough money left on him to pay for her two items.

She was embarrassed to show him Mrs. Peacock's note, but she knew she had to, in case he didn't have the money.

Franklin glanced at the note, cleared his throat and said, "Tell Miss Earnestine to give you two of them," and he pointed at the word Brassiere. Instead of getting to his feet, he reached into his front pocket and pulled out a small roll of bills. He peeled off ten dollars and gave it to her. "This ought to do it," he said.

Annie Laurie kissed her daddy on the cheek, then walked into the store, wondering how a brassiere would feel while wearing it.

She knew they already had some baking powder, so she just bought the two brassieres.

When she came back outside with her purchase in a bag, she saw that her daddy was talking to Mr. Lum.

She noticed how stooped her daddy was. He had to stand away from Mr. Lum and really had to strain his neck to see Mr. Lum's face. She felt so sorry for her daddy, and she knew that he had to stay in pain from the amount of liniment that he was using on his back at night.

She had two dollars left over, so she gave it to her daddy, and he stuck it in his pocket.

"Mister Frank I has strict orders to takes you and de Missus home, specially wit dat basket of groceries," Mr. Lum said.

"Aw, the devil, we can make it," her daddy said.

"Well, you knows how Miss Earnestine is, sides, I done whittled you a gif and I done gots it in de truck," Mr. Lum said.

"Well, if you insist," her daddy said, so Mr. Lum put the basket of groceries in the back of the truck.

He then opened the truck door, and they crawled inside.

When Mr. Lum opened the driver's door, he pulled her daddy's gift from behind the seat. Annie Laurie thought it was the prettiest walking stick she'd ever seen, and it had carvings on it too. They read "Mr. Frank, 1938." On the other side was carved simply "Lum."

"Eyes made it from a sassafras root, it be good and strong. If it bees too long, you can cuts some of it off," Mr. Lum said.

"Mr. Lum, pride comes before fall, I should have been using one of these years ago, and I thank you," her daddy said, as he smiled and continued to examine the walking stick.

Blacky was waiting on them, and he ran out to the edge of the property as Lum stopped. He was eager for them to see what he had in his mouth.

Without exiting his truck, Mr. Lum said, "Look Mr. Frank, dat dog done cotched a rabbit while you wuz gone."

"Yeh, it's his way of telling me that we ought to be hunting," Franklin told Lum.

"He's a smart dog fuh sho," Lum said and laughed.

Annie Laurie crossed the ditch, holding the basket of groceries, along with her purchase by the handle of the basket. The stooped Franklin followed behind her using his newly acquired walking stick.

Franklin rubbed Blacky down his back, and as if the dog understood him, he told the dog that it would be alright for him to eat the rabbit.

Annie Laurie practically ran up the doorsteps, eager to put on her new brassiere, while Franklin was dreading the next day. He knew it was time to start cutting the sugarcane and
Making the syrup. He only hoped he was up to the task, for it seemed that his spine and neck hurt more and more each day. He also hoped that Pete would be up to pulling the heavy pole around in circles to extract the juice from the sugarcane. *"Pete is like me now,"* he thought. *"We're*

both getting old," He knew the mule would stumble now and then as they'd be plowing, and the mule ate less and less.

Annie Laurie did take time to put the groceries up, and she saw that her daddy had bought something new. She saw that he had purchased a can of beef stew. They seldom had beef, it was always some sort of pork or chicken, so she laid the can on the counter, along with a bag of macaroni.

She ran into her room and pulled off her dress. While looking in the mirror she put the brassiere on. It did lift her breasts up, but it seemed like it took forever to get it hooked in the back. The brassiere had very fancy lace on it, and she liked it.

Annie Laurie brushed her teeth each morning, using baking soda, so she ran to her bowl and pitcher. She reached into the box and put a pinch of baking soda under her arm pits, then rubbed it in. *"Mrs. Peacock was right, the odor is gone,"* she thought, so she rubbed a little in the armpits of the dress that she'd been wearing. She smelled, *"No stink."* She wondered why her daddy hadn't told her.

She redressed and looked in the mirror. *"Lord, my breasts look like they're gonna poke through my dress,"* she thought. She felt better though, just knowing she was like every other lady.

It was still too early to start supper, so she left her room to search for her daddy. She found that he'd never come inside of the house. He was sitting in his rocker on the front porch, as he did so many afternoons after he'd taken care of the animals.

"Pull up a chair and let's sit a spell," so she did. He continued, "I know we should be out there weaving more baskets, but I just felt like sitting for a while." He then said something to Annie Laurie that he'd never said.

"Honey, when your mama died, I'll be honest, I didn't believe I could pull it off. Here you are a young lady and I'll be the first to say, a pretty one too. Just goes to show, Annie Laurie, don't ever give up. With the Lord's help the impossible is possible, and you're a prime example of it."

Annie Laurie wanted to tell him that he'd done a good job, but not being able to talk, she wiped the tears from her eyes instead.

He continued to talk about days past. He spoke of his beloved Laurie. "She was different from her sister, Sarie. Your mama was a lady in every way. Sarie ran off and married Rat, but your mama wouldn't marry me until her folks told her it was alright. Lord, I'll miss her until my dying day," her daddy said.

Annie Laurie got up from her rocker and began to rub him on the back.

Franklin realized that maybe he'd talked too much, so he broke the atmosphere by saying something comical. "You know President Roosvelt promised us if we'd vote for him there'd be a chicken in every pot and a car in every garage. I reckon I'll have to build us a garage before we get that car," he said, then laughed.

He then told Annie Laurie if something happened to him, "You go to Miss Earnestine, she'll put you on the right track," her daddy said.

Oh! How she wished she had brought her notebook and pencil with her, so she could comfort him, but all she could do was rub his aching back and neck.

Her daddy talked of several trivia things, then he said something that surprised her.

"Your new brassiere makes your dress look like other girls. Your mama hated them, she only wore one when she was around someone. I guess I should have told you about them when you started sprouting, but I just didn't know how to bring up the subject. The new dress that Mrs. Peacock is making you is for your birthday. I told her to make it a red color."

Annie Laurie stopped rubbing and held out the palm of her hand so he could see it, and with her index finger, she drew the image of a heart.

Franklin then told her. "You know, I would never have been able to slaughter the two hogs last week if Mr. Lum hadn't sent his two nephews over to help me. It was mighty good of them to just settle for the entrails of the hogs, we never ate them anyway. Maybe I should have mentioned the fact that we start cutting the cane in the morning to Mr. Lum."

Annie Laurie then wrote in her palm, "We can do it."

Franklin laughed and said, "I guess we'll have to, but meanwhile we'd better get busy on those baskets."

Annie Laurie noticed that he used his new cane once he got out of the chair.

They each had a straight back chair that they sat in as they weaved the baskets. To weave the tips of your fingers had to be course and tough. First off, you had to find a small white oak tree. You then cut it into, below the limbs, then you used an iron wedge to split the log into several pieces, usually sixteen pieces. The next step was, with your knife blade, you peeled off the strips that you wanted to make your baskets with. Franklin always peeled off the strips, giving Annie Laurie the small flexible ones to make her baskets. The first step was to make the bottom. Sixteen long strips were laid on the ground, then you weaved between them, making a circle, or square, according to the type basket you wanted to make. After you got the size basket you wanted, next, all sixteen pieces we cut in half on the bottom, then turned upward, so you could weave around them. Lastly, when you weaved to the top, the sixteen pieces were cut again, and bent inward. A long piece of white oak strip was put under the sixteen pieces where they were cut, then was wrapped good and tight with long strips. When the baskets were dried in a couple of days, they were tough as nails.

Annie Laurie had time to make one small basket, complete with a handle, before she had to start supper.

On the way to the house, she fed the chickens and gathered the eggs. She had to go through the front door, for the back door was still locked. On the way up the doorsteps she saw that Blacky was having a good time with the rabbit. He'd sling it in the air, then catch it with his mouth.

She'd already decided what she was going to cook for supper. She decided, instead of the pork, she'd use the can of beef that her daddy had bought and make the macaroni stew her daddy liked. She thought of the eggs on the counter, so she put six on to boil, after making a fire in the stove. She figured, after peeling the eggs, she'd slice them into and lay a slice of sweet pickle on top of each one of them. *"It will be something new, and who knows, it just might be good,"* she thought.

She'd finished with supper before her daddy came in, so she went out on the front porch to watch the sunset, and to her surprise her daddy was sitting on the top doorstep.

Not a word was spoken, she sat down beside him, and they watched the day end together.

Later, they ate supper, and after listening to the radio for a while, they went to bed.

Annie Laurie was glad to pull off the brassiere, it was as though the straps were cutting her rib cage. She checked to see if she could adjust it, but discovered the straps were adjusted to their maximum. She thought about cutting the sugarcane the next day and decided she wouldn't wear it.

She thought the concoctions she'd cooked for supper were delicious. Her daddy had thought so too, but she noticed that he ate very little of it. In fact, she'd noticed that for the last few weeks, he'd eaten less and less.

Annie Laurie got the flashlight, fed Blacky at his usual place, then took the leftovers to the springhouse.

About the middle of the morning, the next day, Jesse and Lee came by for a visit. They were on their bicycles, as usual. They saw what Annie Laurie and her daddy were doing. Annie Laurie was cutting the cane as fast as she could with the bush axe. She knew that each stalk that she cut was one less stalk that her daddy had to cut.

Lee and Jesse had never cut cane before, but after watching them for a few minutes they practically took the bush axes away from them.

"You two go over there to the spring and get cool, we can handle this," Jesse said.

Both Annie Laurie and her daddy were glad to oblige them.

Annie Laurie didn't only stick her feet into the water, she pulled up her dress to her knees and stuck her legs into the refreshing cold water. She noticed how course and blonde the hair on her legs had gotten.

Franklin was just satisfied to sit in the shade and rear his back against a big tree, if only for a small while.

Next, Franklin and Annie Laurie came behind the boys stripping the leaves off the cane, then cutting the bottoms and the tops off the cane. They could judge where to cut the stalks by the color of the joints. The tops would be used to plant for the next season.

Both Jesse and Lee pulled off their shirts and swam in the shallow creek while Annie Laurie and her daddy finished stripping the leaves and cutting the stalks.

Next was replanting the cane for the next year. The boys didn't know how to plow a mule, so that was left up to Franklin. The breaking plow was hitched to Pete, and Franklin went down the furrows of the old rows, breaking the ground. Franklin couldn't plow as deep as he usually did, for Pete wasn't able to pull the plow, also since Franklin's neck was drawn down so, it was hard for him to plow a straight row.

For some reason, Frankin called Jesse, "Mr. Jesse," but he still referred to Lee Peacock, as just Lee. The only reason Annie Laurie could think of was because her daddy had watched Lee grow up.

Annie Laurie didn't know where Jesse's parents were building their house, but it must be north of them, and she never went in that direction. They always went north toward Dottelle and sometimes Excel.

Jesse saw what kind of shape her daddy was in though, and he told Annie Laurie that they farmed, and his daddy had two tractors with all the equipment. "Shoot, we should be moved in by Christmas, and I'll be glad to work your garden for you," he said.

Annie Laurie clasped her hands and put them under her chin.

Jesse knew her well enough to know that she was thanking him.

When Annie Laurie had been at the spring, she'd forgotten that she had unbuttoned the two top buttons of her dress and ran her cold wet hand over and under her neck. She noticed that Jesse was practically staring at the top of her dress. She turned around and looked down at the cleavage of her breasts. She quickly buttoned her dress and turned back around, feeling embarrassed. She saw that Jesse had turned around and was walking away, toward Lee. *"Maybe, I'm just imagining things,"* she thought.

The fellows hung around long enough to place the cane chutes in the newly plowed furrows and left, after taking another dip into the cold creek water.

Franklin covered the chutes, by using the mule and breaking plow. He started from the opposite end though, so he could throw the same soil that he'd plowed up back over the chutes. Pete didn't mind that though, for Franklin just skimmed along the top of the dirt, throwing the dirt he'd plowed up over the tender chutes.

They both knew the hardest part of the job was coming up, So Franklin threw a couple ears of corn near the creek and turned Pete loose at the creek. He knew that Pete wasn't going anywhere, for he'd just eat the corn and drink a belly full of the cold water.

Annie Laurie took the leftovers from the night before out of the springhouse, so she could re-heat them for a light lunch.

After lunch, they took a small break on the back porch, then it was time to go back to work.

Franklin walked to the creek and led Pete by the reins to the wagon. After hooking Pete to the wagon Franklin held the ends of the reins but walked beside the wagon until they reached the heaps of stacked cane. Both he and Annie Laurie started loading it into the wagon. When the wagon was filled, they'd take it to the juicer. They wound up with three wagon loads.

"That's a lot of cane, I pray that Pete can walk around in circles long enough to get it all juiced," Franklin said.

Annie Laurie could never remember when they didn't have Pete, and she wondered how they'd survive without him.

They soon had stacks of cane near the juicer.

Annie Laurie told her daddy she'd feed the juicer if he could manage to pour the juice in the vat, so Franklin started the fire under the first vat. He then hooked Pete to the pole, and he started walking around in circles. Annie Laurie poked one stalk of cane behind the other and the juice began to pour out into the cleaned bucket.

It was a hot tedious job for Annie Laurie, for she couldn't get up, she had to stay sitting in one place, or she'd get hit by the pole.

Franklin made sure that she kept plenty of cane to stick in the juicer, and he pulled the squeezed stalks out when they would begin to stack up. When the four-gallon bucket got about ¾ full, he'd pull it out and put an empty one in its place, then pour the filled bucket into the vat. It wasn't long before Annie Laurie smelled the syrup cooking.

Usually, it would take at least three people to make syrup, but they each knew they had to get by with two.

By three thirty, Annie Laurie had ran out of stalks to put in the juicer and boy she was glad.

Franklin, who was busy stirring the syrup to keep it from burning, stopped the mule long enough to unhitch him and put him back in his stable.

After Annie Laurie got the feelings back into her legs, she ran over and began to stir the syrup, taking her daddy's place.

After feeding and watering the animals, Franklin returned with an armload of one gallon tin containers that had lids on them. Looking at the syrup, he made haste to the barn and brought back two skimmers. Annie Laurie began to skim the white residue off the top of the vat, white her daddy started a fire under the second vat.

"I do love the scent of syrup when it's cooking," her daddy said, as he began to help Annie Laurie with the skimming.

Annie Laurie just smiled at him, for both of them was almost smoked black from all the smoke that kept billowing from under the vats.

"I'll be dang, looks like that wind would change directions, this smoke is rough," her daddy said.

Even in her smoked condition, she couldn't help but laugh, for about all she could see of her daddy's face was the whites of his eyes.

Right before the syrup came to a boil, Franklin pulled up the opening to the second vat, and before long they were skimming again. Vat # two's fire wasn't as intense as the first one, so they both got relief from the smoke and heat. They were steady skimming though.

Frankin finally started the fire under vat # three. For the syrup was getting a little ropey.

"We don't want it to scorch, not after all this work," Franklin said, so when he felt like the vat was heated enough, he pulled up the board that led to the opening. They continued to stir in vat # two until all the syrup was out, and into the third vat. Vat # 3 was more or less to just keep the liquid hot, for the syrup was already made. There was very little fire under the third vat, and no white residue at all on the top of the golden colored syrup.

"I think we've really out did ourselves this time, look how pretty it is. It's just about the color of honey," her daddy said, as he began to take the lids off the gallon cans and placing them around the end of the vat.

Several five-gallon buckets stayed at the vats year around, they caught the rain and almost stayed full all the time, so Franklin poured two buckets each into the first two vats.

He told Annie Laurie that she could go to the creek and get cleaned up, "I can handle it from here," he said.

Vat # 3 was relatively easy. There was a hole in the bottom of the side. The hole had a long wooden plug. Franklin just pulled the plug until the syrup began to pour into the buckets below, when the bucket was full, he'd put the plug back in the hole. After that he'd tap the lid on with a stick, for the bucket would be blazing hot. He'd then push the bucket out of the way with the same stick, then replace it with an empty one. He did it all while sitting in a rickety chair.

Annie Laurie pulled off her stockings and shoes, then got the strong bar of soap from atop the springhouse. She stepped over into the freezing water, then waited until she was completely submerged into the water before she took her dress and bloomers off. She bathed from head to toe with the strong octogen soap. Every once in a while, she'd stick her head up for air, then go down again. She had lain on top of her dress and bloomers to keep them from floating downstream. She thought about her brassiere and was glad she wasn't wearing it.

After dressing herself under the water, she stepped out of the creek, shivering. She wanted to wash her stockings too, but she was too cold. She jammed the stockings into her shoes, then picked them up and ran home dripping wet in her bare feet.

"Whew, what a relief!" she thought, after she'd dried herself and was warm again. After putting on another pair of dry bloomers and dress, she walked to the back porch and hung her dress to dry in the morning sun. She hadn't bothered with the brassiere or baking soda for she knew no one would be coming by.

She still had to worry with suppe,r though, so she headed to the sweet potato bank, and brought out three large potatoes. She knew that cooking another one would just be a waste, the way that her daddy ate lately, she thought.

When walking back to house she saw that her daddy was pouring water into the last vat, so she knew that the syrup making was over for another year.

All she could think of cooking with the fried sweet potatoes would be fried pork chops, for it was too late to soak dried beans or peas to cook. *"It's nigh impossible to find something green to eat, especially this time of the year,"* Annie Laurie thought. *"Besides, I'm too tired to fool with anything else."*

She boiled the two pork chops, as her aunt Sarie had taught them, then put them into the hot grease, for she'd already sliced and fried the sweet potatoes in the same grease.

Her daddy had spoiled her, for she rushed through supper so she could sit on the front porch and watch the day's end.

She put the meat and potatoes in one platter, then spread a cloth over things, and headed to the front porch.

She sat in the rocker that she claimed and looked east toward the setting sun and purple sky. She inhaled, as though she could breathe in the tranquility of the evening. Off in the distance she could hear the sound of a lonesome whippoorwill as it called its mate.

Blacky discovered where she was at, so he crept up the doorsteps and lay down by her chair. Once in a while, she'd rub the black dog's ears, something that he dearly loved.

"This is the best place in the world to live, little wonder my forefather had chosen this spot to live," she thought.

In a few minutes her daddy came out, and took his spot, on the top doorstep. He had on clean overalls, and she smelled the octagon soap scent his clean body radiated.

Finally, as the last rays of the sun disappeared behind the skyline, her daddy said, "That's where my Laurie is," and he pointed east.

Annie Laurie felt sorry for him, but there was nothing she could do but rustle his graying hair and go into the house.

When she got into the kitchen, she saw that her daddy hadn't forgotten her, for he brought her a cold quart jar of water from the springhouse, to make her Kool aid with.

Her daddy told her while they were eating that he sure appreciated what the boys had done. "If not for them, I'd still be out there. You know, the Lord works in mysterious ways. I've never grown stalks of cane that big. I do believe all those rain showers we got was the reason for it," he said. After eating a little he added, "We usually make about thirteen gallons; this year we made sixteen. I do believe that I'll take three gallons of it to Miss Earnestine's. We might get enough out of it to finish paying for your dress, and each of us get haircuts."

Annie Laurie smiled and nodded her head.

After supper, her daddy went outside with a flashlight to check on the syrup to see if it had cooled enough to put in the barn, and douse water on the hot charcoals.

Annie Laurie scraped the plates and fed Blacky before she cleaned the dishes. After she'd cleaned the kitchen, she was just too tired and not in the mood for music, so she went out on the porch for some relaxation. She knew it wouldn't be too much longer before the cold weather kept them inside.

While sitting outside, she looked around at the stary sky and wondered what other girls would be doing at her age. She'd see them as they'd come and go at Miss Earnestine's and noticed that most of them would be dressed just about the same. *"The shoes most of them wore sure wouldn't hold up long on a farm,"* she thought. Not one of them seemed to like her, and some stared at her as if she was unhinged or something. *"That's alright though,"* she thought, *"For I sure wouldn't change my life with any of them."*

She'd taken her Aunt Sarie's advice and still was giving her hair a hundred strokes each night. She thought she'd get the jump on it tonight, so she was combing it as she sat in her rocking chair. She'd continued to let her blonde hair grow long and still combed it straight back. All Mrs. Peacock did was trim the ends. Her hair came to her knees, and she thought she wouldn't let it get any longer. She combed her hair as far back as she could reach, then the ends she'd have to put in her lap. Around the house, she'd simply let it hang freely but if she was working in the fields or going to Miss Earnestine's, she'd twist it into a bun.

Aunt Sarie had told her that she looked like her daddy, but she still wished that she had a picture of her mama to look at. Her daddy simply told her that her mama would never allow her photograph to be taken.

There was a picture of her grandma Reed that hung in the living room and Annie Laurie could see some resemblance of her in the picture.

She wished that her Aunt Sarie would come for another visit, but so far, she hadn't. She'd written her several letters, but none of them were answered. She knew that her Aunt Sarie could write, for she still had the old cooking instructions that she'd written.

Annie Laurie's train of thought was broken when her daddy climbed the steps and sat down in his rocker.

"My oh my, what some pretty hair," he said before he turned off his flashlight.

"Honey, we've done it again. It's still plenty warm, but I have all sixteen cans in the crib. I separated the cans, so it should cool on down," her daddy said.

Annie Laurie would've gotten up and lit the lantern so she could see her daddy, but she figured they wouldn't be outside very much longer.

It wasn't long before they heard Blacky barking.

"It sounds like he has something treed at the edge of the woods behind the house," her daddy said, and then added, "I'm gonna get my gun and go see what he has up the tree."

When her daddy left hurriedly, Annie Laurie finished her hundred strokes then went inside for her mama's old shawl, for she was getting cool.

She didn't sit too long before she heard the sound of the gun as it shot.

After waiting on the porch for about thirty more minutes, she was beginning to get worried, so she walked to the back door to look towards the woods. She saw that her daddy had lit a lantern, and she could vaguely see his figure as he moved about, down near the springhouse.

Knowing he was safe, she went to the front and locked the door, for she knew he'd be coming through the back.

Instead of just waiting for her daddy to come in, Annie Laurie thought that she'd resort to her favorite, secret hobby, which was drawing. She'd gotten Mrs. Earnestine to order the thick pad of sketching paper and special pencils for her. Her daddy thought that she had bought the paper to use in order to communicate. She had to admit, it was about the most enjoyable thing she'd ever done, especially after she thought she'd gotten pretty good at it. Finding time to sketch was her problem. The sheets of paper were bigger than a regular notebook and more course.

So far, she thought her best drawings were of Miss Earnestine, Mr. Lum, Miss Lois, who Annie Laurie thought was beautiful. She also had a sketching of Pete, Blacky, her daddy, and Miss Earnestine's store. She had other sketches, but didn't think they were good. Sketching portraits was easy for her. She found that landscapes were harder and took longer. *If only I was good enough to get someone to pose for me,* she thought.

About the only time she found to draw was at night, when she was in her room, and it was done by kerosene lamp. At present she was drawing a picture of their log house, she'd erased so many lines until she'd thought about going to another subject. Sketching the house was easy, it was blending the pecan trees, cribs, and barn that were the problem, but still the main things were "Time, and secrecy."

Before long, she heard her daddy as he did his ritual, by cleaning the bottom of his boots on each doorstep.

She turned her sketch book over, put the lamp back on the table near the door and went into the dining room.

Her daddy was grinning, then said, "Well, we'll be having "Coon" for supper tomorrow night, thanks to ole Blacky."

"Where is it?" Annie Laurie asked.

"I cleaned it, put it in an onion sack, then tied the sack to the springhouse and threw it into the cold water. I only cut him on his belly. I thought I'd tan the hide and make Mr. Lum a hat out of it," her daddy said.

Annie Laurie laughed, then wrote in her notebook that was on the kitchen table, "Haha, I can just see Mr. Lum wearing it."

"Well, it'll be fresh meat, something different for supper tomorrow, and I'll have to admit, you know how to cook wild game," her daddy said.

"Tant to," Annie Laurie replied.

Franklin had noticed over the years, that words that began with a "T" Annie Laurie would attempt to say them. *"Any word that she just had to use the tip of her tongue,"* he thought.

Franklin sat down at the table, and automatically, Laurie Anne poured him a cup of coffee that was left over from supper.

"You're a sweet daughter," Franklin told her.

Again, Annie Laurie stammered, "Tant to."

"Oh, if only I had the money to get her to a good doctor in Mobile!" Franklin thought.

In a little while, Franklin said their nightly prayer, and they went into their bedroom.

Franklin had split the end of a stick and slipped a cloth into the split. He'd pour some liniment on the cloth and rub it on his spine at night. The liniment was very hot, but it seemed to give him some relief from the pain.

Annie Laurie put the lamp back on the table at the side of her bed and picked up where she had left off with her drawing.

Chapter 7

After a breakfast of grits and eggs the next morning, they struck out walking to Miss Earnestine's store. Her daddy had weaved a big cotton basket and two smaller ones. He put the smaller baskets, along with the small basket Annie Laurie had made and the three gallons of syrup in the top basket. The cotton basket had hand holes cut on each side at the top of the basket.

It took all that Annie Laurie could do to hold up her side of the basket, but they made it across the culvert and was nearing the junk pile when Mr. Jordan slowed down and stopped.

"Would you two like a ride?" he asked.

"I believe my daughter would love one," Franklin laughed.

Mr. Jordan jumped from his trunk and helped Franklin swing everything into the back of the truck.

"Hey, these are some nice baskets," Mr. Jordan said. "Are you selling these by any chance?" he asked.

"Oh, yeh! And the syrup too," replied Franklin.

Traffic was sparce on the little road, so Mr. Jordan wasn't worried about anyone running into them, as he examined the baskets.

"These are nice and smooth," Mr. Jordan said.

"Yes sir, we sand every strip," Franklin answered.

"What's the price of them, or do you already have them sold" Mr. Jordan asked.

"The big basket is ten dollars, the other two are eight dollars each, and Annie Laura's is four dollars," Franklin answered.

"Oh, my wife would love the little one," Mr. Jordan said.

"Let's see, that will be thirty dollars," he said, as he pulled out his wallet and paid them on the spot.

"What about a gallon of the best sugarcane syrup that you'll ever eat?" Frankin asked as he pulled his pocketknife out and pried the lid off one of the gallons.

"Wow, that's pretty. Do you mind?" Mr. Jordan asked.

"No, go right ahead," Franklin said, as Mr. Jordan dipped the end of his index finger into the tin can, stuck his finger in his mouth and smacked his lips.

"The best I've ever tasted, how much is it?" he asked.

"Seven dollars, but since your son and his friend helped us, I'll let you have it for six," Franklin answered.

"So, your place is where that rascal was," Mr. Jordan said, then counted seven dollars and gave it to Franklin. "Come on and get in the truck, I reckon y'all are headed to Miss Earnestine's," Mr. Jordan asked.

"Yes sir, That's where we were headed. It's truly a blessing that you came by. I can say one thing, Mr. Jesse is a fine young fellow," Franklin told Mr. Jordan.

"He is a good boy, if I have to say so myself. He'd rather stay on the tractor though than he does a classroom. His mama has to keep an eye on his grades. He and Lee Peacock are good friends. I hear tell that Lee is a straight A student. I was hoping that some of Lee would rub off on him," Mr. Jordan told them.

"Mr. Jesse will do you proud," Franklin said, as they pulled in front of Miss Earnestine's store and stopped.

Franklin sold one of the cans of syrup to Mr. Lum before he made it into the store.

Lum put the can of syrup into his truck, then walked across the road to the fertilizer barn, because that's where Mr. Jordan had backed up to.

Franklin couldn't believe it, but Miss Earnestine also gave him seven dollars for the store's gallon of syrup. She then told Franklin that she'd had a few customers to inquire about his baskets.

Franklin didn't tell her about selling the baskets to Mr. Jordan.

"Yes mam, I'll get on them when we get back home," Franklin told her.

Several people came in ordering ice. She sold the ice in blocks. They'd take the ice and put it into their iceboxes to keep things cool. The Icehouse was also across the road. Lum would use an icepick to chisel the size they'd paid for.

Annie Laurie thought they were lucky, for they had the springhouse.

The blocks of ice were always covered in sawdust, and her daddy told Annie

Laurie the sawdust would help prevent the ice from melting.

Franklin tallied his money and discovered that they'd earned fifty-one dollars, so they treated themselves to a cold Coca Cola. The red box that the drinks were in was also kept cold by a big block of ice.

Franklin learned while he was in the store that Mr. Jordan made a living by buying and selling cows. He'd buy the underweight cows, fatten them then re-sell them.

Mrs. Earnestine said that he sold most of his cows to a big meat company in Brewton.

"Just think, if we had electricity I could be selling meat in the store," Miss Earnestine said.

"Well, he must be making money with it, because he spends money like it's going out of style," Miss Lois said.

"Just thank the Lord that he's spending it here. Those two big cattle trucks that he has drinks some kind of gas," Miss Earnestine told Lois.

Franklin hung around long enough for them to finish their drinks, then they walked over to Mrs. Peacock's.

Lee was on the front porch swing, swinging just as high as he could go. He invited Annie Laurie to join him, but she pointed toward the back door, which led to her small barber shop, and then her sewing room.

Franklin tapped on the door, then they entered.

They found that she had her cutting smock wrapped around Mr. Jerry Watson and was cutting his red hair. She told them to take a seat, so they did.

Mrs. Peacock used a pair of hand clippers to cut the men's hair, she had to work them by hand, which was very tiring to her. Therefore, when she finished with Mr. Watson's hair and he paid her, she shook the smock and called Annie Laurie's name. Cutting with scissors weren't half as tiring. She knew all she had to do was trim Annie Laurie's hair, and it wasn't half as tiring as the hand clippers.

Since Annie Laurie's blonde hair was always immaculately clean it didn't take

Mrs. Peacock long to comb it all to the back of her head and trim the ends.

"Oh, what a beautiful head of hair, now why do these other girls around here want to ruin their hair by burning it with a permanent wave," Mrs. Peacock said.

Since Clark Gable become famous all the men wanted their hair to be cut like Clark's, which was parted on the side and combed over.

Franklin liked his hair combed straight back, making it much easier for Mrs. Peacock to cut.

Mrs. Peacock didn't have a barber's chair, like the barbers in Excel had. She had a regular straight back wooden chair for adults and a highchair for children.

While cutting Franklin's hair she told Annie Laurie that she wasn't quite finished with her dress, "But, I'll have it finished before your birthday on the 26th," she said.

Annie Laurie smiled and nodded her head.

"It seems like everybody, and their brother has been wanting a haircut here lately and it's thrown me behind with my sewing," she said.

She soon finished with Franklin's hair, and he thanked her, then gave her forty cents, because she only charged fifteen cents to trim Annie Laurie's each time.

Lucky for Franklin and Annie Laurie, Mr. Jordan had finished paying Miss Earnestine, and was about to leave, so he gave them a ride back to their house.

As they passed by the junk pile, Annie Laurie saw where someone had thrown away a pile of assorted things. She thought she'd get Blacky to come back with her because she wanted to go through it.

When they reached the house, Franklin offered to pay Mr. Jordan, but he said he was glad to oblige them.

Annie Laurie knew that her daddy was eager to get back to making the baskets, but she wrote in her notebook what she intended to do.

"Okay honey, just take Blacky, watch where you're putting your feet and you'll be safe," he answered.

Blacky was just glad to get away from his domain, so he gladly accompanied Annie Laurie to the junk pile.

Annie Laurie let Blacky do his sniffing around in the pile of junk before she found a stick and carefully walked through the new pile of junk. She didn't realize it at the time, but what she'd find would influence her for the rest of her life.

First, she found several canvases of scattered painting, then a few canvases that hadn't been used at all. She looked at several of the images and realized the person didn't know what they were doing. She then found a small suitcase and opened it. Inside were several tubes of assorted colors of oil paint. Also, there were small paint brushes of various sizes and shapes.

She didn't know a thing about painting, but she was dying to give it a try, so she gathered up all the items and stacked them near the road. She then continued her search, with Blacky in the lead, but all she found was a jar of glass marbles. She didn't have time to play marbles, but she thought she'd get them and give them to Mr. Jesse or Lee.

She knew she couldn't search further for she had to get the racoon out of the spring water and get it in the oven.

She found a string and tied the canvases together, put the jar of heavy marbles in one of her wide dress pockets. She called Blacky away from his investigations and sniffing, then headed toward home. Holding the string that was looped around her arm with one hand and the suitcase in the other. After making it back home she put everything in her room, then headed toward the spring with a dishpan in her hand.

After giving the racoon one more good cleaning, she put it in the dishpan and headed toward home. On her way to the house, she saw her daddy hard at work with the big cotton basket.

After building a fire in the stove, she began to season the "Coon," as her daddy called it. She knew he liked them highly seasoned, so she rubbed the entire racoon with black pepper, then salted it. After waiting for the temperature gauge to reach 325 degrees, she put the racoon into the oven. She cracked open the damper knowing the temperature would rise a little, then headed to the shed to start on her first basket.

"Did you find anything interesting at the dump?" her father asked, without taking his eyes off the basket.

She wondered why her father would ask her a question like that, knowing she couldn't talk. So, she simply drew a heart in the palm of her hand and picked up some of the oaken strips he'd made for her, then went to work.

Annie Laurie kept an eye on the stove flute as she worked with the basket. She knew if the smoke became almost invisible to see, it'd be time to add the sweet potatoes and put more wood in the stove.

There were two different places you'd put wood in the stove. One was directly under the top of the stove. Putting the wood there was when you wanted to cook food on top of the stove. For the oven, you had to open a compartment in front, and to the end to build a fire. Like the top of the stove, the wood set on large wide grates, and the ashes fell into a compartment. There was a metal scoop, you'd scoop the ashes out and carefully put them into a metal foot tub. Her daddy always scattered the ashes into the garden.

Annie Laurie had made one of her baskets and was midway through another one when she noticed the white smoke had almost stopped coming from the flute. She laid her basket down and ran into the kitchen.

She could smell the aroma from the baked racoon the second she came into the kitchen, and it made her mouth water. *"Sure beats pork and chicken all the time,"* she thought.

She used two thick potholders to slide the rack out of the oven and saw that it was baked to a light brown, just the way she wanted it. She then began to peel the sweet potatoes to slice and put around the racoon.

After slicing the potatoes, she slid the rack back into the oven, then added one more piece of wood to the red charcoals. She figured that would be enough to finish cooking the racoon and sweet potatoes.

The pot of coffee that was made that morning was slid to the back of the stove. She checked it and it was hot, so she poured her daddy a cup. She thought he'd really enjoy it, and he deserved a break from all the work.

There was a pancake left from breakfast, so she surprised Blacky with it, as he was lying on the ground beside her daddy.

"Ahh, you know the way to your daddy's heart," Franklin said, as he grabbed the hot cup with his rough hands that were lined with corns.

Annie Laurie saw that he had already ran the oak strips for the next basket through the sandpaper that he'd hold in his hand.

The sandpaper was another good item that they'd retrieved from the junk pile. Years ago, someone had thrown out rolls and rolls of it, so they brought it home and put it in their barn.

Annie Laurie began weaving on her basket again, while her daddy enjoyed his cup of coffee.

They were far enough into the shed to keep the wind off of them. Annie Laurie silently thanked the Lord they prayed to for giving them such a peaceful ending to a day. She thought about what she'd found in the junk pile that day and was excited about it. She didn't have to think about who she would attempt to paint first. It would be the likeness of her kindhearted daddy. She'd heard other people curse, even ladies, but she'd never heard a curse word come out of his mouth. If he'd ever been angry or upset with her about anything she didn't know, or with anyone else that she knew of. *"He was just a kind hardworking man,"* she thought, as she weaved on her basket, thinking how blessed she was.

She had to rush, but she had enough time to finish her second basket, when she realized things in the oven had to be ready to eat.

Annie Laurie hung both her baskets by the vail on some random nails that were sticking out from a board.

Her daddy saw the two baskets and smiled.

"Wow, they're nice, I'm about finished with my second one too, that's twenty-eight dollars we've made this afternoon," he told her, and smiled.

While she had his attention, she rubbed her stomach and pointed toward the house.

"Ok honey, let me put the finishing touches on this one and I'll come on it," he told her.

Annie Laurie ran inside to check on things in the oven.

After pulling the rack out for the second time, she saw that both the racoon and sweet potatoes were golden brown.

"Just right," she thought, so, using the two thick potholders, she picked up the heavy cast iron tray and put it on top of the stove.

"Whew!" she exclaimed, as she closed the door to the oven.

Her next thing was making a fire in the top of the stove, to make her daddy's coffee.

She'd just got the coffee going when she heard someone knocking on the door, which was very unusual, for they seldom had company, so she ran to the door.

Years back, someone had made a small peep crack between two of the thick boards in the door. A small string was pushed into the crack to keep the wind out. When Annie Laurie pulled some of the string up, she saw that it was Mr. Jesse. She quickly pushed the string back in place and opened the door.

"I was about to decide that y'all were gone," Mr. Jesse said.

Annie Laurie, who was still perspiring from the heat of the stove, made a sweeping gesture with her left arm for him to come inside.

"Boy, something smells good," Mr. Jesse said, the second he stepped into the room.

Annie Laurie held up her index finger at him, motioning that she'd be right back, so he stopped.

In just a jiffy she was back with her notebook pad. She quickly wrote, "Daddy's outside, and I just took a racoon out of the oven. "Would you like to eat supper with us?"

"Sure, I've never eaten coon," Jesse answered.

"Good, let's go out on the porch where it's cooler, Daddy will be here in a minute and we'll eat," Annie Laurie scribbled.

"You know Annie Laurie, walking into this house is like stepping back in time. I wish our new house was going to look like this," Mr. Jesse said, as he turned to go back outside.

Along with her pencil and notebook, Annie Laurie followed him out onto the porch, where she had a seat in her rocker. Mr. Jesse sat in the rocker beside her.

"Boy, you're right, it's much nicer out here," he said, then patted her on her hand.

Just his touch on her bare skin sent chills up her spine, but without really thinking, she moved her hand.

She wrote in her tablet, "Daddy and I have been weaving baskets today," then held the book so he could read it.

"Yeah, I know, dad showed them to me. In fact, that's really the reason I'm supposed to be here. Mom wants to put in an order for ten more of the small ones. She belongs to a church group, and she thought she'd get the other ladies one, also," Jesse said.

Annie Laurie tallied in her head and came up with forty dollars.

"Tell your mom to give me a week, if weather permits," Annie Laurie wrote.

"Oh, she'll love that. She also sent a verbal invitation to attend our church," Jesse said.

"What type of a church?" Annie Laurie scribbled.

"Oh, it's of the Baptist faith, and I'll be there," Jesse said.

Again, he grabbed her hand from her lap and squeezed it.

Annie Laurie almost jumped from her rocker, but she didn't, for he only held her hand briefly, because they heard her daddy's footsteps in the house.

Annie Laurie wanted to write in her notebook, "But I can't talk, nor do I have the proper clothes." Instead, she simply wrote, "We're of the Methodist faith."

"Well, there you are," her daddy said, as he stepped out onto the porch holding his cup of coffee.

"Nice seeing you here, Mr. Jesse, would you like a cup of coffee?" he asked.

Jesse didn't want to tell Mr. Reed that he wasn't allowed to drink it. Instead, he just said, "No, thank you sir, but I am planning on having supper here."

"Oh, that's great, there's no way we can eat all of that coon by ourselves," Franklin said.

Annie Laurie got up and went into the Kitchen to set the table and to put the racoon and sweet potatoes on the table. She saw that her daddy had brought some cold water from the spring, so she made a quart of Kool aid.

Before telling them supper was on the table, she decided to open a can of spinach, so they'd have something green to eat. She seasoned the spinach with some smoked pork grease, to give it a good flavor, then put the boiler on top of the stove.

She knew that it would soon be dark, so before she decided to call them to supper, she lit the kerosene lamp in the kitchen and the living room.

Annie Laurie knew it would soon be her daddy's favorite time of the day, so after going back out onto the porch. She decided to wait until the sun set before she'd called them in for supper.

"Wow, we don't have this view from our house. All you can see are the trees," Jesse said.

"I just do imagine that sunset is the reason my grand paw built this house on this very spot, after he came home from the war between the states," Franklin said.

"I'd like to know how old that road is out there?" Jesse asked.

"I can tell you this, it's been here since Indian times. When they traveled the path, it was called, "The Wolf Trail," Franklin replied.

"Wow, it could've been my folks, my daddy said we had Indian in us," Jesse said.

Mr. Jesse and Franklin seemed to be enjoying each other's company, so Annie Laurie just let them talk, before she finally motioned to her daddy that it was time to eat.

Annie Laurie ran ahead of them and poured the spinach into a bowl. The racoon and sweet potatoes were warm enough to set on the table beside the spinach. After the three were seated at the table, Franklin blessed the food.

"Alright, it's each to their own at this point," Franklin said, as he grabbed the long fork and wooden handle butcher knife to cut the coon into portions.

"Mr. Reed, I do love your house," Jesse said, as he stabbed him one of the coon's back legs, then helped himself to a generous portion of the sweet potatoes.

Annie Laurie noticed that Jesse only got a spoon full of the spinach until he tasted them, then he got two more.

It pleased Annie Laurie to have Jesse for supper, and to just see him make himself at home. She could tell that her daddy was enjoying his company too, for she'd never seen him eat so hearty.

Jesse waited until he'd finished eating, then practically swilled his glass of Kool aid.

"Boy, if mama could cook like this. It's the best I've eaten in a long time," Jesse said.

"Huh, she weaved two baskets while she was cooking," her daddy said, as he pushed his plate away from him.

"Mama put in an order for ten of her baskets to give to her church group," Jesse said.

"My goodness, I know what she'll be doing for the next few days," Franklin said.

Annie Laurie gave her daddy his usual cup of coffee after supper, while she began to clean the dishes. She couldn't believe it when Jesse got up to help her.

Franklin could clearly see that Mr. Jesse had a crush on his daughter, and he intended to talk to her after he left.

"Boy, Ole Blacky will have a feast tonight, with all the coon that's leftover. He deserves it though, for he treed him for me." Franklin said, as he sipped his cup of hot coffee.

Franklin wanted to go in the living room to listen to the radio, but he didn't feel like he should leave the two in the room unchaperoned. It wasn't that he didn't like Mr. Jesse, but he knew what was on the young man's mind, for he was young once himself.

"It's going to be pitch dark when you go home, are you sure you can make it?" Franklin asked.

Jesse had finished with cleaning out the dishes, so he sat back down at the table.

"Now who would want to fool with me. I could guarantee you one thing, if they grabbed me, they'd turn me loose quicker than they grabbed me," Mr. Jesse said. He then flexed his biceps and showed his perfect two rows of white teeth. He then laughed and said, "Nah, I'm not brave, but I'm not afraid of the dark, Mr. Reed."

Franklin laughed, and said, "No, I don't imagine you are."

He had to admit, Franklin did admire Mr. Jesse's muscular build and height.

Annie Laurie walked out onto the back porch and fed the anxious Blacky, then dove in on the dishes while her daddy and Jesse talked.

She wouldn't admit it, but she was sure glad her daddy stayed in the kitchen with her, for she didn't know anything about boys. All she knew was they made her nervous.

"How old are you, Mr. Jesse?" Franklin asked.

"Old enough to be a good quarterback, at Excel, but not old enough to get my driver's license. I will be before long though, I'll turn 16 on June 15th," he answered.

Speaking of age, I guess I'd better head toward home. I really enjoyed my supper, Annie Laurie," he said.

Annie Laurie turned around and simulated "Thank you" backwards in the dim lit room.

"My goodness, look at that girl writing to where I can read it. She's a girl Einstein," Jesse said.

"She's a smart one, and you're not going to out figure her either. She can tally numbers in her head quicker that Miss Earnestine can figure on that machine of hers." Franklin said.

"Well, I'm walking, so I best leave before mama has a hissy. Before I go Mr. Reed, I can see that you're not in the best health, anytime I can be helpful to you, you just whistle," Jesse told him.

"Thank you, son, I'll sure keep that in mind," Franklin said, then he saw Mr. Jesse to the front door.

Franklin couldn't help but get tickled at Mr. Jesse, for as he hit the road he began to whistle, "A Ticket, A-Tasket."

Franklin locked the door, and blew out the lamp, in the living room. He didn't quite know how to begin, but he knew he had to do it.

"Is he gone?" Annie Laurie wrote in her notebook, when her daddy sat back down at the table.

"Yes, and while we're talking, let me warn you about boys," Franklin began.

Annie Laurie began to write in the notebook, then held it up to her daddy.

"I know about boys, and I know what they want. As long as I resist, we can be friends, can't we?" she asked.

"Yes, you can be friends as long as you're around a grown-up. No dating until you're sixteen years old," Franklin told her.

"That's fine with me. Guess what?" she asked.

"What?" he answered.

"Mr. Jesse's mama ordered ten more of my baskets. I believe that's really the reason he came by," Annie Laurie scribbled.

"Boy, that's great honey, so I guess we'll be busy for a spell," her daddy said.

Chapter 8

1939

Things had run about as usual, except their mule, Pete had died. He just fell over in the field and was dead by the time he hit the ground.

Franklin was breaking the land for the spring planting. He'd been looking for the occasion, but still, he didn't know what he was going to do with the body of the heavy mule.

He remembered what Mr. Jesse had told him several times, for both he and Lee still stopped by occasionally.

Franklin had enough money stashed back to buy another mule, but he knew he'd just be wasting his money. Franklin didn't feel like he could hold up to break and train a new mule. He hadn't told Annie Laurie, but the pain wasn't just in his spine, it was now behind his shoulder blades too. He was also spitting blood. He knew Annie Laurie had to have noticed it but just hadn't said anything.

Franklin took the gear off Pete and walked to the road. As luck would have it,

One of Mr. Jordan's big trucks came by, and Franklin flagged him down.

Franklin told the man what he wanted. "If you will, ask Mr. Jesse to come down here on the tractor," Franklin said.

"Mr. Jordan, he's in school rat now, but when he gets in, I'll tells him," the driver said.

Franklin thanked him and the driver left.

Annie Laurie felt that if her daddy wanted to tell her about him spitting blood, he'd tell her, so she didn't say anything about it to him. Her daddy was now drawn so until he was bent double, but he never complained to Annie Laurie or anyone else. Annie Laurie just tried to keep a closer eye on him. He ate less and less, no matter what she cooked.

She'd heard the commotion in the field and looked out the back door to see that Pete was lying on the ground. Pete had been around for as long as she could remember. All she could do was go back into the kitchen and cry.

She wondered what they would do without a way to farm, *"After all, we practically live off the land,"* she thought.

About the only enjoyment she had was her painting, and she felt that she had gotten pretty good at it, *"Especially the portraits,"* she thought. She was about out of several colors of paints though, and she knew the only way to keep painting was to buy more paints. She had long ago run out of the canvasses she'd found and was now painting on boards and pieces of flat tin she'd found in the junk pile.

Annie Laurie knew she had to do something in order to buy more paints. She knew it was bad timing, with Pete dying, but she wiped the tears from her eyes and went into her bedroom, wondering why life had to be so hard.

As she randomly arranged the paintings in her room, her thoughts returned to her daddy. They seldomly went to Miss Earnestine's store, for she knew he just wasn't up to the long walk, even though he wouldn't tell her that. Their only source of income was selling the baskets, pecans and eggs. It was tight, but it bought them flour, sugar, rice, coffee, baking powder and other cooking items. The corn meal they used came from their corn patch. Mr. Flowers, that lived near Dottelle had a gristmill and he'd grind your corn and grits for a fourth of your corn. Mr. Flowers gave an option of either paying him or trading a fourth of your corn. Since they always had plenty of it, Franklin just swapped it out with him.

When Franklin made it back to the house, he sat on the doorsteps, in order to get out of the sun, for the house shaded the sun until noon. Franklin had kept sawing his walking stick off to suit his condition.

Annie Laurie shelved the dinner she was cooking to the back of the stove and walked to the front door.

"Daddy, I have something I want you to look at," Annie Laurie told him.

He had to really lean on his walking stick, but he made it to his feet and climbed the steps. He saw that Annie Laurie's bedroom door was open and he knew what she was going to show him. He knew that she'd been painting, for he'd smelled the unusual odor of the paints one day and looked in her room.

Annie Laurie smiled as her daddy looked around in her room in awe.

"Honey, you have some kind of talent," he smiled.

"Thank you, but if I'm going to keep painting, I need more paints," she wrote. She then wrote, "You reckon Miss Earnestine will buy her painting, so I can buy more paints?"

"No doubt about it, especially after I make you some frames for them," Franklin said.

"Well then, now you have a job to do," Annie Laurie wrote, thinking it would keep his mind off Pete.

Franklin borrowed Annie Laurie's notebook and began to take measurements. As long as she could remember her daddy always carried a ruler in his front pocket, along with his razor-sharp pocketknife.

They were forever finding an assortment of boards and lumber in the junkpile and bringing it home to be stored in the barn or stacked under the eaves of the barn.

Her daddy had to stand on his tiptoes, but he hugged his daughter around her waist, and said, "You're the smartest little girl I know," before he left the room.

"My Lord, she might just make it on her own, after I'm gone," Franklin thought, for he didn't figure he would make it much longer. He knew it was useless worrying about Pete. He also knew he wasn't able to farm anymore, so he began to go through the scrap wood in the barn. He sanded each piece of wood before he started to make the frames.

He made the largest frame first. It was a painting of baby Jesus, with Mother Mary swaddling him in a colorful blue and white blanket. The next two were for Miss Earnestine, and Miss Lois. He was just starting on the frame for Mr. Lum, when he heard the sound of a tractor and knew it would be Mr. Jesse.

Franklin stopped what he was doing and hurried to the front of the house as fast as he could go.

Mr. Jesse had stopped the tractor in front of the house and was about to get off the tractor when he saw Mr. Franklin.

Franklin made it close enough to the tractor to tell Mr. Jesse what he needed him to do.

"Do you have a chain?" Mr. Jesse asked.

Franklin told him he had a chain in the barn that was thirty feet long.

"Good enough, you just show me where it's at and I'll get it," Mr. Jesse told him.

Mr. Jesse drove the tractor to the barn, and hopped off the tractor, but left the motor running.

Franklin pointed to the back of the barn, showing him the chain that was looped over some rafters.

Jesse knew that Mr. Franklin wouldn't have been able to reach the chain, so he was glad he had volunteered to get it.

Jesse saw that he chain had a hook on each end, so that would make things easier.

A set of discs were hooked to the back of the tractor, so Jesse unhooked the disc and hooked the chain to the back of the tractor.

Jesse could see the dead mule lying in the field, so he asked Franklin where he wanted him to put the mule.

"Well, it's marked, I have forty acres here, so just pull him to the end of my property, you'll see the markers notched on trees," Franklin said.

"Will do, and when I come back I'll hook up my disc and break your garden for you. All you need to do is get your seed together and I'll come back Saturday and plant your garden for you," Jesse told him. He then added, "If weather permits."

The plow was still standing upright in the field, so Franklin waited until Mr. Jesse had pulled Pete to the tree line, before he made his way to the field. It took all his strength, but he managed to pull the plow back under the shed, by the time Mr. Jesse made his way back.

"Aw, I could have done that," Jesse told him.

"It's the least I could do," Franklin told him, as Jesse carried the chain back to the barn and re-hung it. Jesse made sure he didn't touch the end that he'd wrapped around the mule.

Jesse then backed up to the disc and re-hooked them.

"Now, you just go about your business while I disc this garden for you. I see those cane chutes sticking up, I must admit, I don't know a thing about

sugarcane, so I'll just disc around them,"
Jesse said.

"That's fine, I'm not going to fool with
making syrup this year anyway," Franklin
said.

Jesse had a lift on his tractor, so he let
the disc down when he came to the
garden and began to tear the ground up.

"Uh uh uh," Franklin thought, as he
marveled how quickly Mr. Jesse made his
way through the garden.

Franklin went back to work making the
frame for Mr. Lum's painting and did a lot
of thinking about things as he worked.
He had to admit, he didn't know a thing
about paintings, but in his opinion, he
thought Annie Laurie's were great. Where
she got the talent, he didn't know, unless
it was from her mama. He only knew that
he was so proud of her and had always
been. *"Maybe, just maybe, she'll be able
to make it on her own,"* he thought, as he
coughed up a wad of blood, then
continued thinking. He knew that Annie
Laurie was meant for a bigger realm of
things. *"Maybe the reason she couldn't*

talk was she expressed herself with her paintings and not her voice," he thought.

Franklin's thoughts turned to Mr. Jesse. He believed he was a good young man, and from his actions he was raised right. He also knew that Mr. Jesse had always had a crush on his daughter. He also wondered how his parents would think about the possible coupling, knowing she couldn't talk. They probably already knew how and where she lived. He wondered if they knew she'd never gone a day to school. "Maybe, I should talk to Mrs. Peacock about the clothes that she wears, for he didn't see the other girls her age that dressed the way she and Mrs. Peacock about the clothes that she wears, for he didn't see the other girls her age that dressed the way that she and Mrs. Peacock did. Franklin just knew that he'd did the best that he knew how in the raising of Annie Laurie, and in his opinion, she was turning out to be a good girl. He also knew with her looks and shapely figure there would be a battle ahead for her.

"*Oh well*," he thought, "She still has another year before she can date, and maybe I can hold out that long."

Before Pete fell dead in the garden, Franklin had seen Annie Laurie gathering turnips in the garden. He wondered what his daughter was going to cook that would go along with the greens.

It didn't take Mr. Jesse but about forty minutes to finish breaking the land. By then, Franklin had six frames made.

Mr. Jesse pulled the tractor near the barn and switched it off, then jumped from the tractor.

"What are you making there?" he asked Franklin.

"Something for my daughter," Franklin replied.

"She must be planning to frame some things," Jesse said.

Franklin didn't know whether Annie Laurie wanted him to know about it or not, so he changed the subject.

"How much do I owe you Mr. Jesse," Franklin asked.

"What about supper, is that cheap enough?" replied Jesse.

"Yes sir, that's cheap enough, but there's no telling what it will be," Franklin said.

"I'll let you in on a little secret, Mother can't cook for crap, so we eat out a lot, and of course, there's always sandwiches," Jesse replied.

Franklin laughed and started gathering up the newly made frames.

"Here, let me get those for you, you just get your walking stick," Jesse said.

"We'll go in the back door, so I can tell Annie Laurie we've got company for supper," Franklin said.

Jesse gathered up the newly made frames and followed Franklin to the back door. Franklin opened the door wide, so Mr. Jesse wouldn't have trouble getting the frames through the back door.

"We have company for supper," Franklin told his daughter.

Annie Laurie smiled and nodded her head at Jesse.

"I don't know what it is, but it sure smells good," Jesse said, as he leaned the frames against the dining room wall.

Annie Laurie had guessed that Jesse would be staying for supper, so she ran into her room and strapped on her brassiere. She had just finished frying two extra pork chops when they came in. The bowl of turnip greens, baked sweet potatoes, and cornbread were already on the table. Annie Laurie had timed things just right, as she forked the last two pork chops out of the frying pan and put them on the platter.

Annie Laurie looked at the frames and was about to have a fit to see how her paintings were going to look in their frames.

Not wanting Jesse to look into her bedroom, while the supper on the table was cooling, she began to bring the paintings into the dining room.

Jesse sat at the table in awe to begin with, then asked. "Who in the world?".

"Now Mr. Jesse, you know that I'm not the guilty party, my daughter painted those paintings," Franklin said.

"My Lord, what talent," Jesse said, as Annie Laurie began to place the paintings around in the dining room.

There were twenty paintings, total.

"I see Miss Earnestine, Miss Lois, Lee Peacock, even Mr. Lum. Where am I, for Pete's sake?", Jesse asked.

Annie Laurie pulled his likeness from behind another painting.

"My hair is not that curly, it's almost kinky in that painting," Jesse said.

Annie Laurie nodded her head, that it was. She then plundered through the frames and found one that was right for the painting. She placed Mr. Jesse's likeness into the frame and presented it to him.

"You're giving it to me?" he asked.

Annie Laurie nodded her head.

Always keeping her notebook and pencil handy, she wrote, "For being so good to us."

"My Lord is my mama's gonna flip out, when she sees this," Jesse said.

"I still need to put some tacks in back of the frame, so the painting will be in there good and tight," her daddy told Jesse.

"Well, I can't carry it home on the tractor, so I'll swing by after school tomorrow and get it, but my Lord, what are you gonna do with so many paintings?"

"She's hoping she can sell them," Franklin answered.

Before Jesse could answer, Annie Laurie motioned for them to sit at the table.

"Oh boy, supper looks delicious, but who would've thought you had that kind of talent. Ain't being knock dead gorgeous enough for you?" Jesse asked.

Franklin cleared his throat, blessed the food, and they all ate.

Jesse, knowing he'd stuck his foot in his mouth didn't say another word, he just ate like a starved hound.

After they'd finished the meal, again, Franklin sat at the head of the table and drank his coffee, while Jesse helped with the dishes.

Afterward Blacky was fed the scraps, they all sat on the front porch and enjoyed the cool April breeze of the darkness.

Franklin tried to think of a tactful way of asking Mr. Jesse, so finally he just came right out and said it.

"Annie Laurie needs to get her paintings to Miss Earnestine's, and she needs more supplies. Reckon you can take us down there?" Franklin asked.

"Well, it's according to what Annie Laurie has cooked Friday night, because dad has me lined up until Saturday morning, and I can't waste time then. I have to plant your garden. That won't take long though, if you have the seed ready. I suppose I can spare a couple of hours without him blowing his top Saturday morning. Of course, I'll need to take the tractor back and get my car" replied Jesse.

"Good, that'll give me time to finish the frames," Franklin said.

Of course, Annie Laurie couldn't talk, but she was thrilled to think that her paintings might be on display at Miss Earnestine's.

Jesse soon got tired of just rocking and knowing that he couldn't get anywhere with Annie Laurie with her daddy sitting on the doorsteps, so he soon bade them adieu. He did manage to hold her hand for a few minutes while Mr. Franklin had a coughing spell though.

Not wanting to bother Mr. Franklin, Jesse leapt from the porch to the ground.

"You be careful on that tractor," Franklin said.

"It has lights," Jesse answered.

"Darn, if I could just get her away from her daddy," Jesse thought, as he felt his way onto the tractor and cranked it.

He soon made his way to the front of the house and was soon crossing the ditch that led to the road.

"He's a boy and a half," Franklin said to Annie Laurie.

Annie Laurie just laughed.

The two remained on the porch for a while, listening to the crickets chirp and the frogs croaking. Both of them were just thinking about life, how strange things could happen at the drop of a pin. Of course, Franklin's thoughts were about his health, Laurie, and the future of Annie Laurie.

Annie Laurie's thoughts were about her paintings, her daddy's health, and Jesse.

"Well, tomorrow is Thursday. I have two days to make those frames, so I say we need to turn in," Franklin said.

There was a bowl, pitcher, soap, wash cloths and towels in each of their rooms, so they took a bath each night. After bathing, they'd pour their bath water out of the window. Annie Laurie slept in a long sleeping gown, while Franklin just slept in his boxers. Annie Laurie figured wearing the tight restricting panties in the daytime was enough, so she pulled them off, along with her brassiere and just slept in her gown.

Annie Laurie lay in bed that night with a smile on her face. She thought of the roughness of Jesse's hand when he held hers. She wondered what she could cook Friday night for supper. She didn't worry about it though, for she believed she could tear the leaves off a tree and cook them and Jesse would gobble them down.

Annie Laurie didn't realize It that night as she lay in her bed. She didn't realize how small her world was, but she was contented, so it didn't take her long to fall asleep after saying her prayers.

The next morning, after brushing her teeth with the usual thing, baking soda, then smearing a little under each arm, she put on her clothes to face the day.

After a breakfast of grits and fried eggs, Franklin went outside to get to work on the frames. He'd already gone to the spring and brought back the water for the house. He no longer had to tote water back for the mule, or the hogs, for the last year's slaughter of the hogs would be the last. Franklin only had to bring back enough water for the chickens and the house. He still had to make just as many trips to the spring though, for he could only tote back one bucket at a time. The other hand was used for his short walking cane.

Annie Laurie decided, after she'd cleaned the kitchen, she'd go outside and see if she could be of any help to her daddy.

Her daddy told her he was only making one frame at a time. "I don't want to get the dimensions all messed up," he told her.

Annie Laurie did the sanding of the boards while her father made the frames. She did learn how to make the frames though, because she watched her daddy closely.

They had six more frames made before it was time for Annie Laurie to go inside and start supper.

Annie Laurie gathered the eggs before she went inside, thinking she could help her daddy a little bit more. For, he'd told her she'd helped him tremendously by sanding the wood.

She looked in the cabinet at the meager supply of things to cook. *"It's certainly not like things in the past, for daddy was able to walk to the store then,"* she thought.

She thought about the dwindling amount of pork in the barrels and smokehouse and wondered what they'd do when it ran out. *"We're not fattening any more hogs,"* she thought. She took a deep breath and selected a can of pink salmon. *"I'll figure out something to go with them,"* she decided.

She wound up going to the garden and pulling up two hills of cluster onions, thinking she'd dice them up and smother them down with the salmon.

They kept the Irish potato bed stored under the house, so while she was outside, she crawled the small distance under the house and picked through the potatoes. She Picked out the ones she wanted.

Annie Laurie just hoped that Jesse wouldn't stop by for supper, if he did, he'd probably be disappointed at supper, and too she was filthy from crawling under the house. Another thing that was driving her nuts was her brassieres. She thought they were just too little, her breasts kept wanting to pop over the top of her brassiere. If she sold any of her paintings Saturday she was going to talk to Miss Earnestine about it, because she didn't know.

The first thing she did when she re-entered the house was to lay the potatoes and onions on the table then go into her room and pulled the brassiere off.

After washing her hands and brushing her dress off with the wet bath cloth she'd used that morning. She went into the kitchen to begin supper.

When her daddy came in later, he had eight more frames of various sizes.

"I've just enough time to get a bucket of water to the house, it'll soon me dark out there," he said.

"Daddy, sit down at the table and drink you a cup of coffee. I'm through with supper and I'll get the water," Annie Laurie said.

She poured what was left in the two buckets into the stove reservoir and headed toward the spring.

When she returned to the house with the two buckets of water, she said, "There, see it was no trouble at all."

Her daddy smiled at her.

That night they dined on the stewed salmon and fried potatoes.

After Annie Laurie finished with the dishes, they listened to WCKY on the radio. They sat on the porch in their favorite place. They listened to the beer barrel polka, and other songs, including "Somewhere over the rainbow," by Judy Garland.

That night was the first time that she'd heard the name Adolf Hitler. The newsman told of all the wonderful things Hitler was doing for Germany.

"They'd better keep an eye on that man. Anytime a person attempts to rule a country with an iron hand, you'd better look out. Trouble soon follows," her daddy said.

They soon tired of hearing about Hitler, so they decided to go inside and end the day in bed.

After rubbing the liniment on his spine and upper back, Franklin counted the paintings in his head and figured that he had six more frames to make the next day. His back was so drawn, until he practically sat up in bed, so he scooted as far as he could to the head of the bed and slept on three pillows.

Annie Laurie lay in her bed thinking about the song they'd heard that Judy Garland had sang over the radio. *"Oh! If I could sing like that,"* she thought.

Her mind jumped to Jesse, and she was excited that Jesse was coming for supper the next night. She also thought that Jesse liked his painting and that really helped her feelings.

She really didn't have any idea whether she could paint or not, she just hoped people wouldn't laugh and sneer when they saw them.

The next morning after breakfast, she helped her daddy sand more boards until mid-morning. She'd studied on what to cook for supper, so she asked her daddy if he'd wring the neck of one of the young roosters, so he did.

She had never gutted, plucked, or cleaned a chicken, but she knew she needed to learn sometime. She didn't do as her Aunt Sarie had done. She put the fowl in a foot tub and poured hot water all over him. After it had stayed in the hot water a while, she tied his legs to the clothesline and began to pluck the feathers off. She put the feathers in a sack to prevent making a mess in the yard.

She gutted and cleaned the young rooster while he was still tied to the clothesline. Later, she dashed cold water on the chicken and got it clean enough to suit her.

After it was in the broiler she poured about a quart of water over the chicken and seasoned it with salt and black pepper. Annie Laurie never measured anything. By one o'clock, she had the rooster in the oven, along with six sweet potatoes and a baker of cornbread. On top of the stove, she had a boiler of dried field peas soaking.

After she was satisfied with the stove, she swept the kitchen, dining room, and living room, then mopped and rinsed them. She opened the three doors so the floors would dry faster. Next, she emptied the water buckets into the reservoir and walked to the spring to re-fill the buckets.

There was always coffee on the stove, so when she returned with the water, she poured her daddy a cup and walked to the shed with it.

"Oh boy! Thank you sugar girl," her daddy said, as he reached for the cup.

Annie Laurie put her hand next to her heart.

"I do believe you're cooking up something special for Mr. Jesse," her daddy said.

Annie Laurie didn't have her notebook to write, "There wasn't much to choose from," so she just smiled.

"How do you like Mr. Jesse in his frame," her daddy said, as he reached beside the shed and handed her the framed painting of Jesse.

Annie Laurie held the painting up and looked at it. She knew better than to put her hand to her heart, so she just smiled.

She waited until her daddy finished his coffee, then took the painting and empty cup into the house.

Annie Laurie hung the painting of Mr. Jesse on a nail in the living room, and closed the door, for the floors were dried.

She checked on the cornbread and saw that it was brown, so she took it out of the oven. The sweet potatoes would take about thirty more minutes, she figured. She then built a fire under the dried peas and seasoned them with some smoked bacon.

After throwing another piece of wood into the compartment for the oven. She knew it was nearing three o'clock, so she went to the front porch to see if she could see Jesse's car as it zoomed by, and she did.

Annie Laurie laughed at the carefree Jesse and went back into the house to take the sweet potatoes out of the oven and check on the chicken. She thought she'd let the sweet potatoes cool then peel, slice and fry them.

She took the lid off the broiler and saw that the rooster was just beginning to brown, so she went to the pantry and brought the rice back. After pouring about a cup of rice into the broth, she put the lid back on the broiler and slid the rack back into the oven and closed the door.

By four o'clock, her daddy brought the other frames into the house, and began to match the size of the paintings to the frames, so he could tack them in.

Annie Laurie's supper was done, {Except for frying the sweet potatoes} so she helped him.

Franklin was careful with the tacking, for he wanted to tack the frames and not the paintings.

They were finished with the paintings, and Annie Laurie was frying the baked sweet potatoes when Jesse knocked on the door.

Franklin hobbled to the door and opened it.

Mr. Jesse had a smile on his face a mile wide when he shook Franklin's hand.

His eyes automatically fell on his painting. "Well, would you look at that. I'll be dawg if she ain't got me looking handsome," he said. He then added,

"You know I could probably sell that thing to the ladies and make a fortune."

"I think she has about everything on the table," Franklin said.

Annie Laurie was putting the last slice of the baked sweet potatoes into the platter, when Jesse came into the kitchen ahead of her daddy.

He kissed her quickly, then swung her around in the kitchen.

Franklin missed the kissing part, but he came through the door as Mr. Jesse was putting her down. He did as he had done before, he cleared his throat.

Jesse knew he had to change the atmosphere in the kitchen, so his eyes locked on the painting of Lee Peacock.

"You know, I'd be willing to bet that Miss Lois would give you a mint for Lee's painting, I think she's sort of sweet on him."

The idea that Miss Lois, at her age, was sweet on Lee was funny, so both Franklin and Annie Laurie laughed.

Annie Laurie's knees were still weak from Jesse's kiss, but she managed to make it to the back door and open it. She wiped the sweat from her forehead and fanned her face with her hands.

"It is hot in here. Mr. Jesse would you like to sit on the porch until it cools down in here?" Franklin asked.

"Nah, I'm use to the heat, plus I'm hungry," Jesse replied.

"Well, after I bless the food, we'll give you the honor of carving the chicken," Franklin said.

After Franklin gave grace, Jesse made the carving simple by just quartering the rooster, then putting a quarter in his plate. He then put a big amount of rice and peas in his plate. He avoided the cornbread but topped his plate off with three slices of fried sweet potatoes.

Jesse didn't give the other two time to help their plates before he "Dove in."

"Boy, if mom could cook like this!" Jesse said, as Annie Laurie carved her a wing off the chicken for herself.

Annie Laurie didn't put much on her plate, for she was still so hot from the cooking.

She noticed that her daddy ate well though, for he was enjoying listening to some of Mr. Jesse's stories.

Among Jesse's stories was that he'd come out first place in the three-mile run that day at school. "Shoot, I ran that sucker in four minutes flat," he said.

"Goodness, little wonder you're so hungry. That's like running from here to Miss Earnestine's store," Franklin said.

"This fall, coach told me I'd be the 1st string quarterback. Shoot, I can stand on the 1- yard line and sling that ball 70-yards. I'd give anything if y'all would come see me play," he said.

Annie Laurie was surprised at her daddy's reply.

"The answer to that is not "Would but could. I don't imagine I'd last very long at that football game. I can just see myself tottering along with this stick," her daddy answered.

"I'm sorry Mr. Franklin, somehow, I don't think of you as being in the shape that you're in. Shoot, you can do about anything that you want to," Jesse said.

Her daddy laughed.

After everyone had finished eating, Annie Laurie and Jesse did their usual. They cleaned the dishes, so Annie Laurie could feed Blacky and wash the dishes.

Her daddy and Jesse went outside to sit on the front porch until Annie Laurie finished with the kitchen, then she joined them, after closing the back door.

It was too much moonlight for Jesse to hold Annie Laurie's hand, even though he'd chosen the rocker nearest to hers.

Mr. Jesse didn't tarry that night though, for he said in order for him to plant the garden, then take them to Miss Earnestine's the next morning he had work to do.

"I've got paperwork to do for my dad tonight so that he can take a load of cows to Brewton tomorrow," he said. He then asked about his painting. "Mom's dying to see it," he added.

Annie Laurie ran into the house and got it from the wall.

"Thank you for the supper and my painting," he said, as he walked past Franklin and headed for his car.

"Well, one thing's for sure, Mr. Jesse enjoyed his supper," her daddy said.

Annie Laurie laughed.

The two stayed on the porch and Annie Laurie listened to her daddy's small talk until they decided it was time for bed.

Chapter 9

Mr. Jesse was true to his word, for he was there that Saturday morning with the planters hooked to his tractor.

Franklin had him to plant, corn, peas, beans, watermelons, and squash.

He also made-up a long row for them to put sweet potatoes and tomatoes.

The whole operation didn't take over thirty minutes, then Jesse left to return in his car.

It was a tight fit in Jesse's car, but the three managed to squeeze into it. Reason being it was a 1938 Ford V8 coupe, floorboard shift. They'd managed to get the nineteen paintings into the trunk by putting the smaller paintings on the bottom. Jesse said none of them should get scarred up that way.

Franklin did allow Annie Laurie to sit in the middle and each time Jesse would shift the gears he'd hit Annie Laurie's knee.

Annie Laurie thought the best thing to do would be to spraddle her legs, and she laughed at her thoughts, knowing that would finish her daddy off.

It being Saturday, cars and trucks were parked everywhere, but Jesse squeezed between two trucks. Both she and Jesse toted two each of the paintings, making sure that Miss Earnestine's and Miss Lois's were on the outside, and visible.

"What in the world?" Miss Earnestine exclaimed.

"We'll talk later, we have several more to bring in," Jesse told her.

"Lum, who, like usual, was carrying boxes of items to the vehicles, when Annie Laurie brought his painting out.

"Lawd have Mucy, who done dat?" he asked.

Jesse exclaimed, "Miss Annie Laurie painted that of you Mr. Lum.

"What's she gwine do wif it?" Lum asked.

"She has a bunch of them and she's trying to sell them," Jesse answered.

"Miss Octavia, she be wanting to buys dat un of me," Lum said

"Well, they'll all be inside the store. You can give us a hand if you want to, just be careful and don't bump them into anything," Jesse told him.

"Yassuh," Mr. Lum said, as he reached into the trunk and brought out two.

Franklin made it to the edge of the wide doorsteps and sat down. He didn't know a thing about paintings, so he thought he'd let his daughter and Miss Earnestine handle things.

The three soon had all the paintings inside. They were leaning against shelves everywhere.

Miss Earnestine and Lois were extremely busy with customers, so she asked Annie Laurie if they'd put the paintings in Mr. Riley's office, so they did.

While they were moving the paintings, Miss Earnestine asked Lum if he would step over to Mrs. Peacock's and ask her if she could come over.

Mr. Lum bumped into Jesse's parents as they came into the door.

Annie Laurie had just picked up her painting of baby Jesus and Mother Mary.

"Has someone bought that painting?" Mrs. Jordan asked.

Knowing Annie Laurie couldn't talk, Miss Earnestine said, "I'm going to make her an offer for it when I get caught up."

"One hundred and fifty dollars, and Jesse, you can put it in the car," Mrs. Jordan said. "It's for the church," Mrs. Jordan added.

Hesitantly, Miss Earnestine said, "Well, if it's for the church, you can pay the young lady.

Mr. Jordan peeled off the money and handed it to Annie Laurie.

Annie Laurie didn't know it was that much money in Dottelle, but she quickly stuck it in one of the big pockets of her dress.

Mrs. Jordan then thanked Annie Laurie for Jesse's painting.

Annie Laurie handed the painting to Jesse, then nodded her head at Mrs. Jordan and shook her hand.

"Young Lady, you have real talent," Mrs. Jordan said.

Again, Annie Laurie nodded her head at Mrs. Jordan, then continued to carry the other paintings into Mr. Riley's office.

When Jesse came back into the store, he told Annie Laurie that his dad said he needed to go home. "He said I have work to do."

Miss Earnestine overheard the conversation and said, "That's alright, one of us can take Miss Reed home."

Jesse apologized to Annie Laurie and told her if he could get away from his dad, he'd see her later in the day.

Annie Laurie smiled and nodded.

Between customers, Annie Laurie pulled her notebook out of her pocket and wrote, "I have business with you in private, when you have time."

Miss Earnestine read the message and said, "As you can see my brother isn't here and I'm tied up with customers. When things die down, you know I'll be glad to do business with you. Why don't you get yourself a cold drink and have a seat in Mr. Riley's office."

"Daddy's outside," Annie Laurie wrote.

"My goodness, get him one too," Miss Earnestine said.

"Oh, before you do that, take a page out of your notebook. There are some scissors on Mr. Riley's desk, cut a page out of your notebook, write 40 dollars on each square and put them between your painting and the frame, Miss Earnestine said."

Annie Laurie smiled and nodded her head.

While cutting the squares, Annie Laurie's head was still spinning from the $150 dollars that she had in her pocket. She then tallied 18x40 and came up with $720.00 dollars.

"My goodness, just from having fun," she thought.

After she'd finished labeling all the paintings, she got the two drinks out of the Coca Cola box, opened them and went outside.

She met Lee and Mrs. Peacock, as they came up the steps. She noticed that Mrs. Peacock looked very excited.

Annie Laurie handed her daddy the drink.

"Thank you darling," he said.

"Miss Earnestine is so busy in the store until she hasn't time for me right now," Annie Laurie wrote.

"I saw Mr. Jordan carrying out one," her daddy said.

Annie Laurie wrote in her notebook, $150.00.

$40.00 each for the others, Annie Laurie wrote.

"My Lord almighty, girl I've never had that kind of money, especially at one time," her daddy replied.

Annie Laurie just smiled and nodded her head.

Mr. Lum came up with a piece of clean cardboard and laid it beside her daddy.

"For you Missy, we'se mighty busy dis mawning," Mr. Lum said.

Annie Laurie sat down on the piece of cardboard beside her daddy, and they both enjoyed their drink, in the shade, for there was an awning from the gas pump to the store.

"Mr. Jesse left us, he said that he had work to do at home," her daddy said.

Annie Laurie simply wrote "Miss Earnestine" in the rough palm of her daddy's hand.

The store closed at 1:00 o'clock on Saturdays, and it was a good thing because her daddy had started one of his coughing spells.

They'd already seen Mrs. Peacock and Lee come out and Lee was holding his painting.

"Girl, I was unaware that you had this kind of talent," Mrs. Peacock said, and had thanked her for painting Lee.

Miss Earnestine finally closed the store, after all of the customers had left, and she called Annie Laurie and her daddy inside.

"You said you had something private to talk with me about," Miss Earnestine said, after calling her into Mr. Riley's office.

"Yes Mam, I need bigger cups for my brassieres," Annie Laurie wrote.

"That's no problem, and while we're in here. Mrs. Peacock bought Lee's painting, so here," Miss Earnestine said, as she smiled and handed Annie Laurie forty dollars. She then added, "Little girl, I have always known there was something special about you. Those paintings are fabulous."

"Thank you, but I'm out of paints and canvasses," Annie Laurie wrote.

"I've never ordered anything like that, but I know where I can. You just write down the colors you need and what size canvasses," Miss Earnestine answered.

As Annie Laurie was writing down things, Miss Earnestine continued to talk.

"I noticed that some of your paintings are on tin and wood, I don't know what they'd be worth, but I'm prepared to offer you thirty dollars for each of the paintings. That is your intentions?" Miss Earnestine asked.

Annie Laurie nodded her head and kept writing.

While Annie Laurie was writing, Miss Earnestine carried Miss Lois' painting to her, so she could go home. She then told Annie Laurie's daddy the deal that they'd struck up and asked if it was suitable to him.

Franklin was elated, and told Miss Earnestine it suited him.

"Good, I need to look up some prices for her, so if you'd like, Mr. Lum can take you home and I'll bring Annie Laurie in later.

"That's fine with me, but we need groceries," Franklin said.

"Mr. Lum is coming back here, so he can bring them in for you," Miss Earnestine told him.

"Suits me," Franklin said.

In a few minutes Miss Earnestine returned to Mr. Riley's office and counted out $510.00 to Annie Laurie.

"Now, come on back into the store. I'll get your new brassieres, while you get the groceries you need. While you're getting them, I'll look up the prices for the paints and canvasses," Miss Earnestine said.

Annie Laurie had never put so many items on the counter, for they were out of everything.

Miss Earnestine heard Mr. Lum's truck as it pulled up outside, so she opened the door and let him in. She then told Annie Laurie that her painting accessories were $60.10. She then began to tally up the grocery items on the cash register, including the two new brassieres.

"Ok, your total bill comes to $114.25, that's including the gallon of kerosene" Miss Earnestine said.

Annie Laurie gave her a hundred and twenty dollars, and Miss Earnestine gave her back her change, and thanked her.

Mr. Lum put everything on the counter into two cardboard boxes.

"After you've loaded her groceries and pumped her gallon of kerosene you can come back in and get your painting," Miss Earnestine told him.

Mr. Lum smiled and said, "Miss Octavia, she's gwinna lack dat."

"Just be sure to carry things to the front porch, Mr. Reed's in no shape to be lugging them from the road," Miss Earnestine told Lum.

"Yes Mam, I knows," Lum said.

After Lum came back for his painting, Miss Earnestine and Annie Laurie followed, after Miss Earnestine locked the door and gas pump.

Annie Laurie was carrying her new brassieres in a brown paper bag.

On the way home, Miss Earnestine told Annie Laurie not to be foolish with her money. She then said when Annie Laurie had painted the other canvasses, she should have an expose in Monroeville.

Of course, Annie Laurie didn't respond.

"Uh uh uh, who would have thought, just a young girl, right here in Dottelle," Miss Earnestine said, as they passed New Home cemetery.

When they got to Annie Laurie's house, Miss Earnestine said, "I don't understand why your daddy doesn't get the county to put in a culvert, then you could drive right up to house."

After Miss Earnestine stopped behind Mr. Lum's truck, she reached over and patted Annie Laurie on the hand. "Thank you for your painting of me. You can even see the items on the shelves in the background," she said.

Annie Laurie made the shape of a heart with her hands and got out of the car with her bag.

"My Lord girl, at the groceries," her daddy exclaimed, as he was sitting in his favorite spot, the doorsteps.

Annie Laurie smacked him on the cheek and went straight to her bedroom, to put on one of her new brassieres, as the old one was killing her. She knew she had groceries to bring in and put up, but she also knew there wasn't anything that would spoil.

She adjusted one of the new brassieres in the same position as the old one and put it on.

After hooking it in the back, she looked in the mirror. *"Boy, what a relief,"* she thought as she drew a deep breath for the first time all day.

After she slipped her dress back over her top and hooked it, she looked back into the mirror. She noticed that her dress felt tighter up top, *"But my Lord, do I look big,"* she thought.

Annie Laurie decided then and there that she'd start sewing her own clothes. She had her mama's old peddle sewing machine in her room. *"All I need is some material, thread, zippers and buttons,"* she thought.

She counted her money. "$585.75, that should be enough for them to make it until her new supplies comes in," she said to herself, which was still unbelievable to her. She hid the money inside one of her old shoes, then went outside to drag the boxes of groceries into the kitchen.

Her daddy was bent over on the doorsteps.

"Why don't you come up here in the shade?" Annie Laurie wrote, after shaking him..

"This hot sun is so soothing to my ole back," her daddy said.

"I know it's a little early yet, but after I get things put away, I believe I'll join him," Annie Laurie thought.

Annie Laurie had worn her best dress, and it was made from thick material, so she'd been about to burn up all day, so she thought she'd cook something simple for supper. *"I sure don't feel like being over this hot stove very long,"* she thought. She'd bought several canned items, so she left out the can of salmon. "We'll have that and some fried sweet potatoes," she said to herself.

She then went into her room and pulled off the dress and new brassiere. She plundered through her dresses that hung in the closet and picked out one made of thin material. Putting her new brassiere in a drawer, she walked out on the porch shoeless and wearing nothing but the thin dress.

"I would never have guessed my little girl would be buying groceries for the place, I'm so proud of you," her daddy told her.

"Heck, I found the paints, canvases, and brushes in the junk pile, so all I had in them was my time, and I enjoyed that," Annie Laurie wrote.

"You took that from your mama, she could really draw," her daddy said.

"Really, I've never seen them?" Annie Laurie answered in her book.

Franklin made an attempt to get up, then sat back down.

"Go into my room and look on top of my old chifforobe, you'll find some rolled up together," her daddy told her.

Excitedly, Annie Laurie almost ran into the house.

Sure enough, she saw them, so she reached up and got them, then went back outside.

The paper was old and brittle, so she had to be careful when she unrolled them, one page at a time.

"Daddy, this is you," she wrote, as she held up the drawing for him to see.

"Yep, that's me alright," he said.

She unrolled several more, asking her daddy about them, and he'd tell her.

The very last one was the one she'd longed for since she was a child.

"Don't tell me this is mama?" Annie Laurie scribbled, as she held up the intricate drawing. She had even dated it, January 11, 1924. She held the drawing up for her daddy to see.

"Yep, that's my Laurie Anne" her daddy said.

"Why, she was beautiful, but I don't favor her one iota," Annie Laurie wrote.

"No, you look like my mama," her daddy answered.

"Her hair was red?" Annie Laurie wrote.

"Well, it wasn't red like your Aunt Sarie's, it was mostly blonde with streaks of light red. I know one thing, I was lucky to get her," her daddy answered.

"Why haven't you told me about these?" she asked, by using her hands.

"I don't know, I guess I had other things on my mind," he answered.

"Well, I guess you know when my supplies come in, you two will be the first that I'll paint," Annie Laurie wrote.

"I see you didn't bring any of your paintings back," her daddy said.

"Nope, I sold every one of them," she answered, again with her hands.

Her daddy never asked her how much she got for them, so she didn't tell him, as she carefully rolled the drawings back in the same order as they were and put them back where they came from.

Annie Laurie and her daddy had lived together so long that if her replies were short, she could answer his questions by expressions or her hands, and it sure made it easier on her.

Annie Laurie was still so excited from the day until she didn't feel like cooking just yet, so she went back out on the front porch. *"Supper is going to be simple anyway,"* she thought.

Chapter 10
1940

It was October 26th, Annie Laurie's sixteenth birthday, and boy did Jesse have plans for her.

Annie Laurie had grown up four miles south of Monroeville, yet she'd never been there. She never had a reason to. Her daddy had always left the taxes for the land at Miss Earnestine's, and she turned it in, and gave Franklin a receipt for it.

Annie Laurie's world had always revolved around Dottelle and Excel.

She'd continued with her paintings, for that was how they made a living, as her daddy was now completely unable to work. His spine was so drawn, that Annie Laurie wondered why his spine just didn't snap. The only way that she saw his face was that his neck was drawn upward. She'd begged him several times to go to a doctor, but each time, he just say "Honey, it's no use." He could still get around though, but only around in the house and porches.

Blacky had simply disappeared one day. Annie Laurie's daddy said, he probably knew his time was up and had gone to the woods, a place he loved and died.

Jesse and Lee continued to make their visits, Jesse more often and he still ate supper with them once or twice a week. They were both now seniors at Excel High School.

Miss Earnestine continued to be a God sent blessing, for she bought all her paintings, and that was how they made their living. Jesse had told Annie Laurie that Mr. Riley would take the paintings to Mobile. He said there was an art dealer down there that bought them. Annie Laurie didn't care who she sold them to, just as long as she bought them. She'd even increased the price for most of them. Of course, her first paintings after her new paints and canvases came in were of her mama and daddy.

She felt sorry for her daddy, for he cried when he first saw her mama's painting.

"I'll be dang baby, and you were just a baby when she died, that looks just like," he said.

"What about yours?" Annie Laurie asked.

"Well, all I can say is your mama could have done better," he answered.

"Aw, daddy, you were a handsome man," Annie Laurie said.

The paintings were hung above the fireplace in the living room.

With her daddy being in the shape that he was in Annie Laurie was completely home bound, for he was no longer able to climb into a vehicle.

Miss Earnestine knew her predicament and sent the art supply business address to her house, now Annie Laurie could just order her supplies from the company.

Annie Laurie would wait until she had about a dozen paintings before she'd send them by Mr. Lum. She'd learned to make the frames herself. If she could find a straight limb for a tree, she'd make the frame from the limb, leaving the bark on the limb. Mr. Lum would soon return with her money.

Their groceries were bought once a week. Mr. Lum would come by, and after talking with her daddy for a few minutes, he'd pick up the grocery list. When he'd bring them back Annie Laurie would pay him.

Their garden had really been minimized. About all that Jesse planted was corn, to feed the chickens, peas, and of course, he left a row to plant tomatoes and sweet potatoes.

Annie Laurie was just too busy to get around to everything. She now had to wash her daddy's clothes and do everything inside and outside of the house.

Jesse gave her a copy of the book, "Gone with the wind," it seemed like it had taken her forever to read it. The book was so thick, and it took time away from her painting. She loved the book though, and by chance the movie was showing in Monroeville on her birthday. That was going to be her sixteenth birthday present, Jesse was taking her to see the movie.

Nervousness wasn't a strong enough word for how she felt, and too, she felt guilty about leaving her daddy by himself.

"No, it's your sixteenth birthday, your first date, so you go ahead and go. You're a big girl now, and I'm not worried about you not being able to handle yourself," he said.

"Jesse said it's a long movie, so don't be worried about me," Annie Laurie told him.

Franklin just smiled and said, "Have fun."

Annie Laurie hugged her daddy and kissed him on his stubby face, then ran into her room to finish getting ready. She'd actually bought a small bottle of perfume from Miss Earnestine's store and put a dab behind each ear. She'd already taken a good bath and washed her hair, and it had time to dry.

She decided to not wear one of Mrs. Peacock's "Old timey" dresses. Instead, she was wearing a pleaded brown skirt that she had sewn. The skirt fell well below her knees, a white long sleeved satin blouse, which was bought at Miss Earnestine's. She honestly didn't know what size shoe she wore, but she knew that young girls were wearing saddle oxfords, so she measured her feet, and they measured six and ½ inches long. She wound up ordering size 7, and two pairs of bobby socks. The shoes were white and brown, and she thought they matched her skirt. The shoes wound up fitting just right.

Annie Laurie's long blonde hair came to her knees, and she had brushed it until it had a sheen to it. She didn't wear a dab of makeup, and there was no need of plucking her eyebrows, for they were so blonde you could hardly see them.

Jesse showed up thirty minutes early, and she could hear him and her daddy talking in the kitchen, and hear dishes rattling, so she knew Jesse was finishing up the leftovers.

"Um, um, um, more dishes to wash," she thought, but she knew she wasn't washing them until she got back.

She waited until she figured Jesse was through eating before she came out of her bedroom.

"Oh, putter, putter, putter, putter, my heart is going," Jesse said, as he ran to Annie Laurie and had intensions of kissing her on her lips, but knowing her daddy was in the room, she turned her head. The kiss wound up on her cheek.

"Boy, will Lee Peacock be jealous of me," Jesse said, as he grabbed both of

Annie Laurie's hands and said, "You are beautiful," Jesse told her.

"Thank you, and you are so handsome with that pin striped shirt and new Levi's on, Annie Laurie was bold enough to say.

"Well, we'd better hit the road," Jesse said. He then turned to her daddy and said, "Mr. Franklin, don't you worry, I'll bring her back safe and sound."

"I expect nothing less," her daddy said, and smiled.

Annie Laurie kissed her daddy on his cheek and grabbed her brown sweater as they went out the door.

They walked to Jesse's car hand in hand, and he even opened the door for Annie Laurie and held her hand until she was seated in the car.

After he hurried around his car and got in, he grabbed her around the shoulder and slid her to the middle of the seat. His lips were pressed against hers before she knew it. It was the best kiss she'd ever had. He soon pulled away from her, and said, "Now let's go to the picture show."

"Believe it or not, I've never been to Monroeville before," Annie Laurie said.

"Oh, I believe it, my goodness you've been buried in Dottelle long enough. I plan on taking you places, you just wait and see baby girl," Jesse said.

About a mile from Annie Laurie's, they passed a long while house on the right. Annie Laurie could see it from the moonlight. It was a beautiful house, but of course, she couldn't tell him. Jessie told her that's where he lived.

"By the way, I like your outfit tonight, and you smell good too, Jesse said.

Their shoulders were pressed against each other, and Jesse could feel the tenseness in her for a few minutes, but she seemed to relax the closer they got to Monroeville.

Annie Laurie was just enthralled by all the houses. She wondered how they made a living, for they were too close together for them to have a garden.

As they got near Monroeville, the road was paved and the houses were wired for electricity, and she couldn't believe all the bright lights.

Annie Laurie discovered that the businesses formed around a square and the beautiful courthouse set in the middle of the square. Nearly all the stores had the name of the business wrote on the outside, including the courthouse, which had a sign outside. In fact, Jesse had to park near the courthouse to find a parking space. They saw the long line of people, and Jesse told her they were lined up to see the movie, so they got out of the car and headed toward the end of the line.

All the crowd was unreal, she'd never seen so many people and so much traffic, it was almost as if she was in another world. She noticed the clothing of the other girls and she was so glad she didn't wear one of Mrs. Peacock's dresses.

She was in front of Jesse, and he kept his hands on Annie Laurie's sides until they made it inside the theater. Jesse paid for the tickets, and a lady, about two steps up, tore the red tickets in half and gave them back to Jesse.

There was a huge glass popcorn machine that was popping popcorn before their very eyes. Jesse bought them each a bag. There was also a drink machine that spewed drinks into a paper cup. Of course, Annie Laurie had never seen such, but she later found out they were called "Fountain drinks."

Next, they went through a thick red velvet curtain that parted in the middle. She discovered the floor steadily sloped down, so that people behind you could see the giant screen up front. The room was very dark, but her eyes soon adjusted to it. Jesse finally found them some seats in about the middle of the theater. He held his popcorn and drink with one of his huge hands and pointed where she should sit, so she followed his directions. He was right behind her, so he pulled down the seat for her to sit, for she didn't have a clue.

Annie Laurie finally got to see what Adolf Hitler looked like, for on the big screen it was showing moving pictures of the war in Europe.

Jesse leaned over and whispered in Annie Laurie's ear. "I look for the United States to get tied up in that mess before it's over."

Annie Laurie was so caught up with all the strange things, until everything was hard for her to believe.

Soon, the lights were dimmed even more, and the movie came on. Annie Laurie soon was so caught up in the movie until she forgot about her drink and popcorn until she noticed the couple ahead of them.

Jesse must have finished his soon, for in a short while, he put one of his big hands just above her knee. She didn't do anything until he moved it up higher. She took his hand and moved it back to its original place.

In a few minutes he put his arm around her, and she was satisfied with that, so she could concentrate on the movie.

Right after the battle of Atlanta, the show came to a pause and all the lights came back on.

Annie Laurie thought the movie was over, until Jesse kissed her on the cheek and whispered,
"I've got to go to the bathroom while the movie is on pause."

Annie Laurie had wondered what she was going to do, for she was about to burst, so she grabbed Jesse's hand.

When they reached the lobby, Jesse pointed to the door she needed to go inside. She felt stupid, for above the door was labeled, "Ladies."

She had no idea what was inside, but after entering the room she saw several booths, one of the doors was open, so she went inside and closed the door. It didn't take her long to figure things out, so after relieving herself, she pulled her skirt back up, making sure her blouse was inside. She opened the door, never realizing she was supposed to flush the commode, went to the Fawcett, like all the other girls were doing, she soaped her hands, then rinsed and dried them on a paper towel.

Jesse was waiting for her in the lobby, Jesse held her by one of her hands and they returned to their seats.

While waiting for the lights to be dimmed, Annie Laure drew the shape of a heart in Jesse's palm, then laced her fingers with his.

Jesse kissed her on her hand and whispered, "I'm so glad you're my girl."

For the rest of the movie, Annie Laurie couldn't understand her feelings. It was as though she felt she needed to go home, and then again, she felt as though she could spend an eternity with Jesse. He was a looker, and also tall and muscular, she'd noticed how he'd caught the eye of some of the girls in the lobby though and wondered why he'd chosen her. One thing was for certain, she felt safe with Jesse and that meant a lot to her.

The movie finally ended, and Annie Laurie didn't like the way it ended, but the new things that she'd seen alone was worth the trip.

On the walk back to his car, several young men came up and spoke to him and remarked that he was the best quarterback in the area. Jesse smiled and thanked them but added that he needed to get his date home.

Annie Laurie figured that she'd be mauled on the way home, but all Jesse talked about was how demanding his daddy could be at times. "I mean, I do have school and football practice, then the games," he said.

Annie Laurie just laughed and thought how understanding her gentle daddy had been her entire life.

When they reached her house, Jesse pulled almost into the culvert, then reached over and first he hugged her, then the long kiss was next. Finally, he moved his strong hand to her breast.

She stopped kissing him and pulled his hand away from her breast, and shook her head.

"Wow, so they are real," he said.

Annie Laurie reached for the doorknob.

"Just a minute and, I'll walk you home. I promised your daddy I'd see you safely home," Jesse said.

Annie Laurie leaned over and gave Jesse a chaste kiss on his cheek, then waited until he got out of his car to open the door for her.

They had a long kiss on the front porch. Annie Laurie thought that was the end to a wonderful night, but he followed her inside the dimly lit living room.

"My goodness," thought Annie Laurie as she saw that the lamp in the kitchen was still shining brightly.

Jesse only intended to see her to the living room, but Annie Laurie grabbed his hand and practically pulled him into the kitchen/dining room area, for it was unusual for her daddy to still have the lamp turned so high.

They found his crippled dead body lying on the dining room floor.

Annie Laurie ran toward her daddy, but Jesse could see that he was dead, so he grabbed her hand, and said, "Don't go to him darling, it's plain to see he's left this world."

Jesse cradled Annie Laurie in his arms, while she sobbed.

In a few minutes, Annie Laurie pulled loose from Jesse and ran to her pencil and notebook that was still lying on the kitchen table.

Hurriedly she wrote, "What am I going to do?"

"I believe we need to contact the coroner, Dr. Eddins, but he won't be coming until in the morning," Jesse said.

"Poor thing, he had a hard life, it's as though he waited until I was sixteen," she wrote.

"Isn't that his bedroom over there?" Jesse asked, as he nodded his head.

"Yes," Annie Laurie wrote.

"Well, I'll put him in his bed and cover him up," Jesse said.

Annie Laurie ran into her daddy's room and lit the lamp, then returned to the dining room.

Jesse placed one arm under his knees and the other behind his crippled neck and with the first attempt he picked the cold body up. After squeezing through the door, he put his body in the bed, for Annie Laurie had turned down the covers.

Franklin's body set upright in the bed, so using both hands, he put one on his stomach and the other on his chest and pressed down. He finally got Mr. Franklin's head to where it would lie on the stack of pillows.

"I need to go through his pockets before someone else does," Jesse said.

Jesse went through every pocket in his overalls and shirt. He pulled out her daddy's sharp pocketknife, a roll of string, some change and a roll of money.

Jesse looked at her questionably when seeing the large roll of money.

Annie Laurie pointed toward her mouth, and he understood.

Jesse scooped up all the items and handed them to Annie Laurie, and she put everything into one of her skirt pockets.

After Jesse pulled the cover over Mr. Franklin's face, he blew out the lamp and they went back into the dining room. Annie Laurie closed the door to his room.

Annie Laurie quickly wrote in her notebook. "Poor thing, he could have done better financially but he had to stay home to raise me. I was only three when my mama died."

"I understand," Jesse said.

"What am I going to do now?" Annie Laurie wrote.

"Well, we take one day at a time. First of all, you're not staying in this house by yourself tonight," Jesse said.

"What do you suggest?" Annie Laurie asked.

"Get your sleeping clothes and you can stay at my house," Jesse said.

"No, I don't know your folks that well," Annie Laurie wrote, "I'll just stay here, I'll be alright," she added.

"Baby, a casket will need to be bought, the coroner will need to come out here, his grave will need to be dug. Someone will have to bathe him and put clean clothes on him," Jesse said.

Annie Laurie remembered what her daddy had told her once. "If anything happens to me, get in touch with Miss Earnestine."

"If you will, pick me up early in the morning and take me to Miss Earnestine's, and drive your daddy's truck. You'll need to come early before she goes to church," Annie Laurie wrote.

"Okay, have it your way, Miss hard head," Jesse said.

Jesse looked at her middle finger and saw that she had a knot on it from writing so much.

There wasn't any more kissing, Jesse cradled her in his arms, and said, "I'll be here at eight o'clock."

Annie Laurie followed him to the front door. They embraced once again, and Jesse said, with a smile, "Eight o'clock, and have breakfast on the table." He then went out of the door and headed toward his car.

Annie Laurie locked the door behind him, then blew the lamp out in the living room. Her next move was to mop the spilled coffee up from the dining room floor. She built a fire in the stove, as it was cold in the house.

Annie Laurie ran into her room and brought back her pajamas, after lighting the lamp in her room.

It felt strange getting near naked in the dining room, but after the stove began to project heat, she striped her clothes off and put her warm pajamas on. Attempting to keep her mind off her daddy, she tried to think of other things. She was sure glad that she'd painted the painting of her mama. *"At least he had a short while to look at it,"* she thought.

After she was good and warm, she gathered up her clothes, blew out the lamp and headed to her bedroom, leaving nothing in the dining room but her new saddle oxfords.

After turning down her covers, she didn't blow out her lamp but turned the wick down.

Of course, her mind was on her daddy. *"What will I do without him?"* she thought. He might have been crippled, but at least she felt safe with him being on the porch or in the yard. Really, it was no more than what she'd been looking for. *"You can only cough up so much blood,"* she thought.

The only reprieves she had, was he wasn't in pain anymore, and he was now with his Laurie.

Annie Laurie said an extra-long prayer that night, knowing her life was about to change.

She went to sleep knowing she'd more than apt spend the day with Jesse and thinking about "Gone With the Wind."

Chapter 11

Her daddy had been right. Miss Earnestine handled everything but the grief.

She called the coroner, and got hold of Mr. Lum. He unlocked the store and both he and Jesse toted her daddy's gray casket down the stairs and slid it into the back of Mr. Jordan's truck. Mr. Lum left and brought two of his nephews to Annie Laurie's to dig the grave. Mr. Lum washed Franklin's body and put him on clean underwear, a white shirt and his newest overalls.

Mr. Lum got two chairs from the dining room and stepped off the exact length of the casket, so they placed the ends of the casket on the two chairs.

He and Jesse brought the body out of the bedroom and put it in the casket, but they discovered that Franklin's body was almost sitting up in the casket. Mr. Lum scratched his head, and then an idea came to him. He pulled out his pocketknife and began to cut the cushion from the casket where Franklin's back should be. After cutting out nigh all the padding it looked as though Franklin was laying in the casket. Mr. Lum then closed both lids on Franklin's final resting place. Thinking it would be best for Miss Annie Laurie to not see the body for he was forced to put a quarter over each eye lid to keep them closed.

Annie Laurie had shown Mr. Lum's nephews where she wanted her daddy buried. Of course, his grave was dug beside her mama's.

Miss Earnestine had set the funeral for three o'clock. The young men were through digging the grave by eleven o'clock, so Mr. Lum told Annie Laurie they were going to get something to eat, but they'd be back for the burying.

Annie Laurie had paid Miss Earnestine twenty-five dollars for the casket, and she still had some money left in her pocket. She wrote in her notebook offering to pay Mr. Lum and his nephews for the work they'd done so far.

"Oh no, Missy, you don't owe me a thing, jist gives de boys about five dollars adder dey git finished dis addernoon," Mr. Lum said.

"I'll give them five dollars each," Annie Laurie wrote.

"Nome, jist five dollars. Dey liables to gits in trouble wit moe money dan dat," Mr. Lum told her.

Annie Laurie then did something that wasn't done, she hugged Mr. Lum's neck and thanked him, by using her hands.

After Mr. Lum and his nephews left, they weren't expecting visitors, so Jesse suggested they go to Monroeville for hamburgers. "I'm hungry as a wolf," he said.

Annie Laurie had never eaten a hamburger, but she'd agree to go anywhere to get away from the casket in the dining room. They weren't expecting any visitors anyway.

Annie Laurie had sewn another skirt the same time she'd sewn the brown one, only it was a dark corduroy blue. She had put it on that morning, because it was an overcast cool day.

Jesse knew right where to go. He'd driven back to Monroeville and parked across the road from the courthouse. There was a sign painted on the plate glass window that read, "Home Cafeteria."

Annie Laurie had never eaten a meal away from home, so she decided to just mimic Jesse.

There weren't too many people in the place, so it was easy for Jesse to find them a table.

Soon, a young lady came over and asked them what they would like to eat.

Jesse ordered two hamburgers with everything on them with two sweet teas.

Annie Laurie thought that Jesse seemed so worldly, and so unlike her. She knew that she had to learn though, and she'd made up her mind to do so.

While they waited on their food, Jesse began to talk.

"You know, I noticed when we were in your house, your hair is the same length as your skirt. Don't ever cut your hair Annie Laurie, that's what first attracted me to you. "Of course there's a couple more attributes too, but now isn't the time and place to mention them," he laughed.

"What are your intentions, you're mighty young to stay at that house alone, even though it is a fortress," he asked.

Annie Laurie grabbed Jesse's hand, and in the palm, she wrote with her index finger, "Stay."

"You don't have any kin folks that live near," he asked.

Not turning his hand loose, she wrote, "No."

"I must say, you're taking your daddy's death very well," Jesse said.

"He was ready, he suffered so. He was ready to go be with mama," Annie Laurie wrote.

Jesse smiled, and asked, "So, what attracted you to me?"

"Simple," she wrote, "You."

"Well, I hope it stays that way. I'll try to be a good boy, it's hard though," he said.

Annie Laurie just laughed.

Their food arrived, and Annie Laurie observed him, as how to eat it.

Jesse simply just picked the entire thing up with his hands, so she did too.

She couldn't eat all her hamburger, but he did. She'd never had iced tea, but she loved it. *"It beats Kool Aid,"* she thought.

They both used the bathroom before they left. Annie Laurie didn't feel so alien this time.

The old courthouse clock struck one o'clock as they entered Jesse's car.

"We still have a little time, I'm going to show you around just a little bit," Jesse told her.

He turned right at the traffic light and Annie Laurie recognized the theater as they passed it. Right past the theater were beautiful two-story homes.

"Must be rich folks living in these houses. Probably doctors, lawyers, or businessmen," Jesse told her.

Annie Laurie didn't like it when she couldn't write, for she wasn't able to ask questions or express her opinions. She felt that Jesse knew it for he constantly rattled, telling her what he felt like she'd like to know.

About a mile out of town, Jesse drove down a steep hill, then it leveled off and he drove across a long wooden bridge. "This is "Limestone Creek," he said.

She looked down at the wide rushing stream, and thought, *"It's not clear water like the one at home."*

After crossing the creek, it wasn't long before they began to see houses, then nestled in a little valley were several stores and places of business.

This little town is called Peterman. "Lots of good people live in this little town," Jesse told her.

The roads weren't paved like they were in Monroeville, but Annie Laurie thought the little town looked clean and orderly.

"That wide road there," Jesse pointed, "Goes to Burnt Corn, there was a big Indian battle there, back in the day," Jesse said.

He turned his daddy's truck around at Burnt Corn Road and said, "Well, I guess it's time to get this over with," and they headed back toward Monroeville.

Somewhere, on their trip, Annie Laurie, without realizing it, had lain her hand on Jesse's leg and it stayed there until they got back to Annie Laurie's house.

They didn't see any other vehicles as Jesse pulled off the road.

"If it's the last thing I do, I'm going to see that you get a driveway to your house," Jesse said, then he gave Annie Laurie a peck on her lips.

They'd barely had time to reach the front porch before Lee, Mr. Lum and his helpers parked beside the road. Shortly afterwards Miss Earnestine, and Mr. Jordan pulled up.

Annie Laurie could see that Miss Earnestine had three others with her. She also noticed that Jesse's mom wasn't with his dad.

Mr. Lum's nephews went around the house and headed for the grave.

Annie Laurie unlocked the front door and motioned with her hand for everyone to come inside.

Miss Earnestine introduced her entourage to Annie Laurie after they'd entered the house.

"This is our pastor at Woodlawn, Reverand Hall, the other two are Cecil and Delores Chandler. Mr. Chandler has a beautiful baritone voice, he's going to sing, and this is his gracious wife, Delores. Delores has brought you some food that doesn't spoil easily. We know that you won't feel like cooking right away," Miss Earnestine said.

Annie Laurie nodded and shook hands with each of them.

"Of course, we're already acquainted," Mr. Jordan said, and instead of shaking hands, he hugged Annie Laurie's neck. He apologized for his wife not being there, and said she was in Montgomery concerning a church benefit.

Mr. Lum went to the dining room and the others followed.

Mr. Cecil, Lee, Jesse, and his father carried the casket to the grave.

Annie Laurie could tell that Mr. Lum had done this before, as he had a rope stretched at the foot of the grave and one at the head. Stakes were driven down, and the ropes were tied to the stakes.

The casket was laid on the ropes.

The funeral started with Mr. Cecil singing "Farther Along."

When he'd finished Reverand Hall said a few quotes out of the Bible, then finished with the Lord's prayer.

Mr. Cecil then sang "Down by the riverside."

Mr. Lum's nephews pulled the ropes over the stakes at the head of the grave, then held them firmly, while Mr. Lum and Lee did the same with the foot of the grave. The casket was slowly lowered into the grave.

Annie Laurie cried through the whole ordeal, so when the thing was over Jesse led her back into the house.

Mr. Cecil and Delores went to Miss Earnestine's car and brought back a tray of sliced meats, an assortment of crackers, preserved figs and peaches, with a loaf of hard tack bread.

Annie Laurie settled down some and put on a pot of coffee.

Mr. Jordan didn't stick around long before he gave Annie Laurie his condolences. He said he had cattle to tend to.

Mr. Lum and his crew left right away, which left only Miss Earnestine, Mr. Cecil, Delores, Jesse, Reverand Hall and herself.

They all sat around and talked for a short while before Miss Earnestine made the remark that the church had evening services, so they needed to be leaving.

Delores jumped up and cleaned the kitchen and remarked how clean Annie Laurie kept the house.

Very quickly, Annie Laurie wrote in her notebook, "Thank you for all you did, I couldn't have done it without you," She tore the page out and gave the piece of paper to Miss Earnestine.

Miss Earnestine gently held Annie Laurie under her chin, and said, "Young Missy, you're mighty young to be left by yourself. You can use it to your advantage, or you can wallow in your grief. Undoubtably you're very intelligent, use it to your advantage without, allowing anyone to use you. It's going to be hard, not having a way to go, but just trust in the Lord and he'll see you through, If you need me for advise you know where I'll be."

After those words of advice, the four of them filed out of the house, after Delores hugged Annie Laurie's neck and invited her to church.

Jesse remained seated in the dining room while Annie Laurie saw them to the door.

"Brr, I'm going to need some wood in this house, it's getting cold outside," Annie Laurie thought as she put more wood in the stove.

As if he could read her mind, Jesse said, "I'll bring you in some more wood before I go home, I see that the wood box is getting low. I sure hate to leave you here by yourself, but Dad gave me strict orders to come home, besides I'm in his truck. We use that truck to feed the cattle," Jesse said.

"I understand, and it was sweet of your dad to come to the funeral," Annie Laurie told Jesse.

"Dad's a good man, he really is. It's just that his mind is constantly thinking about money from the time he wakes up until he goes to sleep at night," Jesse said. He then reached over and pulled Annie Laurie into his lap and kissed her.

"Boy, you feel good," Jesse said, after they'd stopped kissing.

Annie Laurie pulled his hands loose and jumped out of his lap.

She grabbed her notebook and quickly wrote: "A simple kiss would have been good enough!"

Jesse retorted, "You can't tell me you didn't enjoy that, it did me a lot of good."

"Maybe if we were married, I'd enjoy it, but not before then," Annie Laurie wrote.

Jesse laughed, and said, "Well let me get that wood in, that'll take my mind off it."

After the wood box was filled, Jesse pulled Annie Laurie into his arms and said, "In time, just you wait and see." He then kissed her briefly and walked to the door. "I'd best get home, it'll be dark before you know it, I have to go. Make sure your doors and shutters are locked."

"I will," Annie Laurie nodded her head, as Jesse walked away, then left.

Annie Laurie closed the door, then locked it.

Her financial situation had been worrying her. She'd been wanting to count her daddy's stash, but just hadn't the time, or someone was always around, so Annie Laurie went into her room and retrieved the money from where she'd hidden it.

Laying the money on the table, Annie Laurie began to unroll the money and count it. She counted it twice to make sure. She found the total to be seven hundred and forty dollars.

"Bless his heart," Annie Laurie thought, *"He'd made this money by the sweat of his brow, and his crippled back to get my tongue seen about."*

Annie Laurie thought of things differently. She decided the first thing to do would be to stop living in the nineteenth century. "No more Mrs. Peacock's dresses, and a way to go, for starters."

She knew Jesse was too busy with football now, *"But once it's over, maybe he'll teach me to drive, after all I can't just be stranded here with no way of going,"* she thought.

They'd been surviving off her paintings for the last few months, and it sure was nice having money to buy things that she needed or wanted. She loved Mrs. Peacock, but her taste in clothing was so outdated, and she realized it now. Making her own clothing was time-consuming, but buying the material was less expensive than paying Mrs. Peacock. She still did her painting at night, so her sewing didn't interfere with it.

Annie Laurie took the money and went into her room. She counted her stash and found that all total, she had one thousand and fifty-five dollars. She stuffed the thousand into three Prince Albert cans, so rats couldn't gnaw through it, and she brought the fifty-five dollars back into the kitchen.

"It sure has been a whirlwind of a day!" thought Annie Laurie. She sat at the table and nibbled at some of the goodies that Mrs. Delores had brought and just thought. She'd seen some small wild sunflowers growing near the edge of the woods, so she thought she'd pick some and put them on her daddy's grave the next day. She realized her life was going to change.

"Oh, if I could just be a leading figure like Miss Earnestine," she thought. *"What would it take?"* She wondered.

Annie Laurie didn't stop to think that Miss Earnestine had given up all hopes of having a personal life, she'd dedicated it to the business and to Woodlawn Methodist Church.

Annie Laurie may have been worried, but she smiled. *"This time of the year we'd be making our baskets,"* she thought.

She put Mrs. Delores' treats in the living room where they'd be cooler, then put two more pieces of wood into the stove, so some of the heat would go into her bedroom. She didn't feel like painting tonight, in fact, she didn't know when she would.

Chapter 12
November 1941

War was raging in Europe. Hitler seemed unstoppable. His army had taken about twenty European countries, including France. The Jewish people especially were paying the price.

It was rumored that millions of Jews were slaughtered or put in work camps, then simply worked to death. The news was all rumored though and no one knew anything definitely, for no one was allowed in Europe.

The news of Hitler and his brutality stayed on the radio and papers. He was constantly bombing the United Kingdom, especially London, but England fought back with everything they had. Winston Churchill, The Prime Minister of the United Kingdom swore to the English people, they'd fight with everything they had. "They'll never take England," he'd promised the people of the United Kingdom.

Churchill had made several trips to the United States in an attempt to get the United States into the war, but so far

President Roosevelt had held off. Roosevelt made promises and delivered war supplies to England.

Annie Laurie stayed worried that Jesse, being so hot-headed, would run away and join the army, but so far, he hadn't. The reason being, Annie Laurie believed, was that his daddy kept him so busy.

They were now dating openly, Jesse kept pushing Annie Laurie for them to go all the way, but so far, she'd been strong enough to hold him off.

Sometimes, at night when she was alone in her bed, she wished that she had succumbed to their desires, but when the mornings came, she'd awake with a renewed strength and was glad she hadn't. Even though Jesse was now out of high school, they only dated on Saturday nights, for Annie Laurie worked at nights with her paintings. Not saying they wouldn't see each other sporadically at Miss Earnestine's, Excel, and Monroeville, and take trips on Sunday afternoons.

Each time they'd meet, Jesse would always be on an errand concerning his dad's business. He'd usually be dressed in jeans, a denim shirt, boots, and always wore a wide brimmed cowboy hat to cover his black curly hair.

Jesse had gotten hold of some old bridge lumber and had made an entrance to her house. Now, a vehicle could be driven to her front yard. Annie Laurie had placed wooden poles around her house in a square and kept the grass hoed. Beside the poles she'd planted a variety of rose bushes.

The two had such a good time with Jesse teaching her to drive, but she'd caught on and got her license on the first try. Afterwards, they stopped at Lee Motor Company and Annie Laurie bought her a 1938 4-door Plymouth. It was dark green in color, and of course Annie Laurie loved it. The Plymouth cost her four hundred dollars. She could now drive to Miss Earnestine's and explore the nearby surroundings. She saw the Alabama River in Claiborne, Alabama for the first time.

Jesse's dad kept him plenty busy. Sometimes when he'd have to go to a nearby town, Annie Laurie would ride with him.

Annie Laurie had kept a promise to herself, one day when she was hoeing the sporadically growing grass in her yard, she looked toward the family graveyard. She wound up not only hoeing the grass, but planting marigolds at the head of each grave. Mr. Lum had made her daddy a nice marker for his grave.

Annie Laurie wished that she knew more about her ancestors. All she knew was that her grandparents were Robert and Minerva Knowles Reed.

Sometimes, Annie Laurie would talk to her mama and daddy. She knew they couldn't hear her, but it made her feel better. She knew that her daddy would be so proud of her and her being able to make it on her own.

Since she had a driveway now, Jesse's mom had made a couple of visits. Her name was Opal. The first time she came inside the house, she offered to buy almost everything in the house, saying, "It would look so nice in her home, this has got to be ancient," she'd say about one item or the other. Annie Laurie declined all offers. Her reason being they had belonged to the family, she wrote in her notebook. They'd wind up looking at her paintings.

Opal, finding it was hard to converse with someone who couldn't talk, made her visits short.

Jesse had taken Annie Laurie to his house a few times, for some reason though, he'd always take her when his mom would be gone. His mom was hard to get to know, but Jesse's dad was different, she really liked him. He'd always put his arm around her waist and tell her how pretty she was, and how lucky Jesse was. Their house was huge, and each room was spotlessly clean.

Jesse had told Annie Laurie that they had a cook, and housekeeper. "Mom can't fry an egg," he said. He then added, "Dad stays onto her, she spends money like it's going out of style."

Annie Laurie didn't comment one way or the other.

She wanted to do something nice for Jesse's dad though. He always wore khaki shirts and pants, so she got Jesse to swipe an old pair.

She made a trip to Miss Earnestine's, after getting the exact size of each item and bought enough material to sew him a new pair of pants and long sleeve shirt. Around the collar and pockets of the shirt she sewed black trimming and also used black buttons for the buttonholes of the shirt.

Mr. Jordan's birthday was November 4th. She wrapped the two garments separately in brown paper and put brown homemade ribbons on each gift.

Jesse took her to the Jordan place, and as usual Opal was gone. Annie Laurie had noticed that Jesse pulled his boots off at the front door. After they got inside, she noticed that Mr. Jordan was walking around with just his socks on.

"Surprise," both Annie Laurie and Jesse said, as they saw him spreading peanut butter on a slice of bread.

Mr. Jordan stuck the butterknife back into the jar and said, "Well, what have we here?"

"It's a birthday present, Annie Laurie made for you," Jesse said.

"Well, my goodness, let me at it," he said, as he sat into an over-stuffed armchair.

Instead of using tape, Annie Laurie used some of the black trimming to tie the paper onto the gifts.

"My goodness, they're almost too pretty to unwrap," he said.

He did though, and then he said, "Excuse me, I'm going into my room and trying these on."

The two sat on the couch until Mr. Jordan returned.

"Now how did you know what size, and this shirt is almost too pretty to wear. Won't I be a doozie at the stockyard now," he said.

"Get up from there little girl and let me hug you," he said.

Annie Laurie stood up, and he not only hugged her, but spun her around in the room, making her squeal from excitement.

"Thank you, so much pretty girl," he said, as he turned Annie Laurie loose.

Using her index finger she wrote in the air, "Welcome."

Annie Laurie noticed they'd finally hung up the portrait she'd painted of Jesse. They'd put it over the mantle board.

"Well dad, if I'm going to tend to the cattle, I'd better get her back to her house," Jesse said.

Mr. Jordan hugged her again before they left.

Annie Laurie had to admit, she'd done a good job with his clothes.

On the way home, Jesse told her that he had to take a load of cattle to the stockyard in Lucedale Mississippi the first week of the next month. You can get married out there without any identification. "Will you marry me?" he asked.

They were pulling into the driveway of her house.

After he stopped, she kissed him and wrote on his leg.

"Yes, but we live here," then pointed toward her house.

"I don't blame you at all darling," Jesse said, then he kissed her.

It was hard for Annie Laurie to concentrate on anything, she was so excited.

"Me, getting married, after all these years loving that boy," she thought. She also considered how her life would

change. It would mean she'd have to go back to cooking and learn to be a housewife, and hopefully a mama.

"One good thing about it, Jesse will eat anything I cook," she thought. Annie Laurie had to admit it, she was getting accustomed to living alone. She could go to bed when she wanted and get up when she wanted. She could also cook when she wanted, unless Jesse was coming over.

The pro's to being married were that she loved Jesse and was willing to do extra things for him. She always wanted a pitcher pump on the back porch, so she wouldn't have to walk to the spring for water. She would have the intimacy that she longed for. She'd have someone to go places with her. She loved his daddy, and she was sure she'd learn his mama's ways and grow to love her too.

She wondered if she'd need a trousseau, or if they'd just get married and come back home.

"Oh well, I have nigh a month to find out," she thought. The main thing was she was marrying the one she loved, he was a hard worker, and he came from a good family.

She figured she'd get back to the matters at hand, so she went outside to feed the chickens and gather the eggs. After laying the basket of eggs on the back porch she walked under the pecan trees and saw they were beginning to fall. *"I'll give them another week, and I'll start picking them up,"* she thought. She then laughed, thinking that was what she was doing the first time she met Jesse.

She knew she wasn't eating enough vegetables, so she carried the eggs inside and brought out the dish pan to go gather turnips. *"They'll be good with some cornbread and stuffed eggs,"* she thought.

In a small while she had the fresh greens, cornbread and eggs cooking, and it was time to sit on the porch to watch the sun set.

It never failed she felt her daddy sitting on the doorsteps. She looked east toward the red glow of the setting sun.

"Daddy, Jesse proposed to me this afternoon, you won't have to worry about me living alone anymore," she whispered. She then went back into the house, locked the door behind her and checked on supper.

She soon found out she had too much on her mind to eat much, so she covered things in case Jesse came by, and went into the living room to listen to the radio. The radio whistled and buzzed for a few seconds, then Kate Smith's voice came on, she was singing, "God Bless America." "It must 've been a special program, for Kate's show had a lot of country singers on. There was Roy Acuff, The Carter family, The Tennessee Cloggers, and last but not least, Hank Williams. Hank sang "Lovesick Blues," and Annie Laurie loved it.

Annie Laurie thought how appropriate it was for Miss Smith to have such a great show on the night of her proposal. When the program went off they began broadcasting about Hitler again, so she switched off the radio.

She'd been working on a painting of Baby Jesus laying down with a lamb, so she went into her room to work on the details, for she was almost finished with it. She was satisfied with everything on the painting but the halo above baby Jesus' head.

As she painted, she thought the events of the afternoon and thought that Mr. Jordan was very pleased with his birthday gift. Jesse had told her he believed it was the first one that he'd ever gotten.

Over the period that she'd been painting, she learned that heat helped dry the paint, so when she was finished with the halo, she propped the painting in front of the oil lamp.

She'd decided that Jesse wouldn't be coming by, so she went into the kitchen and cleaned things up. She then wrapped the leftovers and placed them on the shelf on the back porch, knowing they'd keep in the cool night air.

She went into the living room, blew the lamp out and closed the door that led to the dining room and entered her room. She pulled her clothes and brassiere off, for she still just slept with her panties on, unless the room was cold.

After crawling into bed, she looked at her body and sniggered, "Well, I guess I'll be sleeping butt naked before long."

Annie Laurie pulled the covers up to her chin and she was soon asleep.

The next morning, she awoke and threw on a gown, she quickly fried one egg to eat with her jelly toast. Annie Laurie needed to carry a basket of fresh eggs to sell and buy a few items. She was still exuberant from yesterday's proposal. She knew she wasn't married yet, but she planned to start it off right, she was going to church. It was a place that she'd always longed to go, but for some reason her daddy never went after her mama died.

The doors opened at eleven at the church, and Miss Earnestine opened her store at one o'clock. At ginning time, the gin didn't run at all on Sundays, just the store from 1-5:00.

For the first time it dawned on Annie Laurie how many hours Miss Earnestine and her help spent at the store.

After feeding and watering the chickens, Annie Laurie bathed and dabbed a little perfume behind her ears. She dressed in a two-piece outfit, a brown skirt and long sleeve light jacket she'd sewn herself. She slipped on a pair of brown and white oxford pump shoes over her stocking feet. After brushing her long blonde hair until it seemed to sparkle, she left for church.

The church yard was already full of vehicles when she arrived.

Annie Laurie walked through the wide door, and after looking around she recognized most of the parishioners.

She recognized Jesse's parents right away, so she took a seat on the pew beside Mrs. Jordan.

She noticed right away that Mr. Jordan was wearing the new outfit that she'd made him.

"You look mighty pretty, my dear," Mrs. Jordan said.

Annie Laurie smiled and nodded her head.

She noticed that Mrs. Delano was playing the piano. *"She'd bought a painting from me,"* Annie Laurie thought.

The choir began to sing, and it was led by Brenda Jay, who had bought a couple of baskets from her and her daddy.

She'd seen Mr. Cecil and Mrs. Delores when she came in, and of course, she saw Miss Earnestine and Mr. Riley sitting on the front pew on the other isle.

Needless to say, Annie Laurie felt right at home.

Next came the collection plate. Very few people put in folding money, so Annie Laurie just put in two quarters.

Preacher Hall's sermon was from the book of psalms, and Annie Laurie thought he'd done a good job.

At the end of the service, they had alter call, but no one went to the altar.

Annie Laurie didn't know how popular she was until church was over and everyone was outside. Nearly all the ladies hugged her neck and talked about her paintings or had bought baskets from her.

Miss Earnestine came outside and invited her back to church. Annie Laurie told her she intended to. She could hear money jingling in Miss Earnestine's pocket and figured she must be the one that took care of the church's money.

Having a mode of travel of her own had made a big difference in her life. *"Oh, how I wish Daddy was still on this earth, so he could enjoy life a little!"* Annie Laurie thought.

Mrs. Opal referred to her husband as Jesse, so she learned that her fiancée was a junior. Knowing that Annie Laurie couldn't ask, Mrs. Opal told her that Jesse had Junior working.

After bragging on his clothes again, Mrs. Jordan said they were going out to eat and they left.

Annie Laurie had heard of the town of Repton before but had never been there. She knew it was east of the church and on the same road, so she decided to go see the town before she stopped by Miss Earnestine's.

Of course, the road was gravel or dirt all the way there, except for two wooden bridges.

After getting there, she was surprised at the amount of store buildings and old homes in the town. It, like Excel and Dottelle only had gravel roads for streets, but most of the houses were larger and looked older. A railroad track ran on the west side of the town. After crossing the tracks and driving to the end of the business area, she was satisfied, so she turned around and headed back toward Dottelle.

Miss Earnestine allowed Miss Lois the day off on Sundays, but Mr. Riley, Mr. Lum, along with Miss Earnestine were at the store when she pulled up to the gas pump.

Mr. Lum, as usual was standing on the porch.

Annie Laurie got out of her car, opened the back door and grabbed the handle of the basket of eggs.

"How much gas do you needs?" Mr. Lum asked.

Annie Laurie motioned with her finger, "Fill it up."

Annie Laurie knew that "Miss Octavia," Mr. Lum's wife always cooked a nice dinner and Mr. Lum had it waiting for them at the store on Sundays. They never went home, for when the store closed at five o'clock, they went to the evening worship at Woodlawn,

Miss Earnestine was standing at her usual post, behind the cash register.

"How many dozen, dear?" Miss Earnestine asked.

"Six dozen," Annie Laurie replied, by drawing the number 6 on the glass counter.

The clang of the register made its usual sound when it was opened, and Miss Earnestine laid six quarters on top of the glass counter.

Annie Laurie put the money in her pocket as Miss Earnestine began to take the older eggs out of the store's basket, then began putting the fresher eggs in, and laying the older eggs on top.

Miss Earnestine told Annie Laurie that the art studio in Mobile had made a special trip to the store the day before and were asking about more paintings. Naturally, thinking if they were that interested in them, I went up on the prices. "Ten dollars for your landscapes and twenty-five for your biblical paintings. The lady didn't blink an eye, so you can look for a bigger check the next time."

Annie Laurie smiled, and thinking the last painting should be dry enough by now, so she wrote on the counter with her finger, "Tomorrow, 10 more."

"Wonderful," Miss Earnestine said.

Mr. Lum held up four fingers to Miss Earnestine, meaning he'd put four gallons of gas in Annie Laurie's car tank.

Gas was selling for seventeen cents per gallon.

Both Miss Earnestine and Mr. Riley had college degrees in business, their daddy seen to that. They didn't have to worry about money though, because their father was loaded, and he owned acres and acres of land in the county. Him being a senator kept him in Washington most times and what little time he was home, he stayed shut up in his big white house in Excel. His brother-in-law managed the "Big Store," in Excel.

Miss Earnestine wasn't feminine at all. She was of medium height, slender built, wore no make-up, kept her black hair cut short with bangs. She always wore the same type of dress, with a narrow belt that accented her flat, curve less figure. She was all about money, whether it be a penny or dollar. She lived for Woodlawn Methodist church, the store and gin, and helping people, if it didn't cost money.

Mr. Riley didn't care about anything except dressing nice. He was a good man, but he let his sister run the show. They both still lived at home. Their cook and housekeeper lived in a small tin topped building behind the "Big house."

Annie Laurie wound up with a few items that day and paid for her gas. She had tired of the Kool Aid and began to drink tea, so she had bought a box of tea, five-pound bag of sugar, and flour. Jesse loved her tuna fish gravy, so she bought two tins of tuna. After a few flops, Annie Laurie had taught herself how to make biscuits, and she always had them with the tuna fish gravy. She didn't have to worry much about cooking anymore, unless she knew Jesse was coming over. She ate nick knacks a lot, giving her more time for sewing and painting. She had to admit she was excited about the increased price of her paintings. Her not being able to talk bothered her less and less, for she seemed to being good just as she was.

She wondered how Mr. Jordan was going to make out with Jesse living with her, for he was sure busy on the cattle ranch. She'd found out a little more about Mr. Jordan's business. He'd buy young beeves in large quantities, fatten them, then resale them at a higher price. Jesse spent a lot of time on the road, delivering or picking them up. The animals had to be watered and fed, also Jesse spent a lot of time on the tractor planting different fields of grass to ensure the animals kept plenty of grass to eat. She knew his circumstances all along, and he knew hers. It gave her freedom to sew and paint, being alone. Annie Laurie loved Jesse though, and she wanted a family above all else. She wouldn't dare let Jesse know, but her wants and desires were as strong as his. It was hard, but she intended to hold off until they were married, for she sure didn't want him to think less of her, or think she was cheap.

As Annie Laurie pulled into her yard, she observed how pretty the landscape was. It was the first week of November, and she noticed how pretty the leaves on the sassafras, persimmon, and oaks were. *"No, I could never see myself leaving from my home,"* she thought. She did think if her paintings brought in enough money, she'd see Mr. Lum about putting windows in her house. She'd still leave the outside shutters as they were though. Her first whim though was to have someone put down her a pitcher pump off the back porch.

Mr. Lum was the "go-to" man for most anything, she'd learned.

She carried her few groceries into the house.

It was still too early for her to feed the chickens, so she put on a light sweater and decided to sit on the front porch for a while and think.

She had counted her stash, just the other day and found that she had $1,050.00 in her room. She was hoping to get $600.00 more from her latest paintings. It was costing her more to survive though, for she was having to buy all her wood that she burned in the house. She also had to buy most of her food. About all she had Jesse to plant was corn, a row of peas, and of course, he made up a row for her to set out her tomato and sweet potato plants. Her turnip row, she made herself with one of the hoes.

During her rare idle moments, she thought about her daddy more. She knew he'd be proud of her achievements though and it warmed her heart, just knowing that.

She felt that having her own vehicle was such a relief to her. She'd tired of just sitting at home and depending on someone else to take her places. *"It wasn't so bad until my daddy died,"* she thought. *"Boy, if Daddy could have held on a little longer, they would have had a good time going places together in my car."*

She didn't sit long before she heard the sound of Jesse's car coming down the road.

Sure enough, he pulled into her driveway and almost skid his tires in the yard.

As though he was still sixteen years old, he sailed out of his car, jumped up on her porch, and with one hairy arm he put around her back and the other under her knees. Before she realized it, their lips were locked, and he was spinning her around on the porch. It wasn't long before he lowered his right arm, and she slid out of his arms and was standing.

"My goodness, you are so beautiful," he said. He then continued, "Mom and Dad said they saw you in church today, and that you took the place by storm," Jesse told her.

Annie Laurie just shrugged her arms.

"Boy, it's good to get away from the house, if only for a little while," Jesse said. He then continued, "Do you want to go to Frisco City with me?"

She smiled and nodded her head.

"Well, go change your clothes, you're not going with me all dolled up like that," he told her.

Annie Laurie laughed, then ran into the house to her bedroom. She quickly pulled the two-piece suit off and hung it up, then jumped into a pin striped dress and zipped it up. Then dabbed on a little cologne and put her sweater back on. She went out the back door, making sure she locked it. She very quickly fed the chickens. The last thing she did was to lock the front door.

Jesse, who was already sitting in the car, reached over and opened the door for her, he was also twisting on the tuner knob of the radio. There weren't too many stations to choose from. He finally settled on a station that was playing a Glenn Miller tune.

When they pulled out of the driveway, Jesse told her that his dad was getting the helpers to feed the cattle. "There's a Mrs. Herra, a widow that lives near Frisco City. Her husband died recently, and she wants to sell all the cattle," Jesse said.

As usual, Annie Laurie was almost sitting under Jesse. She'd learned though how to twist her body so that her legs would be on the passenger side.

When Jesse was shifting gears the back of his arm would hit her left breast, but she didn't care, as long as it was just his arm.

Jesse knew he had to hurry, because darkness would soon come, so he didn't waste time going through Excel.

About three miles from Excel, Jesse slowed down for a sharp curve, then he sped down a steep hill and crossed a long wooden bridge. Jesse told her the wide creek was called "Escambia Creek."

Before they were to go up another steep hill, Mrs. Herra's place was on the left.

Annie Laurie just sat in the car, while Jesse walked to the door and knocked.

The elderly lady came out and they walked behind the house. Annie Laurie could see the plank cow lot behind the house, next to a barn.

Jesse wasn't gone but about twenty minutes before he walked back to the car, with a piece of paper in one of his hands.

"What a pitiful sight," Jesse said, after he'd slammed the door to his car.

Annie Laurie drew a question mark on his dashboard

"Prime feeder calves, a dozen of them and not a one of them will weigh 500 pounds. All they had to eat was a little hay, and they were drinking putrid green water," Jesse said. He continued, "We'll worm 'em, and start giving them a little grain to go along with the hay, that'll fatten em up to where we can sellem. I gottem at a good price though," Jesse said, as he flashed the bill of sale before Annie Laurie's eyes.

"Poor things," thought Annie Laurie, remembering how her daddy petted and pampered the farm animals at their place.

Jesse didn't drive as fast going back, and Annie Laurie was glad of it. He was always in a hurry, and sometimes it scared her.

About a mile from Excel, Jesse turned right and went into the black quarters.

Annie Laurie could smell the heavenly aroma before Jesse pulled in front of an old tin topped house.

"They cook the best barbeque here, I'll be back in a minute," he said.

Annie Laurie didn't see how anyone could live in that house, for smoke was everywhere.

Before long, she saw Jesse walk through a cloud of smoke with a bag of sandwiches in his hands.

"I bought mom and pop one too, it's the so-called cook's day off," Jesse said, as he sat down in the car.

Annie Laurie noticed that Jesse wasn't his usual jovial self on the ride back home. He acted as though he was in deep thought about something.

When they reached Annie Laurie's, Jesse kissed her, and said, "You know, I've been thinking. I really haven't been fair to you. What good does it do for a girl to be engaged and not have a ring, it's not right."

Jesse reached across the car and opened the glove compartment.

"As usual, I don't have but a minute, but I have something to give you. Come on, let's go inside," Jesse said.

Jesse left his car lights on and motor running, so they didn't have a problem climbing up the steps, and for Annie Laurie to unlock the door.

It was cold in the living room, so they walked back to the dining room, with Jesse carrying their sandwiches.

Annie Laurie threw a piece of wood into the stove, then sat down at the table and grossed her legs. She then cocked her head, as if she was waiting.

Jesse laid the sandwiches on the table, then reached into his jacket pocket. He brought out a small box and opened it.

"Okay, I don't feel like I need to get on my knees, because you've already told me you'd marry me. This is your engagement ring. I've been making payments on these suckers since I fell in love with you," Jesse said, as he handed her the golden diamond ring that sparkled in the lamp light.

Annie Laurie began crying and put both hands over her eyes.

"Well, stick your left hand out and let's see if it fits," Jesse told her.

Annie Laurie wiped her eyes, and held her hand out, as he had asked.

Jesse slipped the ring on her finger that was wet from the tears, and it was a perfect fit.

Annie Laurie jumped from her chair and hugged Jesse and began to cry again.

"Here, here, you're getting my jacket wet," Jesse said, as he pushed her body away from him and kissed her, long and hard.

When she felt his erectness against her, she pushed him away and pointed at the box that contained the wedding band.

"Boy, you meant what you said didn't you," Jesse said.

With the most sorrowful look in her eyes, Annie Laurie nodded her head.

Jesse put his hand beneath her chin, and said, "You know what, you have character."

Annie Laurie picked up her notebook, and quickly wrote:

"I remember when I was a little girl, I heard my aunt Sarie tell my daddy that a man would never marry me, and here it is, I'm getting the best-looking man around, the only one that I've ever wanted."

Jesse quickly read the note.

"Well, I just hope we can make if financially, the old man only pays me forty dollars a week," Jesse said.

Annie Laurie wrote, "I make money, with my paintings."

"He might fire me," Jesse said.

Annie Laurie wrote, "He won't."

"He might take my car," Jesse said.

'We'll still have a car, food, and a house that's paid for, with fifty acres. You might want to bring your underwear though, he might take them," Annie Laurie wrote.

"I'm not planning on wearing any, at least for a while," Jesse said.

"Me either," Annie Laurie wrote.

"I can hardly wait," Jesse said, then added, "I'd be willing to bet it's 400 degrees in my car, so I'd better get a move on before their barbeque starts to sizzle."

Jesse stuck the small box that contained the two wedding bands in his jacket pocket, then said, "Oh! We'll be leaving here on December 4th, going to Lucedale."

Annie Laurie put her hand to her heart, and scribbled with the other hand, "Now, I'm the scared one."

"Believe me, you have no reason to be scared, you got what it takes," Jesse said, as he picked her up as though she was a little girl and kissed her.

"Good night sweetheart, I love you," Jesse said.

Annie Laurie followed him to the door, and she couldn't resist it, she patted him on his cheeks when he reached the door.

"Hey, my behind isn't yours yet," he said, and laughed, as he went out the door.

"I can't believe I had the nerve to do that!" Annie Laurie thought, and then laughed as she sat down at the table to enjoy looking at her ring and eating the barbeque.

"Wow, what a day," she reflected. *"I went to church, saw the town of Repton, for the first time, received good news from Miss Earnestine, and now I have my engagement ring on my finger."* She

kissed the diamond on the ring and put it up to her face. "Oh, how I love you, Jesse Jordan!" she whispered.

Annie Laurie had been dreading it, but she knew she had to move her art studio out of her bedroom, and into her daddy's old room. She knew the room still smelled like liniment, for she could still get a whiff of it when she passed the door. She certainly knew her bedroom wouldn't do, after they were married.

Her first priority for the next day was to finish framing the paintings. She'd gotten to be good with the framing too. With some of the paintings, she'd use the limb of a tree, but most of them were from scrap boards. It was according to the type painting it was. For instance she'd never use a tree limb or a rat tan vine for a biblical painting. The canvasses were bigger too. She loved painting pictures from the Bible. The paints were of a softer color.

Annie Laura could paint images of flowers, birds, landscapes, etc. but they seemed to take longer.

She thought too, that she wouldn't be able to turn out the paintings as fast after she was married. There's the cooking, more clothes to wash, and she knew they'd probably be going places together, for she intended on putting her marriage first.

After she'd eaten, she finished with the frames and tacking the paintings inside. All she wanted to do the next morning was to put the paintings in the trunk of her car.

After Annie Laurie finished, she thought about listening to the radio, but then decided against it, knowing she'd have to build a fire in the fireplace, so she decided to call it a day.

She put two more pieces of wood in the stove, then ran into her bedroom to get her flannel gown, and bedroom slippers, remembering to leave her bedroom door open.

"It's sure nice stripping my clothes off and changing in front of the heat of the stove," she thought, as she laid her brassiere and dress on the table.

After standing by the stove until toasty warm, she grabbed her slip, dress and bra, then ran toward her bedroom. After hanging her dress into the wardrobe, she turned down the lamp, then crawled into her bed and covered up.

The feel of the ring on Annie Laurie's finger seemed to give a warm glow to her heart and she soon fell asleep, thinking of Jesse and their future together.

Chapter 13

Thanksgiving 1941

Annie Laurie was doing something different for Thanksgiving this year. Mrs. Jordan made a special trip to her house to invite her to celebrate Thanksgiving with them.

Annie Laurie accepted the invitation, then admitted to Jesse a couple of days later that she was scared of the acceptance.

They were in Annie Laurie's dining room when she admitted her feelings to Jesse.

Jesse held her in his arms and said, "Listen to me, there's something special about you, and don't you forget it. I'll let you in on a little secret, mom's father was a sharecropper. Shoot, when dad married her, he had to buy her a pair of shoes to get married in. I think that's the reason he lets her get by with the way she spends money. Just because you can't talk doesn't mean you're not as good as the next one."

Jesse had never brought up the fact about her handicap, but she was glad he did, somehow in the back of her mind she felt as though she was hiding it from him.

"Daddy use to say, they might kill you, but they can't eat you, and that would be the bad part," Annie Laurie wrote.

Jesse laughed, and said, "Now that's a phrase I'm going to remember." He continued to talk, "You know, I really liked your daddy, and I feel that he liked me."

"Oh, he did. I believe he somehow knew we were meant for each other," Annie Laurie said.

Annie Laurie mentioned the fact that Miss Earnestine had paid her seven hundred dollars for her last paintings. "She keeps mentioning it to me that I should take my paintings to Mobile. She says that I'll make more money, but shoot I'd be scared to death driving to Mobile," Annie Laurie said.

"Shoot, we'll take them down there the next time," Jesse said, he then added, "You know that Miss Earnestine and Mr. Riley are making money on those paintings too."

"I feel sure they are, but Lord what would I do without her, especially in the past," Annie Laurie answered.

"Now, what are you planning on doing with seven hundred dollars?" Jesse jokingly asked.

"I talked with Mr. Lum about getting someone to put a pitcher pump off the back porch, and putting windows in the house," Annie Laurie wrote.

"It will be money well spent, especially the pump. I worry about you toting water from that spring," Jesse said.

"It's not that bad, except for in freezing cold weather," Annie Laurie wrote, then laughed.

Jesse laughed with her, then briefly kissed Annie Laurie on the lips.

"You know, you not only amaze me, but everyone who knows you. When your daddy died, I think people around here looked for you to sink like the Titanic, but you haven't, you've actually thrived," Jesse said.

"You know darling, me being like the Titanic never entered my head, for I had you," Annie Laurie hastily wrote.

"Hmmm, that's strange, because you're the reason that I hang on. You just don't know how demanding dad is. Oh, he's not mean or anything like that, but supplying all those packing houses with beef is a task and a half. It's not only a bunch of time on the road, but all those hours in the fields and cow lots," Jesse said.

"Well, I guess all jobs have their drawbacks, but with painting and sewing, it seems to make me unwind," Annie Laurie wrote.

"Well, I know your poor finger is bound to be killing you, with all the writing, so with your permission, I'd better go tend to cattle," Jesse said.

"Au revoir," Annie Laurie wrote.

"Oui," Jesse grinned, then kissed the knot on her finger, then they simply embraced before he practically ran out of the door.

After Jesse left, Annie Laurie knew the only way to get her daddy's old room straightened out was to swallow her emotions and to get in there and do it.

After going into the room, she knew the first thing she needed to do was strip the bed, and bag everything that had the odor of liniment.

She closed the door that led to the dining room and opened the shutters, allowing the cold air to fill the room. She threw the bed sheets, blankets, everything that smelled of liniment through the opening, onto the ground outside. Annie Laurie closed the door to the room after she ran back into the dining room.

She cleaned the dining room and kitchen until it suited her, then went back into her daddy's old room. She closed the shutters to keep the cold wind out, and sure enough, she smelled only a faint whiff of the liniment. Annie Laurie found the stick that her daddy had rigged up to swab his back. It still contained the gauze on the end. *"Poor Daddy,"* she thought, then choking back tears she went back into the kitchen and stuck the whole thing into the burning embers inside of the stove.

Somehow or other, it seemed that Annie Laurie was burning her daddy's pain away, and she suddenly felt better, and she returned to her daddy's old room.

Spreading a clean sheet she'd found in his old chiffer robe, she gathered what few clothes, underwear, and shoes he had and threw them onto the sheet until the chiffer robe was empty. She then tied the corners of the sheet and thought she'd give it all to Mr. Lum.

All that was left in the room was her daddy's clock, and his knives that set on a table at the head of his bed, and an old calendar that hung on the wall.

Annnie Laurie thought of her mama's old drawings that were on top of the chiffer robe. As she tip toed to reach them, she saw a square that was cut into the ceiling with a wooden covering.

Her curiosity got the best of her, so after removing the drawings, she went into the dining room and brought back a chair and a flashlight.

The old chiffer robe was homemade, so it was very stout. She pushed the chair to the side of the furniture, then laid the flashlight on top.

Standing on the chair, she hoisted herself to the top of the chiffer robe. There was only enough room between the top of the chiffer robe and ceiling for her to squat. Pushing hard against the square, she found that it would push up. She soon had the square resting in the loft. Holding the flashlight, she stood up into the cold loft.

The whole house had twelve-inch exposed beams in the ceiling, and it had never dawned on her that the loft was floored.

Annie Laurie was shocked at the things the flashlight exposed.

She saw an old army uniform, it was gray in color, so she figured it to be confederate, two old muzzle loaders stood leaning against the wall of the ceiling near where she stood. She saw women's dresses hanging everywhere, and they were made similar to the ones that Mrs. Peacock made. There were old antique tools. The two things that intrigued her the most were two old oval topped trunks. There was enough room in the middle of the loft for her to stand, so she pulled herself up until she was standing in the loft.

Of course, she walked straight to the trunks and opened them one at a time. She found old folded clothes on top, old tin type photographs were on the bottom, and some of them were framed.

The other old trunk revealed about the same items, except for a set of wedding rings and a cameo locket with a golden chain.

The trunks were of medium size, but she found that it was a struggle scooting them back toward the opening. Luckily, on each end of the trunks were thick leather straps. They barely fit through the opening, but by holding to the leather strap she eased them to the top of the chiffer robe. She had to do them one at a time, in order for her to have room to get back to the top of the chiffer robe.

After she had them on the floor of the bedroom, she climbed back up to the loft and got the two old muzzle loaders and the confederate uniform. She noticed that the old muzzle loaders had rags stuffed in the end of the barrels, and the old packing rods were still in their rightful place.

"Oh, Jesse would kill for these," Annie Laurie thought, as she propped the old firearms against the wall.

After double checking to make sure that both doors were locked, Annie Laurie dipped into the reservoir of the stove and carried a pan of soapy water into the bedroom. The trunks, especially, were covered in dust.

After wiping off as much dust as possible on the trunks, she dragged them into the kitchen, where it was warmer, and she could sit down. Annie Laurie noticed right away that the wood was a beautiful rosewood color. She wondered why they had been stored in the attic and were not put on display or used in the house.

All the old newspapers just crumbled when she picked them up, but she noticed the dates on the newspapers, and the oldest one was dated June 15, 1856. The papers had been used to wrap old vases, glasses, silverware, and such. The silverware was black, and most of the vases were ruby red in color. She finally got to the wedding rings. They were stamped 14 karat gold. She turned on the flashlight and by squinting her eyes she read the inscriptions inside. The lady's band read, "SLK," and the man's ring was inscribed, "JJK."

Next, she opened the beautiful cameo, which was blue and white in color. Inside the cameo was a tintype picture of a man with blonde curly hair, dressed in a confederate uniform. The small picture had obviously been cut, in order for it to fit inside the cameo. Annie Laurie could hardly wait to clean the cameo and wear it on special occasions. The glassware, she thought she'd place in different places in the house. She'd need to buy some silver polish from Miss Earnestine to polish the silverware.

The other trunk contained mostly old dresses, but it did have eight ruby red dishes, saucers, and a bowl that matched the glasses in the other trunk. She went through the pockets on the dresses and found a $5.00 gold coin. *"Lord knows what these things would be worth now,"* Annie Laurie thought.

Annie Laurie was pretty sure the wedding bands belonged to her Knowles ancestors, but why they were put away in the trunk, she would never know. Undoubtably her daddy didn't know of the things in the loft either.

After she was sure the trunks were dry, Annie Laurie polished them with some "Old English" furniture polish, and she thought they were the prettiest pieces of furniture in the house. She then polished the stock and barrel to the two old guns and hung the old confederate uniform on the back porch. She thought she'd give it a good dusting the next day.

While eating her supper, which consisted of two boiled eggs and a slice of bread, Annie Laurie thought of her ancestors. She thought of the men and women who had worn the clothes that were in the trunk. She wondered if they'd had a good life, about their demeanor and what they looked like. From the painting she'd painted, she thought she favored her mama. She was glad that she had a kitchen cabinet with glass doors. She thought she'd wash the glassware the next day and put them on display.

By Thanksgiving, Mr. Lum's nephews had seen to it that Annie Laurie had her windows in and her pump exactly where she wanted it. The pump made things so much easier for her, and the windows, they brought so much light into the house. She had two windows in front of the house, the windows in front were very long. One in each bedroom, and one in the dining room. The total cost for the windows and pump wasn't but three hundred and thirty-five dollars. Needless to say, Annie Laurie was well pleased with everything, and Jesse was too.

Annie Laurie had chosen red material for the curtains in her living room, light blue material for the bedrooms, and brown for the dining room. She'd bought the material from Miss Earnestine's and had sewn the curtains herself. After she had the curtains hung, she sewed the dress and a jacket with ¾ inch sleaves she was planning on wearing to the Jordan's on Thanksgiving. She made it out of the same red material that she'd made the living room curtains with.

In the daytime, Annie Laurie pulled the curtains in the living room back, and now she could look outside without opening the door. She still had her shutters on the outside, in case bad weather happened.

She simply didn't have the heart to throw the old dresses away, so Annie Laurie put them in pillowcases and put them back into the loft. She put the trunks at the foot of the beds in the bedrooms, after she had them polished and looking pretty. The extra bed in the living room was left like it was.

Jesse's mom had stopped by one day and she complimented Annie Laurie on the changes she'd made. She evidently knew antiques, for when she walked into the dining room, her eyes glued to the Ruby red glassware in the cabinet.

"Oh, those are just beautiful, I've never noticed them here before," she said, then picked up the red vase in the middle of the dining room table, as though she was examining it.

"On yes mam, they've been here for ages," Annie Laurie wrote.

"Well, I must say, you've done wonders to the place, and for it to be a log cabin," Mrs. Jordan remarked.

"Yes mam, it's a log cabin, but they tell me it's just as sturdy now, as it was when it was new," Annie Laurie wrote.

Mrs. Jordan hugged Annie Laurie, then said, "Okay dear, remember tomorrow is Thanksgiving, and we're already cooking."

Annie Laurie nodded her head and did a short bow.

Before Mrs. Jordan left, she mentioned that Jesse had sent Junior to Andalusia with a load of cattle.

Annie Laurie had to admit that she felt a little dejected at Mrs. Jordan's last statement, but she knew Jesse's predicament when she fell in love with him.

She knew she should be ashamed of herself, but she breathed a sigh of relief when Jesse's mother pulled her black Cadillac out of the driveway.

Annie Laurie was pretty sure that Jesse wouldn't be coming by, so she decided she'd start on a painting that she had in mind. She was well aware that she'd neglected her painting since she'd sold the last ones.

Annie Laurie had moved her canvasses, painting supplies, and easel into her daddy's old room, and she had to admit it sort of gave her the willies to begin with. Soon she was absorbed with her work though and the feelings soon went away, too, she knew that her daddy wouldn't want her to feel uneasy in the room.

After Annie Laurie had painted the background of the painting she knew it had to dry before she could continue, so she left the canvass on the easel and closed the door to the bedroom.

Annie Laurie seldom cooked a full meal, with conditions being as they were, but she was hungry, so she made her a peanut butter and jelly sandwich and washed it down with some lukewarm tea. Annie Laurie felt like she might be thinking a little extravagantly, but she planned on wearing the cameo neckless to the Jordan's for Thanksgiving. Her engagement ring, she'd just turn the small diamond toward the palm of her hand, like she had done when Jesse's mom had popped in.

After eating her meager supper, she stripped in front of the stove and took a good bath, she also shampooed her hair, so that it would have time to dry somewhat before she went to bed.

After putting on her cotton gown, she thought about listening to the radio, but since Hitler had started bombing England in September, that was about all you could hear on almost every station.

Annie Laurie put more wood in the stove, then leaned forward so her blonde hair would be nearer the heat and commenced to brush it. She thought about Jesse and how enthused he was about the old muzzle loaders. He'd even got hold of some black powder somewhere and had fired them. She thought about how "Happy go lucky" Jesse was and how hard he worked. *"Really, I saw more of him when he was in high school,"* she thought.

Annnie Laurie wound up brushing her long hair by letting it lay in her lap. After seeing the old tintype in the cameo she saw where she had inherited her hair color.

After making sure her hair was dry, Annie Laurie blew the lamp out in the dining room and ran into her bedroom. She'd already pulled the covers down, so after she pulled her slippers off, she crawled into bed.

The next morning, Annie Laurie was dressed and ready to go to the Jordan's by 10:30. By 11:00, she was beginning to get worried. She wondered if she should drive her car, when Jesse came flying into her driveway.

Annie Laurie waited at the front door.

"My oh my, just look how pretty," Jesse said, as he picked Annie Laurie up and swung her around, with their lips locked.

After he put her down, he stood away with his hands on her shoulders and said, "Just think, a week from today we'll be near Lucedale by this time."

Jesse's black hair was wet, so Annie Laurie knew the poor thing had been working all day and had just taken a bath. He was dressed in a new looking pair of jeans and a long-sleeved denim shirt that had snaps on it instead of buttons. Annie Laurie noticed that he was also wearing a pair of new brown cowboy boots.

"You look good enough to eat, but we'd better go, mom is waiting," Jesse said.

They held hands until they reached Jesse's car.

Both Mr. and Mrs. Jordan hugged Annie Laurie's neck as they entered the door.

"My goodness, don't you look pretty, and I love your outfit," Mrs. Jordan said.

Annie Laurie smiled and bowed her head slightly.

"We're just thrilled that you could make it," Mrs. Jordan said, as she led them to the dining room.

Mr. Jordan looked uncomfortable in his tight black suit, but Annie Laurie thought Mrs. Jordan looked radiant in her light blue chiffon dress.

Annie Laurie had never seen such a meal on a table. There was a baked turkey, cornbread dressing, turnip greens, sweet potato or either pumpkin pies, fruit salad, and some other dishes that didn't look familiar to Annie Laurie.

Jesse pulled out Annie Laurie's chair and he took the chair next to her. Mrs. Jordan sat across from them at the extravagant table. Mr. Jordan gave grace while standing at the head of the table, then went around and began to carve the turkey.

After Mr. Jordan finished with the turkey the servant showed up and began to pass the bowls and platters of food around.

The knife, spoons, and forks were placed at her different sides of her plate, and the cloth napkins were rolled and stuck into a beautiful marble ring.

Annie Laurie just did as the two Jesse's did, which was using one knife, spoon, and fork. She did take the cloth napkin out of the ring and spread it in her lap though, for she didn't want to risk ruining her dress.

They even had ice in their tea glasses. Annie Laurie let them know the fact that she wasn't accustomed to having ice in her tea, by shaking her glass and pointing at the ice.

"That's right, you have that old antiquated springhouse," Mrs. Jordan replied.

Mr. Jordan gave his wife a hard look, then she said, "Dear, we just bought a bigger icebox, would you like to have our old one. It's small and won't hold much, but it's a good one."

"Oh, my goodness, yes," thought Annie Laurie as she clasped her hands together and nodded her head.

"Good, someone will deliver it tomorrow. You can't get it too close to your stove though," Mrs. Jordan said.

The tall grandfather clock that stood near the corner of the room struck twelve times when they began to eat.

Annie Laurie was determined not to act timid or shy, so she ate heartily. And for dessert she ate a piece of sweet potato pie. The servant was steadily putting more tea in her glass throughout the meal.

Mrs. Jordan must have noticed how much tea Annie Laurie was drinking, for after everyone ate, the two Jesse's sat near the fireplace and turned the radio on. Mrs. Jordan motioned for Annie Laurie to follow her.

Annie Laurie followed Mrs. Jordan down the wide hall, they soon went into a bedroom, and Mrs. Jordan eventually opened the door to the bathroom. The room looked similar to the one at the theater. *"How could this be?"* she thought, for they like everyone else on the road didn't have electricity." The room was well lit by a small window that was near the ceiling.

Annie Laurie didn't ask questions for she was about to pop. She closed the door, shimmied up her dress, then pulled down her panties and sat on the commode to relieve herself. Afterwards, when she got her attire straightened back out, she washed her hands at the small sink, then dried them with a small paper towel that was conveniently stacked on a shelf with lots of others.

There was a full-length mirror in the room. Annie Laurie made sure she looked presentable, then flushed the commode and stepped back into the immaculate bedroom with the carpeted flooring. Annie Laurie had never seen such luxurious furniture. *"Little wonder poor Jesse worked so hard,"* Annie Laurie thought. There was a big four poster bed with a canopy on top. Annie Laurie had never seen such a long dresser, with two tall dressers to match. *"It's just not fair to her son,"* she thought.

Mrs. Jordan suddenly came out of another doorway. "It's a shame we ladies' bladders are the size of a pea, and I'll swear, I think a man can hold a water bucket full and then some," Mrs. Jordan said, smiling. She then grabbed Annie Laurie's hand and they went back to join the menfolk, who were still engrossed about the news on the radio.

"I still say Churchill will pull us into that war over there. They did it once before and they'll do it again. I'm carrying bullet wounds to prove it," Mr. Jordan said.

Annie Laurie looked at Mrs. Jordan, and she nodded her head in agreement, then whispered in her ear. "He has a wound on one thigh, and another on his left arm. He has a shoebox full of medals," she concluded.

She saw a small paper pad and a lead pencil on the table next to her, so Annie Laurie picked it up and wrote on the top page. "Give me his medals and I'll frame them."

"You know, I've never thought of that, but that would be so sweet of you. I'll bet he'd hang them up over that radio. He stays glued to that thing, especially in the afternoons," Mrs. Jordan whispered.

Something unbelievable came over the radio, they interrupted the news to play the song "Stardust."

"Oh, my goodness," Mrs. Jordan exclaimed as she jumped from the sofa, ran over to her husband and grabbed him by the hand. Mr. Jordan must have known what his wife's intentions were, for he got up from his easy chair and they began to dance.

Jesse rushed over to Annie Laurie's and grabbed her hand.

"Why not?" Annie Laurie thought, and they soon got into the rhythm of the music, as they danced circles around the living room.

Much to her surprise, she thought they were doing very good, and she loved the atmosphere in the room for the first time.

Believe it or not, the Andrews sisters came on next, singing, "The Boogie Woogie Bugle Boy," and boy did they have fun with that one. They couldn't dance, for laughing. Eventually they got tired of trying to keep up with the rhythm and they all sat down. Annie Laurie thought Jesse's dad was hilarious through the whole time he was on the floor.

After things settled down and they'd stopped laughing. Mr. Jordan pulled out his pocket watch.

"Well son, it's a shame to ruin such a delightful time, but you know you must start tending to the beeves at two o'clock. That gives you thirty minutes to get your date back home, do a little wooing and get back home."

"Aw, bologna, just when we were having fun," Mrs. Jordan said.

They had to go back through the dining room, and Mrs. Jordan stopped them.

"Here dear, I had Dolly prepare you a plate to take home. I know you don't have an icebox yet, but it's chilly enough for you to set it on your back porch and it'll keep. Just don't let the sun hit it in the morning though, or it might spoil. I'll see that you get the icebox tomorrow, and get it out of my way," Mrs. Jordan said.

Jesse grabbed the big platter, and both Mr. and Mrs. Jordan hugged Annie Laurie's neck before she went out of the door. "You know you don't have to be invited here, you're welcome just any ole time. We'll team up on the two Jesses together," Mrs. Jordan told her, as she stuck her head out of the door.

Annie Laurie smiled and waved back to her.

Mrs. Jordan was good as her word. The next day, two of their workers delivered the wooden icebox. Annie Laurie put it against the wall that led to her bedroom.

Chapter 14

Lucedale 1941

Annie Laurie didn't know it, but they had to ride to Lucedale in one of the big trucks that was packed with cows. The movement of the cattle in the back of the truck made the thing bounce all over the road.

It was Thursday, December 4,th 1941.

Two of the farmhands were in another truck trailing them. Jesse had picked up Annie Laurie at eight o'clock that morning and driving non-stop they'd reached the slaughter house in Lucedale at 11:00.

The trucks were weighed while loaded with the cattle, then again after they were emptied. Jessie was paid for the cattle with a check, which he stuck inside his cowboy hat. He gave the workers twenty dollars for fuel and food to get back home on.

Jessie then told Annie Laurie to write the short note that read:

Dear Mom and Pop, Annie Laurie and I were married. I'll be back Monday with your check, truck, and my wife. We'll be living at Annie Laura's.

Love you, Jr. and Annie Laurie.

Jesse then folded the note and gave it to one of the workers.

They had noticed a motel that had a café on the way into Lucedale. The place was called "No tell Motel," so that's where Jesse headed after they were married.

Annie Laurie was surprised at how simple it had been to get married, all they had to do was present their driver's license, have two witnesses. In their case, LeRoy and Alvin, the two workers and fifteen dollars. The city clerk married them right there in his cluttered office, he stamped the license, recorded it and handed it to Annie Laurie.

"It's not a requirement, but if you wish, you may now kiss your bride" the old clerk had told Jesse.

"Mister, I've been waiting since I was twelve years old to call this young beauty mine," Jesse said, and he then held Annie Laurie in his arms and kissed her. He broke his embrace after he heard LeRoy and Alvin giggle.

Annie Laurie waited in the big truck until Jesse paid for their room. She knew she had to be starving, for she hadn't eaten all day, but she was both happy and nervous, so her hunger pains dissipated. She made up her mind right there in that truck that she was going to make her marriage work.

In a few minutes, Jesse returned, grinning from ear to ear.

Annie Laurie unlocked the truck door for him.

"Well, honey, room 12 is gonna be honeymoon home until Sunday morning at 9:00 am," Jesse told his new wife.

"I hope that it's warm in there, I've been about to freeze out here in this truck," Annie Laurie said, as she hopped off the running board of the truck.

"Hey, you were supposed to allow me to help you out of that truck, and as far as the heat, we'll soon heat it up in there," Jesse told her.

"Okay then, dutiful husband, I have two sacks of clothes in the floorboard, you can grab them for me," Annie Laurie told him.

Jesse had to park the big truck a good distance from the motel, due to its scent. They made their way to their room though, and Jesse unlocked the door.

Before Annie Laurie could build her nerves to go inside, Jesse laid her sacks at the door and carried her into the cold room. He then ran back to the door to get her things, then locked the door.

"Oh God, give me the strength," Annie Laurie said to herself, then squared her shoulders to prepare being a wife.

There was an electric heater hanging on the wall and Jesse turned it on.

Jesse began to strip, beginning with his shirt.

"Alright, let's see what you've been hiding from me all these years, because you're about to see mine," Jesse said, as he sat on the side of the bed, struggling to get his boots off.

Annie Laurie couldn't help but laugh, as she looked into one of the bags for her flannel pj's.

"Alright, you'd better look, while I'm stripping," Annie Laurie said, as she removed her clothes and undergarments to put her pajamas on.

"Oh, my Lord, they're everything I dreamed of and more. Leave that top part unbuttoned," Jesse said, as he continued to struggle with getting his pants and boots off.

"Settle down, you're in too big of a hurry," Annie Laurie motioned with her hands, as she went around the bed to help him with his boots.

Putting each boot between her legs, she yanked on the heel of each boot, and they came off.

Jesse almost ripped his jeans and underwear off.

It was the first time in Annie Laurie's life that she'd seen a naked man, and she wasn't disappointed. She was surprised at all the hair that started at his pelvic and stopped at his chest.

Annie Laurie wished that they were in the dark, but it was still bright daylight in the room.

"Hop under the cover baby, and let's get this thing on," Jesse said.

Annie Laurie felt that she needed a bath, after riding all day in the stinking truck, but she did as Jesse said.

"Ah, ah, ah, pull those clothes off," Jesse said.

Even though the droning heater was barely warming the room, she again did as Jesse said, then practically dove into bed.

Things were awkward for a while, and Annie Laurie felt that Jesse didn't know any more than she did, and that pleased her.

By dark though, they had it figured out, and Annie Laurie had to admit, making love to Jesse was fun and very enjoyable.

Sex wasn't the only thing they did that night. Jesse talked about things they'd never discussed before.

She learned that Jesse's mom stayed onto his dad about the way he worked Jesse. She also learned that Jesse's dad was saving money to buy more land, help, and cattle.

Jesse told Annie Laurie that his dad looked for Roosevelt to pull them into a war, and that the price of beef would go sky high.

Finally, around midnight things settled down in the bed and they went to sleep, with Jesse's right arm over her waist, and his left arm under her pillow.

Annie Laurie awoke the next morning, and she had to admit, she felt as if the weight of the world was off her shoulders. She didn't feel alone anymore. Strange as it may seem, she never realized she felt that way before. Other than being a little sore in private places, she felt alive and well.

Jesse woke up from her pulling the black hair on his chest.

After kissing and having sex, they both showered together, dressed and left for the café that was attached to the motel. They were both starved, so they ate their grits and eggs, along with jellied biscuits like starved hounds.

Afterwards, Jesse suggested they ride around a little and see parts of Lucedale. Annie Laurie discovered that Lucedale was located in George County, and the county adjoined Alabama on the east side.

Annie Laurie didn't think much of the place, but in her heart it would always be near and dear to her heart. She sat next to Jesse and didn't have to worry anymore if Jesse's elbow brushed against her breast as he changed gears.

"Boy, you sure gave me a hard time over the years, you being so high and mighty. You wouldn't allow my hands past your knees," Jesse said.

Annie Laurie's notebook and pencil were left in the truck, so she hastily wrote, "Now, aren't you glad I did?"

Jesse read the note quickly, and said, "Yes, you were right darling, but I guess that's the way it is with men. I mean somebody has to be the aggressor."

Annie Laurie laughed.

"Now, what's so funny?" Jesse asked.

Annie Laurie wrote, "I was thinking about your mama and daddy," and showed what she'd written.

After reading the note, Jesse laughed too, and said, "Somehow, in their case my assumption just might be wrong."

With that being said, they both folded over in laughter.

After they finished laughing, Jesse said, "You know, we've accomplished our mission here in Lucedale. What do you think about us leaving here in the morning? We'll drive down to Biloxi, take highway 90, along the beach, you'll love that. We'll go home by way of Mobile. That'll make us getting home tomorrow afternoon though."

Annie Laurie nodded her head and smiled. She was pleased that Jesse already considered her place as theirs. She had fed the chickens enough corn and poured them enough water to last them for days. *"The nests are probably running over with eggs,"* she thought.

Jesse's last words sure pleased Annie Laurie; the truck stank profusely. Besides, she was dying to let everyone know she was married. Even though, they probably already knew, for she knew how news traveled in a small town. She dreaded facing Jesse's parents though, for she fully intended on going with him, if she had to follow him in her car.

They didn't eat at the diner that night; instead, they ate at a swanky place. She ate something that Annie Laurie had never eaten, fried oysters, along with French fries and coleslaw. She thought they were very good, smothered in ketchup.

Neither one would admit it, but they both were excited about leaving the "No Tell Motel" the next morning.

That night, as they crawled into bed, Jesse noticed the bruises on Annie Laurie's breast.
He apologized and promised to be more gentle, and he was that night.

The next morning, after eating breakfast, Annie Laurie packed her things back into the paper bags and they left Lucedale, Mississippi as a happily married couple.

"You know the only thing I'll miss about that place is the electricity and the running water," Annie Laurie wrote.

"What about the sex?" Jesse asked.

"Oh, we can have that anywhere," Annie Laurie quickly wrote.

Jesse looked behind him to make sure a vehicle wasn't following them, and picking at Annie Laurie, he slammed on brakes, as if he was going to stop, and she elbowed him in the ribs.

"Well, you said we could have it anywhere," Jesse said.

Annie Laurie wrote on the dashboard, "I love you."

"I love you too, Mrs. Jordan," Jesse said, then patted her on the hip.

Annie Laurie had no idea where they were at, but she could tell they were coming into a town, when she noticed a big sign that read, "Western clothing ahead."

Annie Laurie pointed at the sign and motioned for Jesse to pull in at the place. The thought had never occurred to her, but she had brought five hundred of her stash with her, and she wanted to buy Jesse a new outfit.

It was Saturday and the little clothing store was busy. Jesse had no idea what all Annie Laurie intended on buying, because he'd noticed that things were quite expensive, so he just picked up one pair of brown corduroy jeans. Annie Laurie, after seeing what size he wore, picked out a black pair to add with the brown ones.

"Get yourself two shirts, to match," Annie Laurie wrote in his palm.

Jesse wound up getting a red long-sleeved corduroy for his brown pants, and a black one for his black pants.

Annie Laurie then wrote in the palm of his hand, "Belt."

"If you're sure," Jesse said, and Annie Laurie nodded her head.

Jesse picked out a wide brown belt, size 36" the buckle had a long horn cow on it.

Annie Laurie pointed to the dressing room, so Jesse obliged her by going into the room and trying the clothes on.

"Well, if things fit, I know what size clothes my husband wears, 33x33 in pants, and 1 extra-large in shirts, with 36" belt," Annie Laurie thought.

When Jesse stepped out of the dressing room, he was wearing the red shirt and brown pants. "Everything fits, I think I'll wear this out of the store," he said.

Annie Laurie smiled, "Wondering how she could have captured such a handsome feller."

The total bill was sixty dollars and thirty-five cents, and she was very well pleased.

"You didn't have to do that," Jesse said.

Annie Laurie held her finger to her lips, then held her nose until they were in the truck.

She grabbed her notebook, "When we get home, I'm going to give you a hoe and I want all that manure raked into my garden," she wrote.

Jesse laughed after reading it, and said, "Your wish is my command," and then he tipped his wide brimmed cowboy hat.

They hit highway 90 west of Biloxi and headed east.

Annie Laurie never knew such pretty places existed in Mississippi. Jesse drove along the beach for miles. Annie Laurie sketched a scene in her notebook. She wanted to write Jesse several times, but the traffic was bumper to bumper and with him driving the big truck he really had to pay attention.

Jesse found a cafeteria with a big parking lot in Ocean Springs, Mississippi, so he pulled in.

Annie Laurie began her writing, "Oh, Jesse, this is the prettiest place, I want to come back in the summer."

"You can bet on it darling, you can bring your easel and just paint up a storm, but for right now, let's go inside and eat," Jesse told her, then smacked her on her lips.

After they were seated, there was no need to look at a menu, they both ordered oysters.

While they waited on their food, Jesse told her to keep her sketch pad handy. When we leave here, we'll go over the longest bridge you've ever seen. You'll see commercial fishing boats, a lighthouse, the works," he said.

Jesse turned out to be right, for Annie Laurie sketched until the big truck reached Moss Point.

Before long, Annie Laurie read a big green sign on the right of the road that read, WELCOME TO ALABAMA, THE HEART OF DIXIE.

"Whew, just breathe this good Alabama air," Jesse said, as he rolled the window part way down, for it was chilly outside, then rolled it back up.

Chapter 15
Home

The big truck rolled into their driveway about 4:00 pm. Everything looked as they had left it.

Annie Laurie jumped from the running board of the truck with their sacks of clothing. They had already planned what they were going to do. Annie Laurie set the sacks on the porch, then ran to the barn for a hoe and threw it into the back of the truck. She then unlocked the door and made a fire in the stove, after she'd raked all the old ashes out.

Next, she pumped some water in a pail, and grabbed the egg basket, then toting both things, she headed toward the chicken pen. The chickens looked as they did when she left. She still saw some of the corn on the ground that she'd thrown down Thursday morning. She poured the fresh water into their trough and threw some fresh corn on the ground.

She was gathering the eggs, as Jesse raked the cow manure into the garden. She stopped counting at four dozen eggs.

A few of the eggs were cracked, so she thought they'd eat them.

Annie Laurie washed her hands at the pump before going inside and starting supper. She thought she'd cook the tuna fish gravy that Jesse liked, make a baker of biscuits, and open a can of field peas.

As she was rolling out the biscuits, she could hear Jesse pumping water off the back porch. In a few minutes he stepped into the kitchen, came up behind her, and kissed her on the neck, after brushing some of her hair away.

"I love you my darling," Jesse said.

Chills went up and down Annie Laurie's spine, but all she could do with her hands full of biscuit dough was nod her head and fight back the tears of happiness.

As Annie Laurie cooked their meager supper, Jesse went into her studio room. She couldn't imagine what he'd be doing in there until he came out wearing the Confederate uniform and toting one of the old muskets. The coat was a little tight, but the pants seemed to fit him.

By then, Annie Laurie had the biscuits in the oven, so her hands were clean. She went over to him and kissed him on his stubby cheek, then made signs with her fingers, "I love you too."

"You're a God sent blessing to me baby," Jesse said, as he embraced his wife.

Annie Laurie shook her head and bored her finger into Jesse's chest. She then pushed away from him to check on the biscuits and finish their first meal at home.

Jesse sat at the table and watched her cook.

"You know, I believe I'll wear this Confederate uniform when I take the truck back, he wouldn't dare strike a Confederate sergeant," Jesse said.

Annie Laurie laughed, as she stopped stirring the gravy long enough to take the biscuits out of the oven. Next, she opened the can of field peas and seasoned them. She set the table until the peas came to a boil. In five minutes they were eating.

"Um Uh, boy these biscuits and gravy are good, and best of all, I don't have to eat and run," Jesse said.

Annie Laurie reached across the table and squeezed her husband's hand.

After they'd eaten and Annie Laurie had cleaned the kitchen, Annie Laurie got her notebook and pencil and crawled into Jesse's lap.

"You know, since we're back, I'm planning on going to church in the morning, I'd be very pleased if you'd go with me," Annie Laurie wrote.

"Sure baby, I'll be glad to go, but that means, we'd have to take dad's truck and check to him in the morning," Jesse answered.

"That's really worrying you, isn't it?" Annie Laurie wrote.

"Well, with you by my side, I feel like I could face anything, even Pops," Jesse answered.

"I'll always be by your side, even if we're a thousand miles apart," Annie Laurie wrote.

Jesse squeezed his wife and stroked her long blonde hair with his calloused hand.

"My baby," Jesse said, and before she knew it, his hand fell to his side, and he was asleep.

"Poor baby, he's bound to be tired after driving that big truck all day," Annie

Laurie thought, so she eased out of his lap, and let him sleep.

Annie Laurie sneaked into their bedroom and got out the flannel pajamas she never had the opportunity to wear during their honeymoon, then returned to the kitchen. She checked the water in the stove's reservoir and found it to be half empty. She dipped out what water she could and poured it into long tub that she kept hanging on a nail near the stove and took a bath. She was squeezing out the rinse water from her hair, when Jesse roused himself from the chair.

"Boy, for a split second there, I thought I was dreaming," Jesse said.

"No, my darling, it's just your wife, you can use my water to take your bath, if you'd like, for there isn't another drop of water in the reservoir," Annie Laurie wrote.

Reading the sentence hastily, Jesse replied, "Bathe, honey, I could drink the water you bathed in."

Annie Laurie laughed, and wrote in the palm of his hand, "Silly."

"Boy, these clothes must be made of wool, I'm burning up," Jesse said.

"They are," Annie Laurie wrote, {For she had re-stitched them}.

"Well, before I pull them off, I guess I'd better refill the reservoir," Jesse said, so he heaved himself out of his chair, grabbed the buckets and headed for the back porch.

Annie Laurie brushed her hair dry while she watched her husband take a bath. She couldn't help but laugh at him, as he folded his long legs to fit into the long tub.

They both slept naked that night, but Annie Laurie found that Jesse didn't seem so anxious, he was more gentle and she was glad.

The next morning, Annie Laurie had breakfast on the table at 6:30. She had, grits, fried eggs, and four of the biscuits left from the night before.

Jesse had dressed before he came to the table, but Annie Laurie was still wearing her cotton gown. He couldn't resist running his hand between her legs to hear her squeal.

Jesse took his usual chair, and like always, he ate like a starved hound.

"Now, if I was home, I'd have two boiled eggs and some jelly toast," Jesse said, as he swallowed a drink of hot coffee.

After they ate, Annie Laurie just put the dishes in the sink, letting them soak in water, for she knew that Jesse was anxious to get to his parents.

Annie Laurie dressed in one of her Sunday dresses, while Jesse was dressed in his black cowboy outfit. She followed behind Jesse in the Plymouth.

Jesse drove the truck to where the other two trucks were parked. Annie Laurie waited on Jesse until he got to her car before she got out.

They didn't have time to make it to the house before his parents came out of the door. Mrs. Jordan was in the lead, with a towel wrapped around her head. Mr. Jordan wasn't far behind, wearing just his pants and shoes.

"So, you two are really married?" Jesse's mother asked.

"Yes mam, since Thursday," Jesse answered.

"Oh, if we had only known, y'all could have married right here in the house by

Reverand Johnson," Jesse's mom said, as she put an arm around each one of them.

"Well, we're both under age, and in Mississippi, they don't seem to care," Jesse said.

"How old are you darling?" Mrs. Jordan asked Annie Laurie.

Annie Laurie wrote in the air backward, so the numbers would turn out to be 17.

"Well, welcome to the family baby," Mrs. Jordan said.

Annie Laurie smiled, then nodded her head.

"Of course, y'all will be living here with us," Jesse's mother said.

"No mam, we'll be living in Annie Laurie's house," Jesse was quick to answer.

"Oh, my! Well come on in out of the cold," Mrs. Jordan said, then added, "We need to finish getting ready for church."

Jesse's daddy never said a word, he just stood on the sidewalk, thinking.

As the two followed behind his mother, Jessie pulled the check and envelope from beneath his hat and gave it to his dad.

"I figured you might need this when the bank opens in the morning," Jesse said.

"Thank you son but we've been so worried about you two," Mr. Jordan said. Mr. Jordan, then continued. "I can't blame you two for not wanting to move in here, you need time to yourselves."

"Come on in and let me get a shirt on, we need to talk this thing over," Jesse's dad said.

Annie Laurie had followed Jesse's mama down the hallway to the lavish room she'd been in before. She didn't know the two had separate bedrooms, so after a few minutes she told Mrs. Jordan she was going back to the living room.

"Okay dear but make plans with Junior that y'all are going out with lunch with us after church," Mrs. Jordan said, as she powdered her face generously.

Annie Laurie's intentions were to find Jesse, for she'd promised him, they'd face his daddy together.

After looking outside and not seeing them, Annie Laurie decided to just have a seat in the living room and see what transpired, wherever they were at.

She didn't have to wait but about ten minutes before the two Jesses came into the living room from another direction.

Annie Laurie noticed that Mr. Jordan had a suit and tie on.

"There you are Sugar Pie," Mr. Jordan said, as Annie Laurie stood, and he hugged her.

"I don't think Jug head, could have done any better," Mr. Jordan told her. He then said, "Congratulations and welcome to the family."

Annie Laurie saw that Jesse had the keys to his car in his hand, so she figured everything must have gone alright.

Jesse grabbed Annie Laurie's hand and led the way to the front door.

"See you two in church," Mr. Jordan said, as they went out of the door.

"Everything went fine, I'll tell you all about it when we get home. I'll follow you in my car," Jesse said, as he kissed his wife on the lips, then headed toward his car.

As it wound up, Annie Laurie followed Jesse back to the house.

When she pulled into the driveway and got out of the car, Jesse said, "Honey, it's all going to be alright. I work from eight to five during the week, and I get off at twelve on Saturdays and don't have to go back until Monday mornings. I still have to take the beeves to the packing house twice a week, but I get paid twenty-five dollars a trip. He also raised my pay from forty dollars a week to fifty, and that's not counting the pay I'll be getting from the trips," Jesse said.

Annie Laurie, wrote in her notebook, "You're their only child, he wouldn't want to lose you for anything, plus you're a good worker. Meanwhile, We need to put that basket of eggs in which ever car we're driving to church. I'm selling the eggs and buying a block of ice. I'm dying to try out the icebox."

"Well, since we're going to church, your car Is the cleanest," Jesse said, so Annie Laurie ran inside to get the eggs. While she was in there she got the keys to the house that her daddy had used and gave them to Jesse, who was hooking up the drain pipe to the icebox.

Most iceboxes that Annie Laurie had seen were little squat wooden boxes that were lined with metal inside, but this one was head high, with an opening at the bottom. There a pan was placed to catch the melted water from the ice. *"Leave it to*

Mrs. Jordan to get the best," Annie Laurie thought, for the top had two metal shelves, and was big enough to hold a big block of ice.

Annie Laurie had written so much over the years, she'd taught herself to write at a lightning speed, and it just seemed normal to her.

On the way to church, Annie Laurie wrote to Jesse that his mama had invited them out for lunch, after church.

"Well, I guess that'll save you from cooking, but you know what? I was sort of looking forward to just you and I spending the afternoon alone. I guess we can go with them, then come back to Miss Earnestine's," Jesse said.

They got to church a little early, and they found that word about them getting married, had gotten out, for near every man slapped Jesse on the back and the ladies congratulated Annie Laurie.

The two had picked a pew up front, leaving plenty of room for Jesse's parents, and soon they showed up.

When Jesse's daddy had paid him, he had gone ahead and paid him the fifty dollars, so he had money for the collection plate. Jesse whispered in Annie Laurie's ear about the money.

About the time that Jesse's parents were seated, Reverand Johnson stood behind the podium and services started with everyone standing and singing "Nearer my God to thee."

The collection plate was passed around, then Brother Johnson gave his sermon out of the book of psalms.

After the services were over, Pastor Johnson announced that it had come over the news on their way to church that the Japanese had bombed Pearl Harbor in Hawaii. "It's been reported that over two thousand people have been killed, and several of our ships have been destroyed. May God bless us all, for I can't see our president putting up with this," Reverand Johnson said.

Everyone gasped, and it was as though all the oxygen was sucked out of the church, temporarily.

Pastor Johnson said a short prayer, then made his way to the door to shake everyone's hand as they filed out of church, completely stunned.

After more pats on the back and congratulations, Jesse and Annie Laurie walked over

To his parents Cadillac.

"Oh, my son, I'm afraid you young men are in for it. If my guess is correct, Hitler and Tojo

Will join up together, and we'll be fighting both of them," Mr. Jordan said.

"Oh, Annie Laurie, I'm so sorry, but we'll have to take a raincheck on going out for dinner, Jesse insists that he's going home and listen to the news," her mother-in-law said.

"That's okay mom, we had already had our afternoon planned. I'll see you in the morning at eight o'clock, sharp," Jesse told her.

Jesse sr. was dying to get home, for he fired up the Cadillac while his son was still talking.

Both Annie Laurie and Jesse knew that Miss Earnestine and Mr. Riley would eat dinner that Mr. Lum had brought them before they opened the store. They thought for a few minutes and decided to visit the barbeque house between Excel and Frisco City. They knew Mr. Lum would probably be standing on the porch at the store, so instead of riding around with the eggs in the car, they stopped by the store and Jesse gave them to Mr. Lum.

"We'll be back later," Jesse said, and Mr. Lum nodded his head, after he congratulated them. "I hopes you gits along as good as me and Miss Octavia," Mr. Lum said.

Jesse shook Mr. Lum's hand, and they left.

After they'd gotten down the road a piece, Jesse said, "Now that's one old man, who's respect I hope to never lose."

Annie Laurie made the sign of the cross against her chest.

Jesse turned on the radio, and sure enough, all the news talked about was the bombing of Pearl Harbor.

When they reached "The Smoking House," Jesse brought out four sandwiches, like before.

"I know mom's not cooking the old man anything, so I got them a sandwich too. All he's gonna do is stay glued to that radio," Jesse said.

They didn't tarry getting to his parents' house, for they knew they had to get back to Miss Earnestine's.

Annie Laurie just stayed in the car, while Jesse ran the sandwiches inside to his parents.

It took Jesse about five minutes to make it back to the car.

"It was just as I suspected, he was glued to that radio. I didn't see mom. He thanked me for the sandwiches and was screaming for mom to bring him something to drink when I left," Jesse told Annie Laurie.

Annie Laurie laughed, but somewhere deep in her heart, something told her that the bombing of Pearl Harbor was just the beginning of terrible things to come.

Jesse blew the horn at LeRoy, as they went by the big barn, for he was about to leave with a truck load of hay for the cows.

"Poor fellow, I'll be doing that in the morning," Jesse said.

Annie Laurie sold the five dozen of eggs for a dollar, then bought a fifty-cent block of ice, two pounds of bacon, an ice pick and a quart of milk.

Miss Earnestine looked at her strangely when she ordered the ice.

Annie Laurie wrote with her finger on the glass case. "I now have an icebox."

Miss Earnestine grinned, and said, "Good, I had wondered why you bought an ice pick, and congratulations on the marriage. Reverand Johnson was supposed to have announced it to the congregation, but I suppose the Pearl Harbor thing lay heavy on is mind."

Annie Laurie bowed, in her gesture of, "Thank you."

Mr. Lum and Jesse laid the big block of ice on newspapers in the trunk of the Plymouth, after Jesse paid Miss Earnestine for the remainder of the items. They were both eager to get home to eat their barbeque, for it sure smelled good.

Annie Laurie walked ahead of Jesse with the few items she'd bought at the store, for he was toting the cold slippery ice.

She opened the door to the icebox and Jesse slid the ice onto the top shelf. Annie Laurie put the milk and bacon on the top shelf, then ran to the stove and started a fire. She grabbed he notebook and wrote,

"I'm not going to be satisfied until I make some tea. I want iced tea with my sandwich."

They both changed clothes until the tea came to a good boil. Annie Laurie didn't bother with putting the cumbersome Brassiere back on, for she wasn't expecting company. Of course, Jesse had to rub on her breast a little until she slipped her dress on.

Never having to chip ice before, Jesse got the ice pick and chipped the ice. She noticed that he chipped along the edges.

"Always put the ice pick back on top of the icebox, that way, we won't be searching for it each time," Jesse told her.

Annie Laurie kissed him, then got the strainer to catch the pieces of dried tea leaves as she poured it into her grandma's antique pitcher that she'd already poured water in.

In a few minutes the heat from the stove had the room nice and cozy, while they sat at the table and ate the barbeque while they sipped on their iced tea.

After they had eaten, Jesse built a fire in the living room, and they listened to the news concerning Pearl Harbor.

Jesse didn't dare tell Annie Laurie what his dad had told him, but he didn't look for President Roosevelt to allow the Japs to get away with the bombing.

Jesse sat at the end of the couch, while Annie Laurie lay beside him with her head in his lap. He constantly ran his fingers through her hair and rubbed and patted her.

Finally, Jesse said, "Oh, well the day is wasting, I've been dying to look in your daddy's old shop and barn to see what's in there," he then patted Annie Laurie on the rump.

Annie Laurie grabbed the back of her head to prevent pulling the hair out of her head, then sat up on the couch. She would soon learn that her husband didn't like to just sit around, he liked to stay busy. She was enjoying the coziness of his attention, but she too had things to do.

While Jesse plundered around outside, she put on a sweater and went to the garden with a butcher knife. She picked out a nice head of cabbage and cut it down, then headed to the sweet potato bank and gathered three nice sweet potatoes. She thought to herself as she headed back to the back porch, "It was nice to be cooking again, instead of just eating sandwiches, or quick to prepare meals.

Annie Laurie just couldn't resist it, after she had the potatoes in the oven, she chipped off some more ice and poured more tea in her glass. She sat at the table and thought how her life had changed. *"Oh, if Daddy was still here, he wouldn't believe the changes that have taken place,"* she thought. She knew one thing, she felt safe and secure for the first time since her daddy died.

After she finished her tea, she set her glass in the icebox. After washing the head of cabbage, instead of cutting it into small pieces, she quartered it, and put some of the bacon on it, after she'd seasoned it. All of her cookware was ancient cast iron, including the frying pans. She put a small amount of water in the pot, and after she set it on top of the stove, she put the heavy lid on it.

After the sweet potatoes were baked, she took them out of the oven, while they were cooling, she mixed up some cornbread and stuck it in the oven. She peeled the potatoes, then cut them in halves, after putting bacon on top of them, she slid the cast iron fryer in, next to the cornbread. Everything was ready to eat in thirty minutes, so she slid everything to the back of the stove, so it would stay warm.

Annie Laurie slipped on a coat and decided to see if Jesse had found anything that he liked. She decided to take her notebook with her.

After making it to the barn, she found some things thrown on the ground by the door. Jesse had worked himself to the back of the barn by the time that Annie Laurie stepped inside.

"Boy, Ole Mitch at "Mitch's Pawn Shop" would give a fortune for some of this stuff, and I haven't even made it to the loft yet," Jesse said, holding an old saber that was still in its sheath.

"You're not planning on selling them are you?" Annie Laurie wrote.

"Heaven's no, they're to go to our grandchildren," Jesse answered.

"I've found an old Confederate canteen, a bullet pouch, and now this sword. There's some more things outside on the ground," Jesse said excitedly. "These things are going in the house, after I clean and oil them up," Jesse added.

Annie Laurie thought of the five-dollar gold coin she'd found in the loft of the house.

"Well, since you're collecting things, I have something in the house for you," Annie Laurie wrote. She then added, "By the way, supper is ready, when you get hungry."

"I'm not hungry right now, I have the muskets, uniform, now the sword, all I need is the cap or hat. I even found the old mold they made the lead bullets with," Jesse said.

Well, if you can't find it out here, maybe it's in the loft of the house, I didn't look too closely," she wrote.

Annie Laurie blew him a kiss, then went back inside to the warmth of the stove. She looked in her stash and found the old gold coin, then laid it on the table where Jesse always ate.

While she was still dressed for the outside weather, she went to the corn crib and got four ears of corn and threw it inside the wire fence, after she'd shelled it to the excited chickens. She knew she had to do something with all the roosters she'd accumulated, but she just didn't have the nerve to wring the neck on any of them. *"Maybe Jesse would put all but one in some sacks and give them to Mr. Lum,"* she thought, for all the did was fight.

She gathered twenty eggs that day, and she could hear that Jesse had made his way to the loft of the barn.

After getting back into the house she put the eggs into the bowl she'd always put them, only this time she set the bowl of eggs into her icebox.

Jesse was learning, for in a few minutes she could hear him as he restocked the firewood on the back porch, then him pumping water, so she began setting the table.

She could barely recognize her husband when he came through the back door. His clothes and the kepi hat he was wearing was covered in cobwebs.

Annie Laurie couldn't help but laugh at the image she saw. He had a variety of things in his hands and arms.

"He didn't wear a hat, he wore this thing," Jesse said.

"It's called a kepi hat," Annie Laurie wrote.

After reading her note, Jesse said, "Well, it looks like a cap to me."

Jesse changed the subject real quick when the aroma of supper hit his nostrils.

"Boy, I believe I smell cabbage," Jesse said.

"Go in our room and look in the mirror," Annie Laurie wrote, so he did.

"Boy, I look like I've been through a civil war," Annie Laurie heard him say.

In a few minutes he returned, wearing clean jeans and flannel shirt.

"I'll tell you everything I found while we're eating," Jesse said.

Annie Laurie had laid his plate on top of the five-dollar gold piece, so when Jesse began to put food in his plate, he noticed his plate wasn't level, so he picked it up and saw the gold coin.

"Well, would you look at this," Jesse said, as he picked the coin up, feeling it. He looked for the date. "1864, wow, it looks brand new," Jesse said.

"It is new to you," Annie Laurie wrote.

Jesse stuck the coin in his pocket. "I'm going to show this to the old man, the other stuff I'll tell him about," Jesse said, and he began to put food on his plate.

Annie Laurie had learned that no matter what she cooked, Jesse wolfed it down, and it sure pleased her.

In between bites, he told her of the things that he had found. "I even found a stack of Confederate money in a leather pouch," he said.

"Boy, he was excited about the treasures he had found!" Annie Laurie thought, and she was proud of it.

"I know you cooked that extra potato for me. I'm going to take me a plate for my dinner tomorrow," Jesse said.

Chapter 16

The next day, Roosevelt announced over the radio that the United States declared war on Japan.

Jesse couldn't believe it, but his daddy had been right, for Adolf Hitler declared war on

The United States on December 11th.

Jesse and Annie Laurie had been married for a week, but he knew their time together was limited. Young men across America were lining up in droves to fight for their country. Lee Peacock was pestering him for them to join up with the Buddy System. "That way we can go through basic together, and if the war isn't over, we can fight together," he said.

"Nooo," Jesse told him. "I can't go off and leave Annie Laurie, my goodness we just got married and she depends on me. I've got so many changes planned for our place this spring. It just wouldn't be fair to her," Jesse concluded, so Lee held off, while other young men their ages were signing up to fight.

Jesse kept things about the war hid from Annie Laurie, even though, deep down, he knew she wasn't a dummy, she knew what was going on.

The United States had been supplying Great Britian with war materials for months and Hitler knew it, and that was the reason he declared was on America.

Deep down, Jesse wanted to fight for his country, but he thought he'd give it a little while. Roosevelt had started the draft. He felt like if he was drafted he wouldn't feel like a low-down dog for leaving Annie Laurie.

Besides continuing with her painting, while Jesse worked, Annie Laurie had made a frame from a scuppernong vine. She'd made the inside plaque with red velvet, and stitched Mr. Jesse's medals and ribbons on it. Oh, was he thrilled to get it! He hung it on the wall near his desk.

Mr. Jesse never encouraged Jesse to join the military, but Annie Laurie could tell that he sort of felt let down. Jesse's mom stayed scared to death that he was going to sign up and admitted so to Annie Laurie.

The price of beef fell, yet the demand of it was increasing, due to the military buying so much of it.

For Christmas that year, Annie Laurie and Jesse had gone into Monroeville and bought some Christmas lights for their Christmas tree. Jesse had taken the battery from a tractor that his dad wouldn't use until the spring. He'd got two clamps and hooked them to a wire, then hooked the other end to the Christmas lights and the bulbs lit up.

"It's amazing, people are going to think we have electricity," Annie Laurie wrote.

Jesse's mom stopped by the next day and saw the lights. She couldn't leave fast enough to get to Monroeville to buy her some lights, so Annie Laurie knew what her husband would be doing the next day.

The Holidays flew by. They ate Christmas dinner at Mr. and Mrs. Jordans, with Jesse insisting that she take most of the food. "That stuff that's cooked up there's not worth throwing out to the dogs," Jesse said.

Annie Laurie had never gotten such extravagant gifts. A pearl necklace, complete with earbobs, a long woolen coat that came to her ankles, along with other less expensive things. Jesse got a blue suit, complete with a white shirt and red tie to wear to church. He also got a diamond stick pin for his tie, and a pair of black dress boots. The thing that he treasured most was a leather lariat. "Now, I'll be like Lash LaRue," Jesse said.

"I thought it would help you with the abstinent cattle, once you learn to pop the thing," his dad said.

"No need to worry, I'll learn," Jesse assured him.

On the way home that afternoon, Annie Laurie wrote, "My goodness, If things continue I'm going to need a safe to store all my treasures."

"You know what? I think they truly love you, but I hope we have enough leftovers for our supper. I've never seen them eat so," Jesse said.

"We do, plus I left some in the icebox," Annie Laurie wrote.

For the next month or so, during Jesse's free time, Annie Laurie really enjoyed their time together. They'd go out into the woods and find small dogwood saplings and set them out around the perimeter that Annie Laurie had around the house. "They'll be beautiful once they start blooming," she wrote to Jesse. Annie Laurie soon learned though that she had to walk on Jesse's left side, for he was constantly popping the lariat.

By February, Annie Laurie had finished painting one of the beach scenes and had started on another.

Also by the middle of February, Jesse had covered nearly half the garden in cow manure, and Annie Laurie was ready to plant her early garden.

Jesse brought his dad's small tractor down to break the land.

Annie Laurie started out with the collard plants, then finished the first row with turnip greens. The next row, she planted a row of Irish potatoes.

The weather was still too cold to set out the sweet potatoes, but she had plenty of them in a bed, waiting on the warmer weather so they would sprout. She usually set them out around Easter. The summer garden was always planted on Good Friday, if weather permitted.

By March, on some afternoons, when weather permitted, the two would sit on the front porch, like old times with her daddy and watch the sun go down. Annie Laurie would be thinking of her mama and daddy, while Jesse said one day, "Just think there's a war going on beyond that sun."

Annie Laurie never realized she could love anyone as much as she did Jesse. When he wasn't working, they were together. She spilled her childhood to him, by writing, of course, and he told her about his, which was mostly about him working. Annie Laurie had to work growing up too, but the pressure wasn't put on her, like him.

A few Sunday afternoons, they'd fish from the bank of the river at old Fort Claiborne. A couple times, they caught enough to cook. Annie Laurie had never gone fishing, but she loved it. All she had to do was keep an eye on her homemade cork.

Jesse was surprised that he only had to show her once how to bait her hook.

Fishing, painting, and sewing weren't the only things that Annie Laurie found joy in doing. Jesse also found that his wife loved working in dirt, whether it be their garden, or just keeping the grass hoed out of their yard.

The Collards and Irish potatoes that she had planted earlier were flourishing, and Jesse managed to plant their summer garden on Good Friday. By then, Annie Laurie's sweet potatoes had sprouts long enough to put into the ground, and she set out two long rows.

Jesse loved his mom till death, but she was so hard for his dad to please. With Annie Laurie, she had a way about her to make life simple and easy. Of course, when she was painting, he'd let her paint. When she was sewing, he'd find something outside to do. There was something for sure, Annie Laurie saw there was always food on the table, and Jesse had clean clothes to wear.

By June, Annie Laurie had six paintings. Four of them were the beach scenes in Biloxi, and two of them were paintings of the Alabama River at old Fort Claiborne. She even painted Jesse's image in one of them.

Miss Earnestine didn't mind giving them the address in Mobile where Mr. Riley sold her paintings. Jesse went to work two hours earlier one Saturday morning, and by 11:00 am they were on their way to Mobile with the six paintings in the trunk of her car. The place was very easy to find, after going through Bankhead Tunnel, it was three blocks down, on Government Street.

The name of the place was "Emily's Art Studio." There was three or four ladies in the business. Jesse soon learned that one of them was Emily. He told her who they were and why they were there. After learning Annie Laurie couldn't speak only added the mystic to her paintings.

Both Jesse and Annie Laurie brought the paintings in. After looking at them, Emily offered them six hundred dollars for all six paintings. She then said, what sold the best was the Biblical paintings.

After Emily paid them in cash, she immediately put them on display and one of the beach scenes sold before they got out of the place. Annie Laurie looked at some of the other paintings too. Emily sold Annnie Laurie's painting for $150.00.

Needless to say, they were a happy couple on their way home until they reached a town named Bay Minette. They were both hungry, so they stopped at a hamburger place. After getting a table, they both ordered a hamburger, fries, and a Coca Cola. They had just started eating when a young man stumbled into their table and spilled their drinks everywhere.

"Hey, watch where you're going," Jesse told the fellow.

"I am watching where I'm going, and I like what I see," the fellow said, as he rubbed Annie Laurie's cheek.

Jesse blew up quicker than a stick of dynamite and with his big fist, he stood and popped the fellow between his eyes, knocking him back to the place of entrance. The fellow shook his head and hobbled back to his truck outside and left.

The manager of the place came over to their table with two fresh drinks and apologized. He then told Jesse there would be no charge for their order.

"That fellow got exactly what was coming to him, I saw it all. He's a local bully and maybe he'll stop coming in here," the manager said.

Luckily all of the drinks had spilled on the floor and not them, so Jesse told the manager everything was alright as for as he was concerned, so he resumed eating, as if nothing had happened.

Annie Laurie had never experienced such, so she was just nibbling on her meal.

"You'd better eat, because we have some celebrating to do when we get home, you won't have time to cook," Jesse told her.

Annie Laurie held her finger to her lips, for she knew what Jesse had in mind. Someone had put a nickel in the juke box, and Chattanooga Choo Choo was playing when they left the place.

On the way home, Annie Laurie really thought of her husband's attributes. He wasn't a dummy, for he could add numbers in his head quicker than she could figure them on paper. He also knew all kinds of rhymes and riddles. Things that she'd never heard before would make her laugh.

Annie Laurie had told Jesse where she'd kept her stash when they had married, so on the way home, he asked her how much the $600.00 would make her having In the stash ?"

Annie Laurie was quick to write on the dash "We have $1,550.00."

Jesse cleared his throat, and said, "I beg your pardon, but I believe I have about $40.00 in my pocket."

Annie Laurie laughed, then erased the imaginary number and wrote $1590.00 with her finger.

With his free hand, Jesse reached over and patted Annie Laurie on her leg. "You know darling, you've given me the happiest six months of my life. I just wish there was a way to prove it to you." Jesse said.

Annie Laurie elbowed Jesse in the ribs, then wrote on the dash. "Just keep coming home."

When they reached home, Annie Laurie wanted to finish digging the Irish potatoes in the garden, but Jesse had something more intimate in mind, and of course, if Jesse was eager, so was she.

It was late afternoon when they left the house to go to Monroeville. Jesse said that he had built up an appetite.

There was an open pit barbeque that had opened near downtown Monroeville, so Jesse struck out for the place. He was driving his car, so of course, the radio was blaring.

After arriving, Jesse decided to just get a rack of ribs, and waxed box of potato salad.

"Shoot, maybe we can make it back home to eat from the front porch and watch the sunset" Jesse said.

Since they'd gotten the icebox, Annie Laurie always kept a pitcher of sweet tea sitting on the top rack.

After arriving back at the house, Jesse told Annie Laurie to just have a seat in her rocker and he'd bring her a plate, so she did.

Not forgetting the tea, Jesse chipped a small amount of ice for each glass, for the block of ice had shrunk to the size of two bricks. Jesse then cut the ribs, putting three on her plate and four on his. After dipping a large portion of potato salad for each plate, he wrapped them a fork in a napkin, and rushed them outside, while they were still warm. After giving Annie Laurie her plate and putting his in the rocker next to hers, he ran back inside for the tea.

"Ahh, you can't beat this," Jesse said, as they ate while watching the sun go down behind the tall pines in front of their house. Of course, Annie Laurie's thoughts returned to her parents, and she knew where Jesse's thoughts were.

The two didn't tarry on the front porch long, for both Jesse and Annie Laurie were constantly slapping mosquitoes.

"I could sit out here till morning if it wasn't for the insects," Jesse said, so the two hurried inside, and Annie Laurie pulled the curtains together.

While listening to the radio, Jesse said, "Well, we've had a good day, you sold your paintings, and the lady acted as though she was eager for more. We ate two meals, and you didn't have to cook them, plus I've spent most of the day with the prettiest girl in these parts."

Annie Laurie made a fist with her hand and swung it into mid-air.

"Oh, that. It wasn't anything to that bully," Jesse said. Then added, "I wasn't going to let him disrespect my wife."

After all of the excitement, driving, and marital things, they both slept like two logs that night.

The next morning, after breakfast, the two dressed for church, and they were in for a surprise when they entered the door.

Brenda Jay, the choir leader, always sat near the door at the end of the pew. She stopped them that morning and asked Jesse if he'd join the choir. "You have a beautiful baritone voice," she said.

"Sure," Jesse answered, not realizing he'd start that very morning.

"Oh, that's great, get you a hymnal, and go stand beside poor ole Lee. I know he gets tired of being the only man up there, and the hymns y'all will be singing are in the program.

"If you're sure," Jesse said, and he looked at the program and saw they'd be singing "Nearer my God to thee," and "He set me free."

Annie Laurie was shocked, but also proud of her husband, as she took her usual seat beside her In-Laws.

"Junior is singing in the choir?" his mom asked, and Annie Laurie nodded her head.

Brother Johnson started the services by mentioning everyone who was on the prayer list and praying for them, plus all the young men who were serving in faraway places. After his prayer, the choir sang, "Nearer my God to thee," and Annie Laurie could hear her husband's voice m plain as day.

"Oh boy, he did great!" his mom whispered in Annie Laurie's ear.

The choir stood on the stage until it was time for their next selection.

Brother Johnson then mentioned things in the near future the church would be involved in. The collection plates were passed around. Mr. Jordan and Annie Laurie each put in a dollar.

By this time the choir was getting tired of standing, so after the collection, Mrs. Delano began with the fast tune of "He set me free." And the choir began.

Again, Annie Laurie thought Jesse did great. The choir got a huge applause as they stepped from the stage.

Jesse took his place beside his wife and was ready for the sermon.

"You amaze me," Annie Laurie wrote in Jesse's palm.

Jesse just looked at her and smiled.

Brother Johnson had preached so many years, until he seldomly opened his worn

Bible. He could quote scripture after scripture. That day he preached out of the book of Revelations, in an attempt to get everyone stirred up.

Brother Johnson would preach a while, then cut loose on a song, knowing that a person's attention span would only last so long.

After the alter call, he asked Terry Faulk to say the closing prayer, as Brother Johnson made his way to the front door.

After shaking hands with everyone at the front door, some hung around the church and talked.

Jesse's parents invited them to lunch, but Jesse turned them down, saying that Annie Laurie wanted to go home.

Annie Laurie wanted to get home so she could gather the eggs and change clothes, for she intended on selling the eggs and get another block of ice.

After Annie Laurie changed into something cooler, she gathered the eggs, she and Jesse walked across the well-fertilized garden and found that the pea and bean vines were just loaded.

"They'll be ready to pick in about two weeks, and some of the corn is ready to pull now," Jesse said.

"I know what I'll be doing in a couple of weeks," Annie Laurie wrote in Jesse's palm.

"Uh uh, that's the reason I fertilized them so, you can get someone to gather things for you on halves. I don't want my wife bending over in this hot sun picking anything," Jesse said.

"Yes sir," Annie Laurie wrote in his palm, grinning at her husband's sudden authority.

"We can pull Mr. Lum a dozen ears of this corn and take it to him though," Jesse said.

They figured Miss Earnestine would be open by the time they'd gathered the corn. Jesse put the eggs and corn on the backseat of his car, and they headed out, for they both was wanting some iced tea.

Jesse stayed on the outside, while Annie Laurie went inside Miss Earnestine's with her eggs. That's when Jesse told Mr. Lum they needed someone to pick the beans and peas. "From the looks of it there's going to be plenty of them there," Jesse told him.

"Jist lets me knows when it be time," Mr. Lum said, then he continued, "I really appreciate the corn, and he thanked Jesse for it.

When Jesse told him they had six roosters they needed to get rid of, and he could have them if he came after them, Mr. Lum really thanked him again.

"I'll wait until dey goes to roost tonight. Dat way they'll be easy to git," Mr. Lum said, then added, "Miss Octavia, she'll fatten em up and we'll be eating chicken foe you knows it," Mr. Lum said.

Jesse laughed, then ordered the .50 cent block of ice, about the same time that Mr. Riley stuck his out of the screen door and told Mr. Lum to get "Miss Annie Laurie a fifty-cent block of ice. They both laughed, and Mr. Lum said "Yassuh."

Mr. Lum always put at least one sheet of newspaper with the ice, so the customer would have something to pick it up with. Even though Mr. Lum always used a set of ice prongs to handle the ice with.

Mr. Lum had just set the block of ice in the trunk of the car when Annie Laurie came out of the store.

After getting into the car, and them leaving, she wrote Jesse that she'd seen a few ripe tomatoes on the vines. "We'll have spam and tomato sandwiches, along with some fresh corn out of the garden, and of course, some cold iced tea for supper."

"Sounds good to me," Jesse said, and then he told her that Mr. Lum was coming over after dark and get the roosters.

"Good, I'm going to see if he can get his nephews over to screen in the front porch," Annie Laurie wrote.

"Now, that will be nice," Jesse said.

They were passing by the junk yard, and it never failed, Annie Laurie looked to see if there was anything she could use.

After they got home, Jesse brought the ice in, while Annie Laurie brought in the few items she'd bought. After changing their clothes, Jesse decided to dig Mr. Lum a big "Mess" of new potatoes and give them to him when he came that night. He knew Annie Laurie couldn't resist digging in the dirt, so in a few minutes, she joined him. They didn't stop until they were nigh halfway up the row.

Jesse got a wash tub that hung from the back of the house to put the potatoes in. After filling the tub with the potatoes. They were too heavy for Annie Laurie to pick her side of the tub up, so Jesse slid them across the ground until they reached the house.

"Whew, I feel like having a glass of iced tea," Jesse said, as he sat down on the back porch, then leaned against the house.

Annie Laurie smiled, and washed her hands at the pump, then headed inside for the tea.

The sun had gone over to the front of the house, so Jesse was quite comfortable as the breeze blew across the porch. *"So unlike the barn, fields, and pastures where I work. You burn up in the summer and freeze in the winter. The beeves had to be fed and watered on holidays and Sundays," Jesse* thought.

In a few minutes, both Jesse and Annie Laurie were enjoying cold iced tea on the back porch.

Annie Laurie had thought of something, so she grabbed Jesse's hand.

"Why did a preacher Hall preach daddy's funeral?" Annie Laurie wrote in Jesse's palm.

"I asked mom that and she said Brother Johnson had gone overseas somewhere to buy jewels. You see he not only preaches, for he owns a jewelry store in Monroeville also . That's where I bought your rings, and I'd be willing to bet that's where your pearls came from," Jesse told her.

"Oh," Annie Laurie answered, by putting her thumb and index finger together.

Annie Laurie wound up by putting her head in Jesse' s lap, while he tenderly rubbed her upper torso and told her of some funny things that Lee and he had did together while they were growing up.

"Once, we were on top of dad's barn. All we had on was our underwear and a pair of cutoff jeans. We made a bet to see who could slide down the hot tin roof first. So, we got side by side of each other and made a push, while holding our bare feet off the tin, because it was so hot. Well, I made it to the bottom first and jumped to the ground, with my butt on fire. It turned out that Lee's pants and underwear were snagged by a nail and were ripped from him. He hit the ground butt naked. He was lucky he didn't break his neck," Jesse said.

Annie Laurie was laughing so hard, she had to sit up.

Finally, she stopped laughing, and sat against the wall beside him, hoping he'd tell some more stories, and he did.

"Shoot, we sneaked into the spring back there so many times, we had that black dog of y'all's trained. He wouldn't even bark at us," Jesse said.

Annie Laurie grabbed Jesse's had and wrote, "Two Messes."

"I suppose we were, but that all changed though when I turned thirteen, dad put me to work. Shoot, I loved playing sports, but I had to work like a dog after practice, and I'd already be bone tired. It was different during game night though, boy I loved that. I could sling a football eighty yards with accuracy.

Suddenly realization popped back into Jesse's head. "Oh, well, enough day dreaming, we'd better get back to digging taters, before they get so big that'll bust open."

By late that afternoon, they had all the potatoes dug and stored under the house. They'd also pulled six ears of corn for their supper. Mr. Lum's sack of potatoes was in a big grocery bag on the back porch.

They'd already eaten supper by the time Mr. Lum showed up with a croaker sack and a flashlight.

Jesse went outside to see if he could help Mr. Lum and give him the sack of potatoes.

Mr. Lum was right, the roosters barely made a racket as he picked them up by their legs and dropped them into the sack. Jesse told him which one Annie Laurie planned on saving.

After they had the roosters secured in the sack, Mr. Lum told Jesse that he'd just left his nephews, "And dey say, dey wives will be glad to helps wit de garden."

"That's great, she also wants your nephews to screen in the front porch too" Jesse told Mr. Lum.

"Dey needs de werk. Dey be gitting three of dese roosters, so I'll tells dem tonights, and I magine you'll be seeing dem in de mawning," Mr. Lum said.

Jesse gave Mr. Lum the sack of potatoes before he left.

Chapter 17
The Card

Mr. Lum was right, his nephews, Theodore and Connie pulled into the driveway in their raggedy old truck right after Jesse left for work.

After quick measurements they told "Miss Annie Laurie" what materials she'd need, and roughly what the materials would cost.

"Jist de materials will be around thirty-five dollars, and our charge will be twenty dollars," Theodore said.

Annie Laurie went into the house and brought back seventy dollars. Handing it to Theodore, hoping he could read, wrote, "You never know what the price of things will be with this war going on."

Theodore looked over the note, tipped his hat, and said, "Yes Mam, we'll bring you a receipt for everything."

After they left, she thought she'd surprise Jesse with something when he came in. She never cooked him a dessert, and she'd found the recipe for "Tea cakes" in an old magazine. They were more like cookies, and all she needed was flour, eggs, baking powder, lard, milk, vanilla flavoring, and sugar. The vanilla flavoring had been in the kitchen cabinet since her mama had died, but it still smelled powerful.

She soon discovered that it was about like making biscuits, only she pinched the dough off in smaller pieces. After putting the small clumps into the greased pans she flattened them out with the top of her fingers. They didn't have to bake but about five minutes and they were golden brown. By the time she was finished, she had enough tea cakes baked to feed Pharoah's army.

Theodore and Connie pulled into the yard, as she'd pulled the last baker out of the oven. Annie Laurie decided to sample one, and she thought they were very good, so she wrapped six in piece of brown paper sack and took them outside for the young men.

"Yessum, after our pay, you still have ten dollars and some change left over," Theodore said, tipping his hat again.

Annie Laurie nodded her head, took the money and receipt, then handed him the tea cakes.

"Thank you mam," they both said in unison, and they didn't waste time gobbling them down.

"Poor things, they're starved," thought Annie Laurie, as she went back into the house, knowing what she was going to do after she put her money in a secure place. She went through the back door and headed to the corn patch. After pulling eight ears of corn and shucking them. While the oven was still hot, she put the corn into the oven, after greasing each one.

She had planned on painting that morning before she started supper, but with all the hammering and banging going on, she knew she couldn't concentrate.

In a few minutes she knew the corn would be done, so she snapped open a brown paper sack, and with a long handle two prong fork, she dropped the corn into the sack. After sprinkling a little salt into the sack, she took the corn outside to the young fellows.

She was shocked at how much work they'd completed. They'd even built a door and had it hanging in place over the doorsteps, All it needed was putting the screen on. They were nailing some posts up when she gave them the corn.

After looking into the sack, Theodore thanked her profusely, then tore the sack open, and Connie joined in when it came time to eat.

With the young men being busy outside, Annie Laurie thought she'd get busy inside, before the inside of the house became so hot. First, she put on a bag of dried lima beans in a pot to soak. She then began to sweep out the house, starting at the front door. After she'd swept the kitchen and dining room, she saw that she needed to mop those two floors.

She was on the back porch pumping water into the pail when Jesse's mom came around the corner of the house. Annie Laurie could see that she'd been crying, so she stopped what she was doing and set the pail of water on the shelf.

"I couldn't come through the front, but oh, honey, look what came in mail at the house.

Mrs. Jordan handed her the small card, and it read:

Congratulations, Jesse Jordan!

You have been selected to take a physical in Montgomery, Alabama with hopes of being inducted into the armed forces.

You are to meet the bus in front of the courthouse in Monroeville, Alabama at 8:am on June 19, 1942. Do not bring extra clothes.

Sincerely, draft board of Monroe County, Alabama.

Annie Laurie felt the contents of her breakfast rush to her throat, so she ran to the end of the porch and threw up.

She was embarrassed of her actions, to say the least.

Clutching the card in her right hand, she ran to the pail of water and splashed some cold water on her face.

Jesse's mom ran to her, and they embraced each other, with Mrs. Jordan crying, and Annie Laurie praying.

In a few minutes, Annie Laurie led her mother-in-law into the dining room, she wanted to be near her notebook.

Mrs. Jordan sat down at the table, while Annie Laurie chipped them some ice and poured them some tea.

"What are we going to do?" Mrs. Jordan asked.

Annie Laurie pushed a platter of the tea cakes toward Mrs. Jordan, then wrote, "There's nothing we can do but hide our weaknesses from Jesse."

"I know, but I don't know if I can hold up or not. That Hitler, why hasn't somebody already killed him, and now, we have Japan against us too. We've never done anything against them," Mrs. Jordan said.

"No, not that I'm aware of, but all I know to do is let's pray about it," Annie Laurie wrote, as Mrs. Jordan nibbled on one of the tea cakes.

"Boy, these things are good," Mrs. Jordan said, after eating two of the cookies.

"I've baked enough of them, as you can see, so take some of them home with you when you leave," Annie Laurie wrote.

"I sure will, Jesse will love these," Mrs. Jordan said.

"Does my husband know anything about this card?" Annie Laurie wrote.

"No, he and his dad have gone to Miss Earnestine's after a load of cow feed," Mrs. Jordan said.

"Good, please allow me to tell him," Annie Laurie wrote.

"Sure, I'm afraid I'd just be an ole crybaby anyway," Mrs. Jordan said, then added, "Of course, I'll have to tell dad though."

"Thank you," Annie Laurie wrote.

Annie Laurie found another brown bag and handed it to her Mother-in-law. "Help yourself to the tea cakes," she wrote.

After Mrs. Jordan left, Annie Laurie laid the card on the table and mopped the dining room and kitchen. She then took the ten dollars that Theodore had given her back in the change and decided to go to Miss Earnestine's and buy some pork chops.

She took a look at her front porch, and she loved it. She liked the way they were tacking thin strips of lumber over the posts to hide the nails, making things look so much neater. The screen door was completed and already hanging, and it looked like they were about halfway through with the porch.

"Maybe Jesse and I will get to sit a few nights out there, before he leaves," she thought, for the thought of him failing the physical never crossed her mind. *"He's healthy as a horse."* She knew she was thinking ahead of herself, but deep down she'd been looking for it, and she believed Jesse was too.

She'd contemplated on telling Jesse, but she still wasn't for sure, but she'd missed her monthly period, or she was two weeks late, one or the other. Now, with circumstances as they were, she didn't want to give Jesse anything else to worry about, so she decided to wait until she knew for sure.

Miss Earnestine's looked busy for it to be on a Monday, so Annie Laurie was glad that she'd fixed up some.

Meats and other items that needed to stay cold cost more at Miss Earnestine's than in Monroeville. Annie Laurie figured it was because she had to use the expensive ice to keep things cold.

Annie Laurie had fell in line with the other customers and finally made her way to the cash register.

"Three pork chops and two pounds of bacon," Annie Laurie had written on a piece of paper and gave it to Miss Earnestine.

Miss Earnestine didn't waste time, for she was back in a jiffy, with the meats wrapped and in a bag. After weighing things separately, she rang things up on the cash register and Annie Laurie paid her. They each smiled at each other and Annie Laurie left.

Mr. Lum, who had worked up a sweat had taken his usual stance at the end of the long porch.

"Mr. Lum, Theodore and Connie are doing a fabulous job on my front porch," Annie Laurie wrote in her pad, hoping he could read.

"I knowed dey would, and dey wives will do a good job picking dem beans and peas too," Mr. Lum said.

Suddenly, Annie Laurie had held it back all she could. Mr. Lum was like family. She began to wipe tears from her face.

"Oh, Mr. Lum, Jesse doesn't know it yet, but he got a card to report for his physical to go into the army this morning," Annie Laurie wrote.

Mr. Lum read the message, and replied: "Missy, eyes gwinna tells you something my pap tole me, Jist believes in de Lawd and eberthang will turn out alright," Mr. Lum told her.

Annie Laurie gave thought to Mr. Lum's words, she thanked him, then squared her shoulders and walked toward her car.

The doors to the Woodlawn Church were never locked, so when she came to it she went straight to the alter and fell to her knees and prayed like never before. She must have been there fifteen minutes when she thought about the meat in her car. Annie Laurie rose to her feet. *"Thank you, Sweet Jesus!"* she thought to herself, and when she walked out of the doors, she felt a lot better than when she came in.

After reaching home, Annie Laurie went into the house through the back door, she didn't want to disturb the young men. She changed into some working clothes and went outside and headed to the sweet potato bank. It was a bright sunny day, *"Just right for cleaning out the sweet potato bank,"* Annie Laurie thought.

The sweet potatoes had gotten scarce, but it would soon be time to dig this year's crop, so Annie Laurie threw every sweet potato she could find through the little door her daddy had built.

Annie Laurie thought she'd give Theodore and Connie the majority of the potatoes and put the other few in the house.

After putting more water in the soaking lima beans, she went back outside and raked all of the old pine needles out. Annie Laurie then took the wheel barrel and rake and headed to the pine trees in front of the house. After raking two big loads of pine needles, she refilled the sweet potato bank with the fresh straw.

"Just anything to stay busy," Annie Laurie thought, as she went back into the house to start cooking supper.

She thought they'd have Lima beans, fried sweet potatoes, fried pork chops, and cornbread for supper. Annie Laurie had seasoned the Lima beans, along with other vegetables with smoked bacon. She had everything cooked and was waiting for her husband when he'd come in from work.

"Just think, I can now leave the front door and not have to worry about insects coming into the house. Maybe it'll be cooler in here," Annie Laurie thought, as she wiped the sweat from her face.

About that time, Theodore tapped on the front door. Annie Laurie took the sack of sweet potatoes, along with her pencil and pad with her and opened the door.

"Yes Mam, we wound it up, come out here and see what you think of it," Theodore said.

Annie Laurie handed him the sack of sweet potatoes, and after looking inside, he thanked her.

"Oh, I just love it, and you even swept the sawdust up," Annie Laurie wrote.

"Yessum, we aim to please," Theodore said. He then added that they'd looked over the garden and their wives would be back in about two weeks.

"That's great," Annie Laurie wrote.

"Yessum, if you needs us again just let Uncle Columbus know," Theodore said.

Annie Laurie nodded her head, and they pulled away in the old truck.

Any other time, Annie Laurie couldn't have resisted the temptation, she'd had a seat in her rocker and enjoy her new screened in porch, but her mind was on one thing, "The Card."

Annie Laurie almost closed the front door, by habit, then pushed it open, thinking maybe a breeze might come through the front and cool off the kitchen area.

She did the Army Card the same as she'd done the gold coin, when she set the table, she put it under Jesse's plate. Annie Laurie then set the food on the table, for she heard his car in the driveway.

Jesse headed straight for the pump on the back porch, she knew he was washing up for supper. The towel where he had shaved that morning was still hanging in the same place, so she knew he had something to dry with.

"How's my girl this afternoon, the one with the pretty screen porch?" Jesse asked, as he kissed her and sat down at his usual place.

"Your girl has been busy, and just worried sick," Annie Laurie said.

"What's wrong with my girl?" Jesse asked, as he stood from his chair.

"Look under your plate," Annie Laurie said.

Jesse picked up the plate and read the card, and Annie Laurie could have sworn she saw a flicker of a smile cross his face.

He sat back down in his chair and said, "Well, it's no more than I've been looking for. Nearly the whole county of draft age has already signed up or been drafted already. You're the only reason I didn't enlist at the beginning. It might be a shameful thing to say, but my love for you was greater than for my country," Jesse told her.

"Oh, my darling husband, I love you so," Annie Laurie said, then she added, "Well, let's eat while it's at least still warm."

"And what have we here?" Jesse asked, as he pulled the towel from the platter of Tea cakes.

"It's Tea cakes, I made especially for you. Don't start in on them now, or it'll spoil your supper," Annie Laurie told him.

Just as they'd finished supper and Jesse was about to start on the Tea cakes, they heard a knock on the door. Jesse went to the door with one of the Tea cakes in his mouth.

Annie Laurie recognized Lee Peacock's voice at the door, and he sounded excited about something.

"Say, these things are good," Jesse said, as he popped the last bite of the Tea cake in his mouth, as he made his way back into the dining room.

"Lee was right behind Jesse, as he grabbed a hand full of Tea cakes and handed Lee a couple of them.

Annie Laurie got up to prepare Lee a glass of iced tea.

"Lee's stopped by to tell us that he got his notice in the mail today too," Jesse said.

"Yep, there's a bus load of us that'll be leaving Monroeville Friday morning, from what I hear," Lee told Annie Laurie, and he too boasted on her Tea cakes.

"Here you go, a little something to wash things down. Y'all eat all you want. I have another platter of them." Annie Laurie wrote in her tablet.

Annie Laurie soon found out all they wanted to talk about was the war, so she took her glass of iced tea to the front porch and sat down in her rocker. Even though the sun lacked a far piece being to the top of the pines, the new screen helped shade the porch. She decided to let Jesse enjoy the company of his long-time friend.

Annie Laurie couldn't help but over hear them laughing and talking about things in their past and even their future.

Annie Laurie heard Lee tell Jesse that if the Army allowed him to get within a hundred yards of Hitler with that M-1 rifle, "He'll be a dead duck."

"Wouldn't that be something, a hometown boy killing Hitler. You'd get the Medal of Honor for sure," Jesse told Lee.

"That goose stepping and the way they salute, I think it's ridiculous," Jesse said.

"Now that nut, Benito Mussolini from Italy has joined up with Hitler," Lee said.

"Oh well, we may as well knock both of them off, if we can make it over there before the war ends," Jesse told Lee.

"Well, the British and French haven't been able to stop Hitler. It's hard to believe the Germans are sight-seeing off the Eiffel Tower," Jesse said.

"Well, I guess I'd better get going, before I get sugar shock from eating all these cookies. By the way, I love your screen porch," Lee told Jesse.

"Well, I'm about to go sit out there," Jesse said, as he followed Lee to the porch.

Jesse sat down in his chair next to Annie Laurie on the porch, after Lee left.

"He's a mess of a Lee," Jesse said, as he tinkled the ice in his glass.

Annie Laurie didn't bother to bring her tablet outside, so she just patted her husband's free hand.

"That was a fine supper, and you hit the nail on the head with those cookie things," Jesse said.

Again, Annie Laurie patted Jesse on the hand and smiled.

They watched as the sun went down over the pines and then it eased beyond the horizon.

Annie Laurie sat and listened to Jesse talk until darkness fell, after kissing her husband on his stubbled cheek, she went inside and cleaned the kitchen, leaving Jesse to his thoughts.

That night, they slept as usual, with their arms thrown across each other.

They both would be in for a surprise the next morning.

Jesse hadn't been gone but about twenty minutes before he returned to the house.

Annie Laurie heard his car in the driveway, so she went to investigate.

"Guess what, Dad has given me three days off with double pay," Jesse said, as he walked up the doorsteps.

After he made it to the porch, Annie Laurie threw her arms around him, and they kissed.

The next three days were spent, fishing along the riverbank. Walking through the woods in back of their property, with Jesse never failing to take his lariat, in case they ran upon a snake. Jesse had shown her how he could pop the whip and cut a sapling into.

Jesse told her there would be no cooking. All she did was to keep the tomatoes picked and tend to the chickens.

They went to the movie theater on Thursday night and saw, "Mrs. Miniver." After watching the movie, Jesse said, "Those Nazi's have got to be stopped."

They ate out every night, and Jesse said on Thursday, before the movie, "I must admit, I miss your cooking."

Friday morning came too soon. There was hardly a place around the Courthouse to park.

Jesse saw a lot of his football buddies that would be catching the bus that morning, among them was Shane Jay, with his pregnant wife, Kayla, who was crying. Richard Jordan was also there, just to name a few.

Of course, Jesse's parents were there, with his mom crying the entire time. Annie Laurie had made Jesse a promise that she wouldn't cry.

The head of the draft board told them at 8:00 o'clock to load up, and the young men began to get on the bus. Jesse gave his mom a kiss on the check and hugged his Dad. He gave Annie Laurie a long kiss and stepped onto the bus. In five minutes the bus left from the square and headed toward Montgomery, leaving behind a lot of crying ladies, including Annie Laurie.

Chapter 18

October 1942

As it turned out, only a few of the young men that left from Monroeville that day failed the physical and returned home. Jesse and Lee passed with flying colors, and were sent directly to basic training at Fort Benning, Georgia. When they finished the six weeks there, they were sent directly to Fort Gordon, which was in Augusta, Georgia, to train for their military occupational specialty. Both Jesse and Lee were trained to be military policemen.

On September 20th, they were flown to New York, where they were shipped out on the U.S.S. W.O. Darby, and docked in Southampton, England in nine days.

Annie Laurie received letters from Jesse about twice a week, he always mentioned they were extremely busy. That's when he was in Ft. Benning, and Ft. Gordon, but after they got overseas the letters were very infrequent. Jesse had warned Annie Laurie and his Mom of such.

Jesse had written Annie Laurie that both he and Lee had won medals for firing experts with the m-1 rifle, then when they were in Ft. Gordon they were awarded expert medals for the .45 pistol. "Been in the army just a couple of months and already have two medals," Jesse had written.

They had a couple of days layover in New York, so both he and Lee had toured the Statue of Liberty. One of his buddies had taken pictures of them at the location and he intended on sending them to her, but they were deplored before the film was developed. "I never dreamed the statue was green in color," Jesse had written.

Of course, Annie Laurie wrote back, telling him of the happenings around the area, but she held back the fact that she was pregnant. She didn't want him to be worried about her and a baby. She wanted him to keep his mind on the job.

Jesse had written that he wanted a photograph of her, so she bought a good camera and film at Miss Earnestine's. Hazel showed her how to load the camera. "By all means, while loading the camera, don't expose the film to light," she'd warned. Hazel loaded the camera and took several pictures of Annie Laurie, making sure none of them would show her waist. The roll of film had 24 negatives on it, and Annie Laurie made sure all the negatives were taken. She took two pictures of Mr. Lum, one of the buildings, one of Miss Earnestine, and one of Hazel, plus the ones of her. Miss Hazel took the roll of film out and put the roll in a thick brown envelope, to be sent off for development. "It'll take eight or ten days," Hazel said.

When the photographs came back, Annie Laurie sent Jesse two of her and one of Mr. Lum.

Mrs. Jordan got to where she was visiting more, especially, now that she was going to have a baby.

One day in October, Annie Laurie was busy painting, when Mrs. Jordan stopped by. Annie Laurie stuck the brushes she was using into the jar of paint thinner she was using, so she could visit with her some. She had grown to like Mrs. Jordan more and more. She had to just learn her ways. One day they were talking and Mrs. Jordan admitted to her that her real name was Hattie, and not Opal. "I just thought at the time that Opal suited me better, so I became Opal," Mrs. Jordan had told her.

This visit however, Mrs. Jordan gave her some good advice.

"You know, I've been giving this some serious thought," Mrs. Jordan said, "It's none of my business, but don't you think it's time for you to do something about your speech?" I mean you'll be having the baby in January or February, and that baby is going to mimic you. It would be so much better if you could talk. Please don't take offense by what I'm saying," Jesse's mom said.

Annie Laurie gave it some thought, and wrote, "No offense taken," and hugged her mother-in-law's neck.

"Whew! I was so scared you might take offense," Mrs. Jordan said.

Annie Laurie shook her head, "No."

"So, are you still painting," Mrs. Jordan asked.

Annie Laurie had been painting day and night, knowing she wouldn't be able to paint after the baby came, so she took Mrs. Jordan into her studio. She had completed five biblical paintings and was busy on another one.

Mrs. Jordan gasped, as she looked at the paintings.

"My Lord, how do you do this?" Mrs. Jordan asked.

Annie Laurie just shrugged her shoulders.

"Just think, you never went a day to school, yet you can do this, sew, and write, using good grammar too.

Annie Laurie, wrote in Mrs. Jordan's palm, "Daddy."

"Your daddy taught you how to read and write?" Mrs. Jordan asked.

Annie Laurie nodded her head, "Yes."

"Well, he must have been amazing, like you," Mrs. Jordan said.

Again, Annie Laurie nodded her head.

"Well, I've said my piece, so it's on you now, I'd better run this errand for Senior," Mrs. Jordan said, and laughed.

Annie Laurie saw her to the front door, then resumed her painting, and thinking of Jesse. All she knew was they were camped near a small town near Chesire, England.

Annie Laurie took what Mrs. Jordan had said to heart, she suddenly wanted to talk. She certainly didn't want her child to babble, she wanted him or her to be normal.

Annie Laurie was using Dr. Eddins, due to her pregnancy and she was taking the vitamins that he prescribed her. He was the only doctor she knew, therefore she made a visit to him the next morning about her tongue. Although, she felt sure she'd wind-up in Mobile, as she'd always been told.

Annie Laurie didn't have an appointment that morning, so she had to wait in the lobby about an hour before she made it into the doctor's waiting room. She made sure she had her tablet with her and had already written some of the questions down.

Doctor Eddins read Annie Laurie's questions.

"So glad you've made up your mind to do something about this, you're so talented to let this hamper you, so open your mouth and let's see what we can do," Dr. Eddins asked.

Annie Laurie opened her mouth.

"Wider," Dr. Eddins asked.

Annie Laurie opened her mouth wide as she could.

"My, what some pretty white teeth," Doctor Eddins said, as he probed under both sides of her tongue with a wooden tongue depressor.

In less than a minute, he removed the depressor and said, "Hmph, and to think this has kept you from talking, or possibly singing all these years. The operation looks minor to me, but it is in a delicate place, so I'm going to send you across the road to see Doctor Stallworth. "He's a surgeon," Doctor Eddins added.

Annie Laurie smiled and shook Doctor Eddins hand.

After paying Miss Pauline, his nurse and also clerk his fee of $2.00, she walked across the street to Doctor Stallworth's office.

Annie Laurie found that Doctor Stallworth's office was open. After writing down why she was there, and filling out a form, Annie Laurie was escorted by his nurse to the doctor's waiting room.

Doctor Stallworth was going over some papers when Annie Laurie and his nurse entered the room.

"Doctor, this is Annie Laurie Jordan, she can't talk and wants you to look at her tongue," the nurse said.

"Have a seat on the cot, and let's see," Doctor Stallworth said, so Annie Laurie did as he asked.

"Now open your wide, and let's take a look," Doctor Stallworth asked.

When Annie Laurie had opened her mouth as wide as she could, the doctor slipped a small wooden block between her teeth.

After using a large, sterilized instrument and a flashlight to look beneath Annie Laurie's tongue. Dr. Stallworth went right to work. He used a spray to deaden beneath her tongue.

"The operation itself is minor, you might see a little blood, but don't let it frighten you," Doctor Stallworth said. He then added, "Miss Florine has some cotton balls and tweezer to prevent anything running down your throat."

"Now lift your tongue high as you can and try to keep it that way," the doctor asked, so Annie Laurie did, which wasn't very far. There was a flap of skin that grew to the end of Annie Laurie's tongue.

Doctor Stallworth held to it with a pair of tweezers and using a scalpel he cut beneath her tongue and the bottom of her mouth until he reached her saliva glands. He then removed the extra skin he'd cut out and covered it with a cloth that he'd placed on the cot behind her.

"There's a little blood coming from the bottom of your mouth that'll require a couple of stitches, the bottom of your tongue looks great," the doctor said.

After putting in the sutures, and giving everything a final check, he removed the block of wood, and said, "The stitches will go away in a few days.

"Now don't think you'll be talking as well as the normal person right away, start with simple words, and in a few months you'll be talking as well as your Mother-in-law," Dr. Stallworth chuckled.

Before Annie Laurie left the room, the doctor told her to open her mouth, and she did. He opened a small bottle that had a dropper attached to the lid and put two drops under her tongue.

"This is Sulphur drops, it'll heal that tongue. Put two drops under your tongue in the morning and when you go to bed at night. Eat soft foods for a few days. It'll be sore for a few days too, but nothing you shouldn't be able to handle. If you do have trouble with it, you know where I'm at," Doctor Stallworth said, then smiled.

Annie Laurie smiled too, and touched her heart then his, and left the room.

The nurse had returned to the desk.

"That'll be twenty-five dollars," she said.

"What started at a thousand dollars wound up to be twenty-five dollars," Annie Laurie thought as she walked back across the street to her enter her car. Instead though, she walked about two doors down to the drug store and ordered a strawberry milkshake, as usual she had to point to the menu.

After getting her order, she stuck the straw as far back in her mouth as possible, and oh, how good it was. Even the baby kicked when the cold drink hit her stomach.

On the drive home, she couldn't help herself. "What would be the first words she would speak?" She did some serious thinking, then said, "Jesus, I love you." Now she was shocked how plain the words came out. She had to try it again, "Jesse, I miss you," she said. Tears almost sprang from her eyes, tears she'd held back since Jesse left, so much so until she had to pull beside the road. The infrequent letters she received from Jesse and the twenty dollar check she received from the Army each month just wasn't enough; she wanted her husband, home.

A passing truck blew its horn and brought her back to her senses, so instead of stopping at her in-laws, she drove on home.

The weather was turning colder, but she decided to sit on the porch for a while and just think. *"The painting can wait,"* she thought. She went inside and got a thick shawl and returned to the porch.

Annie Laurie felt ashamed of herself about the crying jag she'd had. *"I have so much to be thankful for, the crops are gathered and either stored or canned in pint jars,"* she thought. Jesse was safe, the baby was coming, and she could talk!

Chapter 19
January 1943

Speech had come easily for Annie Laurie, by the first of the year she was talking as normal as anyone in the community, yet, for some reason she didn't have the southern drawl. Her words came out sharp, yet short. Hattie, who would always be Opal to Annie Laurie, said she envied her speech.

Since Jesse's departure, his Mom had become Annie Laurie's best friend. A week before Christmas, she'd asked Opal if she'd like to go to Mobile with her to sell her paintings.

Her mother-in-law accepted the invitation, providing they go in the Cadillac, and for Annie Laurie not to be picking up any of the paintings. "Honey, you're getting too big for that," Opal said, so Annie Laurie agreed, for she'd noticed that her ankles would be swelled at night.

Annie Laurie learned things on the trip that she didn't know. Opal had told her that Mr. Jordan just couldn't produce the amount of beef that some of his competitors could, therefore he'd lost the contracts. She also told her that one of the workers had to be laid off. "Now, it's just Senior and LeRoy doing all that work. We had to cut back in the house too. Now I just have Jewell, the housekeeper two days a week. I never was much of a cook, so we just eat simple," Opal said. She then continued, "Thank God what we do have is paid off, so no one can run us out of the house."

"I'm sorry, but I've been so busy with the paintings and just everyday things, I was unaware," Annie Laurie said.

"That's quite understandable honey," Opal told her.

"Well, I can cook, I just don't have anyone to cook for, and thank the Lord I don't owe anyone," Annie Laurie said.

"I could've told you that," Opal said.

"Let's find some music. You might think I'm old, but I still love music," Opal said, so they listened to music until they reached the art gallery.

Annie Laurie was paid two hundred dollars each for six of the paintings, and three hundred for the painting of Adam and Eve. As before she was paid in cash.

"Congratulations about your baby, thank you, and I'll see you the next time," Miss Emilie said.

Annie Laurie didn't want to change the perception of herself, so she just nodded her head, and they left.

"Well, at least I won't have to worry about you financially," Opal said, as they drove away.

For Christmas that year, Annie Laurie surprised her in-laws with a good wholesome meal of chicken & dumplings, corn meal dressing, vegetables, and of course, a platter of tea cakes.

The two thanked her profusely, as Opal had plans of them just eating out of cans. They ate too, which pleased Annie Laurie. Of course, they talked about Jesse most of the time that Annie Laurie was there. The subject changed though, when the baby began to "Kick up a storm," and Annie Laurie picked up Mr. Jordan's hand and laid it on her stomach.

"Boy, Junior just thought he was a football player," Mr. Jordan said and laughed.

The day was cold, and Annie Laurie didn't want the house to get cold, so she soon left, just taking a plate of the food with her. She didn't bother with the Tea cakes, for she had more at home.

They both hugged Annie Laurie, then thanked her again, before she went out the door, all bundled up with the plate of wrapped food.

On the short trip home, she said aloud, "I'm thinking of your honey, and I hope you're having a good Christmas."

Theodore and Connie saw to it that she kept a good supply of wood to burn. They even stacked it on the back porch for her, and Annie Laurie was glad of that.

The new year rolled around, and Annie Laurie had an appointment with Doctor Eddins on the 2nd, which was on Friday.

After the examination, Doctor Eddins gave her two more weeks. He then told her to have plenty of diapers.

"I have stacks of them, and I'm so ready to see my baby," Annie Laurie told him.

Dr. Eddins laughed and said, "For Pete's sake try to have this baby in the afternoon. I'll be tending to my patients. Those night deliveries are what's rough on us doctors. Up all night and having to work the next day."

"I'll try," Annie Laurie said, then laughed.

Annie Laurie stopped by and told Opal what the doctor had said.

"Well, I'll be coming so often until you'll get sick of me," Opal said.

Annie Laurie laughed and said, "I hope so."

Her next stop was at Miss Earnestine's, both she and Hazel were thrilled to hear the news.

While Annie Laurie was there, she bought an abundance of easy to prepare foods, for she knew she wouldn't be up to cooking for a few days after the baby came, and Opal couldn't cook.

It was too cold for Mr. Lum to be on the front porch, so he couldn't help but hear her news. When he put her groceries inside her car, he said, "Missy, leaves yo water buckets on de back porch, when Theodore and Connie is there getting yo wood, dey can pump yo water."

"Thank you Mr. Lum," Annie Laurie said.

On January 15th, Annie Laurie started having labor pains around noon, by four o'clock, she sent the nervous Opal after Doctor Eddins.

Jesse Threy Jordan came into the world at 5:45 pm, a fine baby boy, with a head full of blonde hair.

Chapter 20
June 1943

Jesse had been gone for a year, but in Annie Laurie's heart, he'd been gone an eternity. Annie Laurie continued to check her mail box each day, about all she knew different was that Jesse and Lee had graduated from paratrooper school. Her monthly check she received from the Army had increased to twenty-seven dollars a month, as both Jesse and Lee had been promoted to corporals.

Many of the words that were in Jesse's letters had been blackened out and sometimes the letter hardly made sense. He always ended his letters with "You loving husband Jesse," but the word husband was always blackened out.

She had sent him the two pictures of herself, and Mr. Lum and miraculously he'd gotten them. He'd written back how beautiful she was, and that he knew Mr. Lum was looking out for her. He'd written that he put one of her pictures in her wallet and taped the other two in the lid of this foot locker.

For reasons that she couldn't explain to herself, she'd never written that she could speak, and he was the father of a beautiful son.

Threy, was growing and learning each day, and he was absolutely adored by both Opal, Jesse Sr. and of course, Annie Laurie.

Threy was like his daddy, he'd eat anything, most especially candied yams, and apricots, they were his favorites.

Annie Laurie produced more than enough milk for her son. In fact her breast were swollen and sore until Opal told her that was common, so she bought a pump from the drug store so that Annie Laurie could pump some of the milk out. It was such a relief to Annie Laurie.

The yard at Annie Laurie's was so bumpy until it would've been hard for Annie Laurie to push Threy in a stroller, so she bought him a red wagon. After putting a small pillow behind and in front of her son, on pretty days, she'd pull him around in the yard and he loved it.

Annie Laurie didn't plant a garden that year, for she still had plenty left over from the year before.

Opal made Annie Laurie's trips to the store to begin with, but as the weather warmed, Annie Laurie would wrap Threy good with a blanket and she'd drive slowly to Miss Earnestine's. Of course, everyone in the store was in awe of Threy. Miss Earnestine even put a stick of peppermint in his mouth, while Annie Laurie shopped. Threy sucked on the stick of candy until it was sharp as a pencil. Of course, he did a lot of slobbering along with the sucking. Everyone in the store had to hold Threy, even Mr. Lum.

Opal helped Annie Laurie as much as she could, especially while she did the washing, especially with all of the diapers, and cooking. In fact, it had become a habit for Senior and Opal to eat supper at Annie Laurie's about three times a week. It suited Annie Laurie, for with both of them tending to Threy it gave her more time to tend to the house.

Annie Laurie introduced Threy to Woodlawn Church when he was three months old, and they made a habit of it.

By June, Threy was crawling, so Annie Laurie had to be careful where she laid things.

Of course, everything Threy did was just like Jesse had done, and Annie Laurie couldn't help but laugh at them, for his hair was still golden blonde. She did believe that Threy was going to have Jesse's height though, for when he began to walk in September, his head came above her knees. By then he was on solid foods, and she was so glad of it.

Jesse's dad had sold one of the big trucks, just for the need of money, for he had to pay LeRoy each week, whether he sold any cows or not. Fields still had to be tended to, along with what cattle he had. Senior and Opal continued eating supper with Annie Laurie about three times a week, and sometimes, Opal would bring groceries with her.

Annie Laurie hadn't painted anything in a year, but she still had all the money from her last sale and then some, for she tried to be very conservative. She made most of her clothes and little Threy's too, and they ate from the things that came out of the garden. Both Senior and Opal had

Threy spoiled to the bone, and Annie Laurie believed they'd move in, if she offered.

Opal was right about one thing, Annie Laurie was so glad she could talk. At night was her favorite time. She and Threy slept together, and Annie Laurie would always sing softly until Threy fell asleep.

Two days before Christmas, Annie Laurie received a picture in the mail of Jesse and Lee standing in front of a big Cathedral. On the back was written, "Merry Christmas, love, Jesse and Lee."

"Would you look at that," Annie Laurie whispered to herself, for it was the first time she'd seen them in Army clothes.

Threy was the only one with gifts under the tree, that Christmas morning. Annie Laurie tore the Christmas paper for him. He wound up getting a "Jack in the box," a duck that walked and quacked when wound, and a dump truck to push around.

Opal came early that morning to tend to Threy, while Annie Laurie cooked Christmas dinner. Of course, all Opal did was wind the two toys for him. Annie Laurie waited until Jesse's dad got there to show them the picture that she'd gotten in the mail.

"Just look at our son," Opal said, as she ran the tips of her fingers across the photograph.

Senior was glad that their son hadn't stood in front of a blown apart building, for he listened to the news.

They ate about the same that Christmas as the others, except Annie Laurie made a chocolate pudding with a meringue topping and everyone loved it, especially Threy.

It turned out to be a cold windy day outside, but they all stayed warm with the stove going aand the fire in the fireplace.

It turned out that Senior and Opal stayed on and ate supper with Annie Laurie, and Opal even helped with the dishes.

Mr. Jordan was worried about the cows, but Opal assured him that LeRoy would handle things, so he settled down and kept winding the toys until near dark.

Before the Jordan's left, Mr. Jordan reached in his coat pocket and pulled out a $100.00 U. S. Savings bond and handed it to Annie Laurie. "This is for little Threy," he said.

Annie Laurie tried to refuse it, but Mr. Jordan wouldn't hear of it.

"It's for little Threy's education," he said, so Annie Laurie stuck it in her apron pocket, reluctantly, for Opal told her constantly of their hardships.

Annie Laurie was holding Threy in her arms, and Opal gave him one last kiss before they rushed out of the door into the cold night.

The cold weather lasted an entire week. The new calendar from Miss Earnestine's noted that it was January 2, 1944. When they finally got out of the house, except for feeding the chickens and collecting the eggs. Of course, Annie Laurie's first stop was at the mailbox, and all she found was two sales papers.

Even though the day was warmer than usual for the time of year, Annie Laurie had so many clothes on he found it difficult to walk, so Mr. Lum picked him up and sat him on the counter. Mr. Lum pulled two cents out of his pocket for two peppermint sticks, but Miss Earnestine shoved the pennies back to him.

While Threy enjoyed his candy, Annie Laurie did her shopping. They'd stayed shut up so long until Annie Laurie had to buy more food items than usual. Even though Threy had cut four of his front teeth, she still had to mash up most of the things she cooked in order for him to eat them.

When it came time to leave, Mr. Lum carried Annie Laurie's groceries to her car, so she ran ahead of him to open the back door, leaving Miss Earnestine to watch after Threy. He screamed like a banshee when she took the candy out of his hands so she could wash them. He settled down quickly though when Miss Earnestine stuck a half-peeled banana in his hands.

"If it wasn't for that head full of blonde hair, that boy would look just like his daddy," Hazel told Miss Earnestine, after Annie Laurie and Threy had gotten outside.

"Dem boys keeping you plenty wood on the porch?" Mr. Lum asked Annie Laurie.

"Oh yes, and I've been burning it," Annie Laurie answered.

"We all has, it's been cold," Mr. Lum replied.

"They drove off the last time and forgot to collect their money," Annie Laurie said.

"Dey tole me, dey say it wuz too cole fuh you to open de doe," Mr. Lum replied.

"How thoughtful of them, well, tell them they can stop by any time," Annie Laurie said, as she finished peeling the banana for Threy and plopped him on the front seat, then crawled in, herself.

Chapter 21
May 1944

Annie Laurie didn't think spring would ever come around, but it did, and she got Mr. Jordan to plant her garden, for things in her cupboard were low, since she missed the last year.

The chickens were laying again, for they hardly laid in cold weather.

The card from the Army came on May 15th. It read:

Dear Mrs. Annie Jordan:

Do not be alarmed, but your husband is about to be engaged in a top secret mission for at least six months and the War Department is sorry, but there is no way you can contact each other, for Sgt. Jordan is no longer at the same address.

Respectfully,
General Marshall

Annie Laurie's first thought was that the Army was finally going into Germany.

"Oh, my poor baby, look over him Jesus," Annie Laurie prayed aloud.

After receiving the card, Annie Laurie's check from the government increased to thirty dollars a month, due to his promotion. Annie Laurie put the check in the old chest, along with the others, including little Threy's savings bond.

After getting the card in the mail, Annie Laurie listened to the news over the radio more often, hoping to keep up with the movement of the military, and it came on June the 7th. The invasion into France actually took place the day before, but the radio didn't announce it until the 7th. The American Army was met with strong resistance by the Germans, when they landed on the beaches of Normandy, France.

Annie Laurie didn't know it, but Jesse, Lee, and a hoard of other paratroopers had parachuted out of planes ahead of the landings, behind the enemy lines. Their objective was to come in behind the Germans where there were bunkers and shoot as many as they could. In hopes of eliminating as many as possible, so they couldn't fire on the soldiers as they landed on the beaches.

On June 9th, Annie Laurie heard that the U. S. Military had taken the beaches and were continuing to move over land.

Annie Laurie and her helpers had already gathered and canned or preserved everything in the garden before she'd heard anything else of importance. On August the 25th it came over the radio that the French and American Army had driven the Germans out of Paris.

From then on, it was just one battle after the other in Germany, during the winter months of 1944-45.

Little Threy continued to grow and learn. By his 2nd birthday, he was wearing underwear instead of diapers. Annie Laurie also gave him his first hair cut on his second birthday. She just cut his hair shoulder length with a pair of scissors. Annie Laurie couldn't stand the idea of sweeping the golden locks out of the back door, so she swept them in a big envelope and sealed it.

Threy had begun talking, using simple words, like mama, and dada, by the time he was two he was jabbering up a storm. He was Senior and Opal's heart, for it wasn't a day they didn't stop by and see him. Threy called them, "Ganma, and Papa." He learned to say dada by Annie Laurie pointing at Jesse's picture and saying "Daddy."

Families around the county were being notified of their son, or husband's death, but so far Annie Laurie hadn't heard a word. The church and its members stayed in constant prayer and vigilance.

On May 1,1945, it came over the radio that Adolf Hitler had blown his brains out, aand Berlin was in complete shambles.

On May 7th, Germany surrendered and the war in Europe was over.

Word got out that Monroeville would be hosting a dance in the street that night. Annie Laurie didn't go, but Senior and Opal did. Annie Laurie told them she'd be dancing when she heard that her husband was alright.

The letter came on Friday, June 15th, Annie Laurie's heart jumped to her throat when she recognized Jesse's handwriting.

She slowly opened the thick letter, expecting to read anything.

Little Threy was trying his best to throw rocks over the dirt road, for she never left the mail box.

The letter began:

My Darling Annie Laurie,

First things are first. I pray this letter finds you well.

I'm safe and sound. The Germans tried their best, but I was too fast for them.
Boy, Germany is one big ruin. Hitler fought until he knew he was whipped.

Lee, he's alright too. That rascal made company clerk. That typing class we took in school sure came in handy for him.

I can't help but feel sorry for the people over here, especially the children. They have nowhere to live and nothing to eat.

The people are surprisingly friendly, the ones that are left.

The Jewish people really paid for Hitler's stupidity. I'll explain it more when I make it home.

Tell Mom and Dad, I send my love, and tell Pop, I'll compare my medals with his any time.

Be seeing you
Your loving husband, Jesse

Inside the envelope was a jagged swastika. Annie Laurie didn't know it, but Jesse had cut it off a German's coat that he had shot.

Annie Laurie got a few more letters after that one, but none compared to the first one.

One day in the middle of July, Annie Laurie was canning her peas from the garden.

She knew she'd need more jars, so her first stop was at Miss Earnestine's, only to find she had sold out that morning, so Annie Laurie drove to "The big Store," in Excel.

They had the jars, so Annie Laurie bought two boxes of them. On the way out, she saw the bus as it pulled away from the bus stop, which was about 100 yards away.

Among the people that got off the bus were three soldiers.

"Oh my Lord in Heaven," Annie Laurie mumbled to herself, she'd know that loping walk anywhere, it was Jesse!

"Look!" Annie Laurie said to Threy, as she let go of his hand and pointed toward Jesse, "That's daddy," she said.

After putting the jars in the backseat, Annie Laurie cranked her Plymouth and headed Jesse's way. He was walking toward Dottelle, with his duffle bag slung over his shoulder.

When Annie Laurie got near Jesse she reached over and rolled down the passenger window and stopped the car beside Jesse.

Jesse looked at Annie Laurie, then Threy.

"Going my way soldier boy?" Annie Laurie asked.

"Dada," Threy said, as he pointed toward Jesse.

Jesse smiled and asked, "Annie Laurie? Boy you've got some explaining to do!" He then put his duffle bag on the back floorboard and opened the passenger door. After throwing Threy into the air a couple of times he crawled into the familiar passenger seat.

"When did this come along and when did you start talking?" Jesse asked.

"Oh, about six months after you went away," Annie Laurie answered.

Epilogue

Excel, Dottelle, and the surrounding areas finally got electricity in 1948.

Even as tight as Miss Earnestine was with a dollar, she lit up the store like a Christmas tree.

Next was Woodlawn Church, then poles and electric lines headed up Jesse and Annie Laurie's road. By September the log house had electricity. That's when Annie Laurie cashed the checks the government had sent her from Jesse's pay. Her first electric appliance was an iron, then a stove and refrigerator.

By 1948 Jesse and Annie Laurie were the parents of two sons, Threy and Richard.

Senior never was a big-time cattleman anymore, he just kept enough cows for them to survive on reasonably.

Jesse got a job selling life insurance and stayed with it until he retired.

After the boys started to school, Annie Laurie began to paint again. She and Jesse even made a trip to New Orleans once for an expose' of her paintings and they couldn't believe how much money they brought back.

Lee went to work at the local newspaper and made quite a name for himself.

Even with all their modern conveniences, Jesse and Annie Laurie's favor time was sitting on the front porch, watching the placid sun as it set behind the tall pines.

www.ingramcontent.com/pod-product-compliance
Lightning Source LLC
Chambersburg PA
CBHW050915030726
47503CB00007BB/2303